'BEVERLEY HILLS' BROWNING

Peter Corris was born in Stawell, Victoria, in 1942. From 1964 to 1975 he taught history at Monash, ANU and the University of Melbourne. He has been a professional writer since 1975 and was literary editor of the *National Times* from 1978 to 1980. He has three daughters and lives in Sydney's inner west.

By the same author

The Winning Side
Pokerface

In the Cliff Hardy Series
The Dying Trade
White Meat
The Marvellous Boy
The Empty Beach
Heroin Annie
Make Me Rich
The Big Drop
Deal Me Out

In the Richard Browning Series
'Box Office' Browning

'BEVERLY HILLS' BROWNING

From tapes among the papers
of Richard Browning,

transcribed and edited by

Peter Corris

ISBN-10: 0140107398
ISBN-13: 9780140107395

FOR THE MEMORY OF
J. W. 'Jim' Davidson

CONTENTS

INTRODUCTION

A patient search has revealed the batch of cassettes following on from those which record the early life of Richard Browning (published in 1987 as *'Box Office' Browning*). Formerly stored in a box which had contained Old Grandad bourbon whisky, the cassettes are now in the process of being sorted through, labelled and copied.

As indicated in the Introduction to the previous book, Browning's recording methods were erratic. The chaos now seems worse than was originally thought, particularly in the later stages of the taping. Browning appears to have used different tape recorders at different times and in different places, and he sometimes leaves off his account on a cassette in one machine, resumes on another and then returns to the first still later. Not until all the tapes have been transcribed will a fully accurate version of Browning's long journal be possible, but these recollections of his early years in Hollywood appear to be coherent and complete.

There is, however, the matter of self-correction. When it pleased him or when he hit upon a stray memory, Browning corrected a statement made earlier, frequently abusing himself for having got something wrong. Thus in the course of the narrative on another tape (provisionally labelled Tape 12/i), he says that it was not Rudyard Kipling whom he chauffeured in London in 1919, but Conan Doyle, and he adds a significant detail:

The worst part of that job was the uniform — military style jacket, boots and cap. The get-up produced an image too close to that of Corporal William Hughes, 1st AIF, for me to feel comfortable in it.

Readers of '*Box Office*' *Browning* (see especially pp. 116-20) will know just how uncomfortable Browning (recently a deserter under the name of Hughes) would have felt.

As in the previous book, it has sometimes been necessary to add a note of explanation or clarification to Browning's text. Once again, indistinct passages, occasioned usually by drunkenness, are present, and these are indicated. Punctuation and elision are designed to convey Browning's tone and manner of speech.

P.C.

Sydney, 1987

CHAPTER ONE

We couldn't have been very far off the coast of New South Wales when I crept out of the sail locker of the *Sternwood*. I just couldn't take the smell any longer – lock yourself for a few hours in a closet along with some sheets that the cat has pissed on and you'll have some idea of what it was like.

I stumbled across the deck trying to keep my balance as the ship heaved and tilted. I had my bag in one hand and was groping for the rail with the other when a voice cut through the steady hum of the wind.

'Hey! You there!'

Like a fool I dropped my bag and put my hands in the air. Then I fell over and slithered along the messy deck. When I got my face out of the salty slime I looked up to see a black giant looming over me.

'Why'd you put yore hands up like that, man?'

I grinned foolishly. 'I don't know. I thought you might have a gun.'

He threw back his head and laughed. He seemed to have about fifty teeth the size of tombstones and the colour of cue balls in his head. 'Gun. Man, why would I have a gun?'

I climbed to my feet and retrieved the bag. 'I'm, just nervous. I'm a stowaway.'

'You don't say. We'd better go see the Captain. Less'n you fancy swimmin' home from here?'

He pointed at the sea; his hand was pink-palmed and about the size of a shovel. I shook my head and got a grip on my bag.

'Least you ain't sick. Las' one we had, why he was sick all over that locker. Took him a day an' a night to clean it up.'

'Then what?' I said.

'I disremember. Come on, the Captain down here.'

I took a look to the west before we went down the companion-way but I couldn't see land. Just grey water and white tops. If I'd been wearing a hat I would have doffed and waved it. *Stay on the boat at all costs, Dick,* I thought. That's the ticket.

The smells below deck reminded me that I hadn't eaten for around fifteen hours. Sea air and the movement of a ship gives me an appetite rather than the reverse. Also I was parched after the first hour or two because I'd swigged down all the brandy I had with me in an effort to control the fear. And I had a bursting bladder. I clattered down the iron stairs after the negro thinking that I'd give one of my gold sovereigns for directions to the toilet, and a mug of tea with a good dose of rum in it to follow.

My discoverer hammered on a door at the end of a narrow passage.

'Who's that?' The voice was deep, slurred and slow, either by booze or sleep.

'Bosun, Cap'n. Jesse.'

'Are we sinking, bosun?'

'No, Cap'n.'

'Then go 'way.'

'Got a stowaway here, Cap'n.'

'How old?'

Jesse looked enquiringly at me. 'Twenty-four,' I said.

'Twenty-fo', Cap'n.'

'What size?'

'Big, Cap'n, looks strong.'

'Feed him and put him to work. If he talks English tell him the first stop's Honolulu, if he don't just put him to work.'

Jesse rolled his eyes at me and we backed away from the door. 'Sounds like a decent chap,' I said. 'What's his name?'

'Captain Clancy. He all right, long as you ain't drunk when he sober or vice versey.'

'So I work my passage, is that it?' I tried to sound nonchalant but I probably didn't succeed. I had an awful feeling that this big black ran the ship and could do pretty much what he pleased. Like all Australians at that time (and since for the majority), I wasn't used to black people having any authority. That was scary enough, but I also had a bursting bladder.

We climbed up onto the deck again. The wind was strong and a couple of hands were busy with equipment. They looked incuriously at Jesse and me. 'That's it,' he growled. 'What's yore name?'

As always I thought quickly before answering that question. No reason to lie. 'Richard Browning, Dick.'

'Well, Dick, my man, first thing you do is hand over that valise there.'

'What?'

'The bag, man. You a stowaway, maybe you got the Crown jools in there.'

I gave him the bag. He opened it and rummaged through the contents. The .45 pistol came up smoothly; it looked like a toy in his big hand as he cocked it and sighted out over the rail.

'Careful,' I said, 'it's loaded.'

He nodded. He looked at my book on card playing and the new pack of cards I'd thrown in the bag at some point. 'You gots to realise the delicacy 'a yore position, Dick,' he drawled. 'Here you are, an illegal person at sea . . .' Suddenly, he lunged forward and jabbed at me with the pistol. The muzzle hit the money belt around my middle and coins clinked. He nodded again and riffled the pages of the book. I was sweating although the wind was cold. Spray lashed my face; I realised the delicacy of my position.

Jesse stripped the wrapping off the cards and did a fast one-handed shuffle. He held up the cards in one hand and the gun in the other. 'Yo gets yore fun with which one a these?'

I gulped, painful with so dry a throat. 'The cards,' I said.

The cards literally disappeared and he held out an empty hand. 'Welcome abo'd, Dick.'

I got hold of a couple of fingers and shook them. 'Thanks. Your name is . . .'

'Jesse Bill.' The cards re-appeared and he dropped them and the pistol into the bag. 'The *Sternwood* runs on work an' play.'

'Great. Any chance of a feed before work begins?'

'I like yore style. If you can keep down our cook's breakfast you a natural-born sailor. Ain't yore first time at sea, is it?'

'No.' I was hobbling by this stage and didn't have time for the niceties. I rushed to the rail and unbuttoned. As blessed relief came, I thought about the troopship *Wisden* that had transported me to the madness of the Somme and the P & O cruiser that had taken me back to Australia and a welter of troubles. It seemed to me that I was at sea as a free man for the first time. Of course, a first class berth with champagne of an evening and some bad card players in the smoking room would have been better, but bolters[1] can't be choosers.

. . .

The crew of the *Sternwood* was a good bunch, easy and friendly the way Americans are (those that aren't treacherous, murderous swine, that is). I was Dick to all and sundry within a day or two and they were 'Chuck', 'Hal', 'Jerry' and so on to me. The work was damnably hard and they were all glad of an extra hand; that was one reason for my good reception. Another was my rotten bad luck at cards.

Within a week they'd lowered my gold supply alarmingly. Jesse, who was the bosun and had authority over the white men, which was unusual in those days, was a big winner. He'd flash his teeth at me as he raked in a pot.

'You sure there ain't another one like you in that sail locker, Richard? I'd sure admire to meet him.'

'The luck'll change,' I said grimly. But it didn't and after the first week or so I'd only play for tiny stakes. I didn't want to land in America broke.

As I say, the work was hard. I shovelled coal, cleaned boilers, greased machinery, peeled potatoes and stood watch. The food was monotonous – salt meat, hard tack, rice – but I'd had worse in Long Bay Gaol and other places, and I wolfed it down to fuel the body for the work. The main trick to surviving was to stay out of the way of Captain Tom Clancy.

Clancy was an eccentric. Now, eccentrics, for my money, belong in mansions surrounded by servants who can stop them doing things that make other people unhappy. Clancy was in the worst possible position for an eccentric – ruler of a small universe which is what a ship at sea is. He was completely unpredictable; nice as pie one day and roaring for the times when he could have given his men the lash the next. It was he who'd appointed Jesse bosun, a highly eccentric act although a brilliant one because Jesse was the perfect man for the job. But he was also capable of enormous folly, like trying to rid the ship of cockroaches or ordering the men to attend prayer sessions on certain saints' days.

He was a rabid Baptist, a renegade Roman Catholic, addicted to Biblical quotation.

'Browning,' he boomed at me one day when I was attempting to lash something down on the foredeck. 'You are remarkably clumsy at that. Can you say with Gershom that you are "a stranger in a strange land"?'[2] He was a broad, stocky man with iron grey hair, yellow teeth and a cast in one eye that made it hard to tell where he was looking.

'Beg pardon, Cap'n,' says I. 'Must get below to the boilers ...'

'Hold hard, man. "The disciple is not above the master, nor the servant above his lord".'[3] His mad, off-centre eyes glinted and his hands worked convulsively, clenching and unclenching around the ship's rail. We had brilliant sunshine and calm weather, worse luck. I prayed for a wave to cover him with spray or for a marlin to break the surface, anything.

'What caused you to become a stowaway, Browning?'

My mind raced. You're usually safe with some kind of anti-woman sentiment with sailors. None of them has the least idea of what women are about. But there was no knowing with Clancy – his views on the Virgin Mary were unorthodox, or so a Catholic in the crew had told me.

'Woman trouble, Cap'n,' says I. 'The whole continent of Australia could not hold her and me.'

He stared out at the ocean. We were nearing the tropics. Flecks of phosphorus danced in the water.

' "It is better to live in a tree top, than with a brawling woman in a house",'[4] he said glumly.

'Quite,' I said.

He turned on his heel and went below. I breathed a sigh of relief and got back to work. At least he'd been sober; when tipsy the quotations could spew out for an hour and I once saw him have to be restrained when he went for a crewman shouting, ' "If thine eye offend thee . . ." '[5]

. . .

But all things considered the run across the Pacific to Honolulu wasn't too bad. The ship handled the going pretty well; the cargo didn't shift and I didn't get seasick. There was just enough rum to give a man something to look forward to, and to an old soldier like me (albeit one who discharged himself a little ahead of schedule), enforced abstinence from women wasn't a new experience. I'd had enough of women for a time anyway. I had occasional dreams of my dear wife, Elizabeth, in which she got fatter and fatter and her voice got louder as she expanded. Terrifying.

...

Honolulu, in the 1920s, was a wide open town. What else could you expect with sailors landing there every day after months at sea? Add to that the beachcombers, the land dealers, the money lenders and the gamblers and you had the makings of a hell-town. A hell in Paradise of course. The islands appeared to me to the most beautiful part of the world I'd ever seen as we steamed towards Oahu. I don't think so now; I'd have to give that award to parts of France. But then I'd only seen France as a bloodstained, body-strewn sea of mud. After my trials military, filmic and marital, I was ready for some relaxation and Honolulu looked like the perfect place for it.

I only knew one way to relax and that was with a bottle and a woman, or several bottles and women. I intimated as much to Jesse just before we went ashore. It was hot on board in the late afternoon. We were tied up at a wharf that had seen better days; the timbers creaked alarmingly and the fish and bugs in the water seemed to be eating the planks away. There were plenty of bugs in the air, too.

'You want Long Jack's saloon, my man,' Jesse said, 'but you ain't got a lot of time to fit all those sinful recreations in. We's off in the mo'ning of the day after tomorrow.'

'Hardly worth stopping,' I said.

'Naw, I wouldn't say that. Cap'n got radio messages to send about the cargo, 'n we need water and food.'

'Well, that's a day and two nights.'

Jesse let out his best *basso profundo* laugh. 'No, man, it's *one* night. Tomorrow we be cleanin' this ship stem to stern. She gotta pass inspection in 'Frisco. We'll all get drunk tonight fo' sure. An' we be sorry tomorrow. "Drink no longer water, but use a little wine for thy stomach's sake and thine often infirmities." '[6]

'You've been on this ship too long, Jesse,' I said.

CHAPTER TWO

But that's how it was. Long Jack's was a lantern-lit dive a short stagger from the wharves. The flimsy shack leaked people and music and smoke and noise. Since the crowd in the street seemed to be composed entirely of whores and pimps (I suppose there might have been a cardsharp or pickpocket or two), it didn't matter much whether you were inside or out. I rolled up, already oiled by a few tots of rum on board, about eight o'clock, with Jesse and a big Swede named Ingemar whom everyone called 'Dinge' on account of the whiteness of his hair and the paleness of his skin. He was a tigerish fighter in the fo'c'sle and I figured that I'd be safe in a war zone with this sort of company.

The Volstead Act didn't apply in Hawaii so there was no restriction on the selling of booze. In Long Jack's they'd have sold rye whisky to a ten-year-old who said he was a midget with a high voice – *if* he had the price of the drink. The place was rollicking along when we got there; someone about the same shade as Jesse was hammering a piano. The smoke was so thick it seemed to sit on top of the drink in your glass and the men and women were shouting as if that was the only way they ever conversed. And drinking, and dancing, and swearing, and putting their hands where the bishop shouldn't see.

'Yee-hah!' Dinge yelled and he plunged straight towards the bar pushing and shoving, eager to spend his money, some of which, I might add, he'd won from me.' Jesse sidled up to the piano player and they exchanged whispers. I grabbed a table and looked up at Jesse.

'Did you ask him if you could take over? Is that another thing you do well, Mr Bill?'

'No, suh. You come into a place like this and the first thing you check for is the ol' Jim Crow.'

I looked around. Some of the women were dark, some of the men were Orientals or looked as if they had island blood, but Jesse and the pianist were the only outright blacks.

'What did he say?'

'Said seein' I was big enough and in big white company it should be all right, long's I kept my hands off the light skin gals.'

Dinge was pushing back towards us carrying shot glasses of whisky and steins of beer. Big as he was, blind loyal to Jesse and a hell of fighter, I didn't fancy getting in the middle of a lynching party, even with him along.

'And will you?' I said anxiously.

Jesse grinned. 'Dey's all pink inside. Let us drink!'

We drank and drank some more. The pianist was joined by a horn man and a guitar player and they whipped up a storm. I got a tall, slant-eyed woman to dance with me but my British and Australian dancing style wasn't up to this action and she dropped me after one stumble through. I've always known when to fish and when to cut bait. I sat and watched while the people danced; mostly it was the women showing the men what to do but Jesse drank quietly for a while and then got up and cut a dark woman out of the herd by the bar. They swirled and jumped and he flipped her through the air and the crowd cheered. Then the pianist got up and did the same with the same woman. Dinge was deep in conversation with a girl about half his size over at the end of the bar. She stroked his white hair and nibbled his ear.

I looked up from my beer and Jesse, the pianist and the dark dancing woman were sitting opposite me.

'Havin' a good time, my man?' Jesse said.

'Oh, sure, Jesse, sure.'

'Good, well, me 'n Washington here are goin' to see this lady home.'

I reached over, grabbed the woman's brown hand and kissed the palm.

'He's cute,' she said.

'He sure is,' said Jesse. 'See you on bo'd, Dick. Say goodnight to Dinge for me.'

I nodded. They went out. I looked over to the bar and saw Dinge's broad back and the girl's narrow one disappearing through the beaded curtain that hung over one of the side doors. It was after midnight, the place was still jumping but I was all alone. I bought another beer and settled down to feel sorry for myself over it.

'Lonely, sailor?'

I glanced up from the froth; the women was thin-faced with drawn-back dark hair and enormous eyes. She was wearing a loose blouse and scarf around the neck fastened with a strangely shaped clasp. There was a flurry of cloth marked with stars and crescent moons as she flicked at her long skirt and sat down. The fingernails, wrapped around her glass, were long and blood red.

'Good evening,' I said. I was about half a glass short of the maudlin stage. 'I'm getting lonely. My friends have left. How did you know I was a sailor?'

'Are you joking?' Her accent was American, not harsh like Clancy's and the other Yankees I'd recently encountered, but softer and slower, more like the Southerners. 'You can tell a sailor from his walk. You roll like a log in a river.'

Really? thinks I. Have to get rid of that before I hit Hollywood. I smiled at her, admitted I was ashore for the night and bought her a drink. Her name was Atlanta Adams and I was too polite to ask her what she did for a living. It seemed to be obvious. I was more than a little stewed and it wasn't long before I had her on the dance floor and then in a clinch in a dark corner. She seemed oddly reluctant.

'Let's go to my place,' she said. She was looking deep into my eyes with what I took to be sexual interest.

'Yes,' I said. I would've looked into her eyes too, but they wouldn't stay still. 'Less have 'nother drink first.'

I got two more drinks and bumped into a man in a spotless white suit as I carried them back to the table. The liquid splashed his suit and he grabbed at me.

'You clumsy fool!' He waved a fist in my face. I saw a big, face-cutting diamond ring on one finger and flinched back.

'Sorry,' I said. 'Only beer, 'n juice, 'n, 'n . . . wha' was that drink, A'lanta?' I tried to find a handkerchief to mop him down and I split some more liquor on his shirt. He punched me on the shoulder. I dropped the drinks on his white shoes. He roared, swung, missed me and hit a man standing beside me. *He* swore and punched back. The man in the white suit swung a chair. I ducked and put my hands over my head. The floor started to feel like an ice rink. Atlanta Adams struggled through flailing, cursing bodies and grabbed my belt.

'Come on,' she said. 'Don't fight. Don't hurt your hands.'

She supported me as we stumbled out. The fight was going full swing and so was the music; there was a white piano player now but the beat was still black. I nearly gagged on the fresh air outside but it helped to sober me. 'How far?' I said.

She guided me out of the path of a sugarcane wagon and held me up on the corner of two muddy roads. There had been some rain evidently while we'd been in the saloon.

'This way.' She guided me to the left past shops, two more saloons and down a narrow street lit only at one end, the end we were leaving. In different company I'd have been alarmed, but she talked on quietly as we walked. Couldn't for the life of me remember what she said, but she inspired confidence. Let's face it, after some weeks at sea, being deserted by my pals and with the liquor I'd stowed on board, I'd have gone home with Eleanor Roosevelt.[7]

She got a key out of a pocket in her skirt and unlocked a door directly on the street. I expected the usual thug at a desk, or a table under a naked, fly-blown light, but instead there was a well-lit short passage and a set of stairs, also well-lit and carpeted, leading to an imposing door which she opened with another key. The room was large and cool; a fan was turning in the ceiling and I could see a large bed half-hidden by a partition made of woven cane. There was a balcony off to one side. *Ideal for a drink afterwards,* thinks I and I started to propel her towards the bed.'

She was a tall strongly built woman, I now noticed, and when she resisted she was hard to move.

'None of that,' she said. 'You have a most interesting pair of hands – I just want to tell your fortune!'

CHAPTER THREE

I was too surprised to protest. She hustled me into a small room off to one side and sat me at a round table. It was dim but I could see paintings and markings on the walls that recalled the decorations on her skirt. She looked into my eyes again and I felt oddly relaxed. The hard, straight-backed chair felt comfortable too. She produced cards from somewhere, larger than the sort of pasteboards that must have cost me a couple of million dollars through my long and chancy life. She started to lay them out, muttering the whole time and clicking her tongue.

'Well now, anything to drink?'

'Shh. I've got to concentrate.'

Concentrate she did, for what seemed like an hour. You might think I'd be bored, sitting there, sobering up and with a good-looking woman who'd very clearly given me the hands-off, playing gypsy queen. But I wasn't – you see, all the muttering and exclamation, all the gasps and long silences were about *me*!

She laid the cards out in different patterns, picked them up according to some system or other, shuffled and spread them again.

'A long life,' she said. She took my right hand and examined the palm carefully. Her hands were smooth and cool.

'Oh, good. Healthy, I hope?'

'Long, very long, if certain dangerous obstacles are overcome.'

'Ah.'

'Money.'

'Good, good.'

'Much earned, much spent . . .'

'I chuckled. 'None saved, eh?'

'Much wasted, thrown foolishly away.' She was right there, by God!

'An adventurous life – travel, speed, crowds of people and . . .'

'Yes, yes?'

'Periods of loneliness, terrible loneliness. I can't quite understand.'

'Let's not bother. Stick to the good stuff.'

'It is puzzling. There are horses and . . . slaves, it is as if you lead several lives and many of them not of this century.' She gasped.

'What? What?'

'Reincarnation! You are my first! A genuine reincarnate, carrying the aura of other lives. The cards tell it all.'

'Steady on. Don't get carried away.'

'I could hypnotise you, take you back to those earlier lives.'

I pushed back my chair and stood up. I reeled and nearly fell. 'Oh no, you don't. Nothing like that for Dick Browning!'

'Sit down, please. That is another strange thing. I've worked on the name Richard Kelly Browning and it reveals much about you. But there are contradictions, as if you have many names . . .'

'Yes, quite, well . . . very interesting.'

She riffled through the pack again and flicked three cards out. 'Beware of the Israelite and strong drink.' She flicked the third card with her long red nail. 'And the number fifty-two is very unlucky for you.'

'Avoid Jews, whisky and poker,' I said. 'I'll remember that.'

I was still standing; she stood up and moved towards me. She reached for my hand again, probably wanting to check the life line again, but I chose to misinterpret the action. I put my arm around her and pulled her close. I kissed her hard, she started to respond, then drew back quickly.

'Ah, no, no.'

Why the devil not?'

'You forget that I have seen your life, laid out right there on the table.'

'So?'

'There are many women and you do harm to them all. You are very attractive to women but you do not make them happy.'

'I say, that's a bit hard. I . . .'

'No. Your life is drenched with women's tears.'

Well, that was a facer, to be sure. It took the sap out of me and no mistake. I moved towards the door.

'There is one more thing.'

I spun around. *Some good for old Dick after all in this mumbo-jumbo?* thinks I. Change of heart?

'Ten dollars, please – for the reading.'

. . .

Somehow I found my way back to the ship. It wasn't that I was drunk; all the talk of dangerous obstacles and Israelites and women's tears had fixed that, but I didn't know in what direction to head. The woman had taken me away from the docks area and I walked along the dark streets, brushing aside fragrant bushes and slipping on wet roads and generally making heavy going of it until I decided that the night was mine and I'd enjoy the walk. Besides, it was my first time ashore in the tropics and everything was unfamiliar to me.

I can feel it now as I sit here in this damned farmhouse with the sun beating down on the roof and wild dogs howling in the foothills – in Hawaii the air was sweet and heavy and seemed to get inside my shift and run down my ribs as sweat. The trees and bushes had strong smells, some sharp like a sliced lemon and others soft and subtle like expensive perfume. That was one of the things that gave me steering problems – no smell of the sea over all those essences.

The rain had cleared leaving a sky with a high, bright moon and stars that seemed closer to the earth than they did in Australia. There were a few people in the streets, mostly wearing white clothes so that they looked ghostly in the moonlight. People murmured goodnight to each other in the soft voice that seems characteristic of Hawaii. Not in the taverns, the drunk tank or police stations of course, which is where I've spent a good deal of my time on sub-sequent visits. I think that was the most relaxed time I ever spent there in fact, that night, strolling back to the ship. I even heard, and hummed along with, some soft gospel singing from a house high above the street and half-hidden in the palm trees.

But when I spotted the whore, in the cloth of gold dress, with her back to the building on the corner and expelling a stream of smoke into the starry sky, I knew I was back on course. Ordinarily, I might have engaged her in conversation to see whether she was to my taste or not. I'd had a disappointment but it wouldn't have been the first evening of my life that the course of commercial love had taken a turn or two. But, somehow, I wasn't in the mood. Perhaps it was my old fear of the pox (that could be seen as an 'obstacle' surely), or maybe I just wasn't in the mood. I can't believe it was the gospel singing.

The only bed I got into that night was my bunk on the *Sternwood*.

. . .

Jesse hadn't exaggerated about the work. Those of us who'd slept on the ship were roused out at dawn and given cleaning, scrubbing, scouring and painting tasks that looked, at the beginning, as if they would last a week. As the others straggled aboard they were pressed into service. Some of them were grey and shaky and looked as if they could scarcely stand let alone climb, lift, and crawl through holes the way they were obliged to. Odd thing was, no one protested and every hand did his share. Sailors are like that; in the midst of all the abuse they direct at each other and the world, there's a terrific cameraderie and co-operative spirit. All redounds to the profits of the owners of course.

Jesse and Dinge were there by midday, pitching in and sweating the booze out of their systems under the high Hawaiian sun. I'd secured a relatively soft greasing job and squatted down near to where Jesse was chipping off rust and old paint the consistency of concrete.

'Good time last night, Jesse?'

'The best, man, the best. You?'

'I met a woman.'

'Felt sure you would.'

'She told my fortune.'

Just then Tom Clancy saw me bludging[8] in the shade and roared for me to come forward.

'I ain't never heard it called *that* before,' Jesse shouted after me.

The work wasn't going fast enough for Tom. 'Did I see you having breakfast this morning, Browning. One of the few?'

'Yes, sir.'

'I was surprised, I'll admit. Thought you would be a carouser.'

'No, sir.'

'Well, "If any would not work, neither should he eat."[9] Come with me.' He led me to the bow where a rough harness had been rigged to allow a man to lower himself over the side and down to the water line. He handed me a paint pot and brush. 'Paint the name on bold and bright, Browning. Bows and stern, and have it done before the shadow falls across or you'll make a mess of it.'

'Aye, aye, Cap'n.' It sounds easy but in fact I put in a couple of the hardest hours I've ever worked in my life. You had to lower yourself with one hand while balancing the paint pot in the other, and then it was a matter of leg-bracing yourself against the side of the ship sufficiently far out to wield the brush. Going over the letters was easy enough – although I very soon wished the damned boat had been called the *Ian* or something such, straight up and down and short. I had to haul myself up after every letter, move the mechanism along, and lower down again.

Jesse paid me one visit. He spat over the side and missed me by a whisker.

'Hey!' I yelled.

'Oh, sorry, man. Didn't know there was anybody there. Hope none o' dem big harbour sharks takes a fancy to yore ass just suspended above the water there.'

That gave me something else to think about.

I did a good job though. Clancy came as close to paying me a compliment as he ever did, when he looked over the side with me, be-spattered with paint, sunburnt and panting beside him.

' "A good name is rather to be chosen than great riches." '[10]

'I wouldn't say that, Cap'n,' I said.

I was an exhausted man when I threw myself down on the bunk that night. The usual things were going on in the fo'c'sle – cards, toenail paring, smoking. 'Denver' Jefferson was playing his guitar and moaning softly:

As I walked out on the streets of Laredo,
As I walked out on Laredo one day . . .

'Say, Jesse, where's this Laredo?' I asked.

'Not sure, Dick – Mexico, maybe, or Texas.'

'You spent much time in California?'

'Born and raised in Bakersfield.'

'Ever been to Hollywood?'

Jesse sat up abruptly and slapped his naked black thigh. 'I knew it! I just knew it! Boys, Dick here goin' to Hollywood. Gwine be a movie star.'

'Denver' quit plucking the strings. 'Had a sister went to be a movie star,' he said softly.

Dinge took his little finger out of his ear and used his pocket knife to excavate the wax. 'Hope she's prettier 'n you. How'd she make out?'

'Denver' picked up the guitar, adjusted the bridge and strummed a mournful chord. 'Not so good. She's a whore in Tijuana last I heard.'

'You hear that, Richard? Maybe you should stick to the sea. You did jus' fine today. Cap'n Tom practically pattin' you on the back.'

'And tomorrow he could be knocking me over the side. No, mates, I'm getting off in 'Frisco. I'll invite you all to my first big party in Hollywood.'

'I'll hold you to that,' Jesse said quietly. 'I'd sure like to see how those Chaplins and Fairbanks and Keatons 'd take to old Jesse rolling up with his hand out for a martini.'

'Good luck to you, Dick,' 'Denver' said. 'And when you get to Tijuana look up my sister. Her name's Billie Sue.'

Jesse rolled off his bunk and opened his hand to reveal a new, sealed pack of cards which nestled snugly in his big, pink palm. 'What about a few games of chance. If'n you win, Richard, you could arrive in Hollywood by chauffeur-driven limousine and make a big splash. Now I *know* you got a little gold put by. Why not use it to underwrite your future?'

'How will I get to Hollywood if I lose?'

'You can use your thumb,' 'Denver' said, 'or you can ride the rails. That's the way half the Hollywood stars got there in the first place.'

I was tired and my vision was blurry. After working the ratchet on the harness and painting STERNWOOD three times I could hardly open and close my fingers, but I felt lucky. I was heading for the USA, Hollywood and a million dollars.

'Deal the cards, Jesse,' I said.

CHAPTER FOUR

I lost all my gold to Jesse and the others on the *Sternwood* of course. They took pity on me and remitted a few dollars. Clancy gave me ten dollars saying that he calculated it was what I'd earned over and above my passage. He tried to persuade me to stay on for another voyage.

'Round the Horn,' he said. 'The experience of a lifetime.'

I shook my head. He shrugged and filled in a paper which stated that I had been hired on as a seaman in Australia and had committed no crimes and suffered from no communicable diseases.

' "The hireling fleeth, because he is an hireling, and careth not for the sheep." '[11]

I wished I'd paid more attention at Dudleigh so I could've topped him with a line of Shakespeare or Milton. They were very big on Milton at Dudleigh. But nothing came to mind so I just tipped my cap and left the ship. Armed with my passport and that paper from Clancy, entry to the United States of America was a piece of cake. I may have stated that I'd be seeking a berth on a ship back to Australia within a month or something such, but I've entered and left under so many names and in so many different circumstances (including inside the trunk of a '48 Cadillac at El Paso), that I don't exactly recall.

The thing was that I was in California and only around four hundred miles from Hollywood. But those four hundred miles proved to be hard to cover. San Francisco was booming; buildings were going up everywhere. Some of these may have been simply repairing the earthquake damage but a lot of the activity seemed to be looking forward rather than backward. The Panama Canal had not long been opened and that, plus the end of the war, had boosted the city as a place for goods to pass through. Boom towns are expensive. I stayed in a hotel near Fisherman's Wharf for a few days to get the feel of the place, but it soon became obvious that I'd have to move on and watch every dollar, as well as earn a few, on the way to Hollywood.

I started out by hitchhiking which was unknown in Australia at that time but it had already become a common practice in the States. No thumbing, though. The technique was to stand by the side of the road with a sign telling the drivers where you were going. I didn't know the geography so it took me a while to get the hang of this. It was no good holding up a sign saying HOLLYWOOD. No one was going that far. From San Francisco you had to indicate Stockton or Modesto and from there Merced or Madera. I learned this in a roadhouse where I stopped for coffee and bread, the cheapest stomach-filler available.

I stuck it for a while, getting less than halfway and wearing my boots thin. It was hard to keep clean; the roads were dusty one stretch and muddy the next. I slept in a barn one night and nearly froze. I ran out of tobacco and had a miserable time. I was so intent on getting to Hollywood that I didn't notice my fellow travellers for those first few days. I tramped along looking for cars, feeling my sore feet and dreaming. When I got on the road for the fourth or fifth day, wearing the beginnings of a beard and feeling like death, I was suddenly aware that I wasn't alone. I was squatting by the side of the road brushing the dust off my sign when a hand appeared over my shoulder offering a piece of charcoal.

'Here, friend. If they can't read it they won't stop worse than they won't stop if they can read it.'

I looked up. He was a tall, thin character with a prominent widow's peak and an even more prominent Adam's apple. His clothes were like mine – derived from some other trade, gambling perhaps, dusty and road-stained.

'Thanks.' I took the charcoal and blacked in the word.

'Dwight Springfield,' he said. He held out a hard-knuckled hand which I shook. 'You headed for Mexico?'

I shook my head. 'Why would anyone be going to Mexico?'

'Excuse me, I hear that you're a foreigner. British?'

I made the usual quick check, no danger, all right to tell the truth. 'Australian,' I said.

'That so? You a veteran?'

'I beg your pardon.'

'Were you in the war? Seems to me there was something military about you – the way you walked. Not much, mind, but a little bit.'

'Yes, I was in the war.'

'Thought so.'

A car whizzed by just then throwing up dust; I thought I caught a glimpse of a single occupant. This was the most propitious arrangement for getting a ride and I cursed Dwight whatever-his-name-was for distracting me. 'Why the hell would I be going to Mexico?' I said impatiently.

'Easy friend, no offence. I just thought, you being a soldier and all, that you might want to get into the war down there?'

'I didn't know there *was* a war down there. The war's been over for two years.'

'This is a revolution, *hombre*. Both sides need skilled military men. I was in it from the first battle of the Marne to the second.[12] Them was the days.'

I was still feeling testy about missing the possible ride. 'Not as an American you weren't.'

'No, you're dead right there. I was with the British at first, joined up over there, and later under Pershing . . .'

It was one of those many times in my life when I should have just tipped my hat politely and sloped off, but I didn't. After the close comradeship of the *Sternwood* . . . [on the tape Browning coughs, splutters and mutters something about 'piling on the shit here'. This suggests that his account of fo'c'sle life was very selective. Ed.] . . . I found life on the California road lonely and the company of a fellow human being, even a madman like Dwight Springfield, preferable to being on my own.

'I was on the Somme mostly,' I said. 'NCO – Corporal, Acting Sergeant.' That was stretching it a bit; the night the three stripes had been offered I'd deserted. Still, distance lends enchantment.

'Let's walk along together a spell,' Springfield says. 'We've got things in common.'

'Long as we don't talk about the war,' I said. I didn't want to get into discussions of units and times and places, seeing as how I'd waited the bloody shambles out safe in a bolthole in Switzerland.

'I understand,' Dwight Springfield said. 'Real fighters aren't talkers.'

We tramped along and the sun got higher in the sky but it was March or April and the air was moist and warm. We were fairly high up, in prime agricultural country, mostly given over to grape-growing. There was no need to go hungry around there if you could jump a fence, but the few farmers I'd seen – long-jawed, rawboned characters in denim overalls and big boots – kind of discouraged the idea.

'I don't believe I got your name, sir,' Springfield says.

I stopped and scanned the horizon for the small dust cloud that indicated an approaching car. I told him my name.

'Well, Sergeant Browning, I think this is a most propitious meeting.'

'Less of the "Sergeant",' says I. 'I'm a civilian and proud of it.'

'Nonsense.' Springfield proceeded to fill me in on the struggle in Mexico as we walked, stopped, displayed our signs – his read

Bakersfield, which showed that he was an optimist – and walked on. I listened against my will, mind, but as I say I was glad of his company and he had cigarettes in his pocket which probably helped to keep me attentive. The names all sounded like cigar brands to me – Zapata, Carranza and so on – but I gathered that General Something was recently installed in the top job and that the hills were full of people waiting to overthrow him.

'It's the national sport,' Springfield said, 'toppling governments. It's a game to them, really.'

I accepted a Fatima and a light. 'Do people get killed in these games?'

'Only peasants.'

I grunted and we moved on as Springfield explained how the rebels were supplied with guns they couldn't use while the government had conscripts they couldn't train. Springfield pulled his wide-brimmed hat down to get a little more shade from the climbing sun. He walked with a long, easy stride and carried his carpetbag as if there was nothing in it although I'd have been willing to bet there was at least one firearm – he was that sort of man. 'A guy could work for both sides, I bet,' he said, 'and get rich.'

He was talking urgently by this time and the word 'rich' had fired my imagination as it always would, so we didn't notice the flatbed truck that had passed us and pulled up a little ahead.

'Hey, you fellers!' A man wearing overalls and a straw hat had got out of the truck and was waving to us impatiently. It was a newish truck but he looked like a hayseed so Springfield and I took our time.

'Heading south,' the farmer said, squinting at our signs. 'How'd you like to ride a few miles and earn a dollar?'

'I'd rather ride a mile and earn a few dollars,' Springfield said.

'Haw, haw! That's a good 'un. Well, depends on how you can work. You there, you look like a workin' man.' He meant me, dressed still as a sailor in knit cap, blue denim shirt, canvas trousers and heavy boots.

'I can work if I have to,' I said. 'What've you got in mind?'

'Got a whole truckload of jugs of wine and a bunch of deliveries to make. Nigger who usually helps me run off.' He took off his hat and wiped a high, balding forehead. 'Not that I'd insult you by offering you work only a nigger'd do. I help him, I'd help you.'

'Do what?' Springfield said.

'Why, unload the jugs. Finish up just this side of Fresno – get you boys on your way.'

Springfield pulled at his moustache; like me he wore a full moustache which was accompanied now by a couple of days of beard growth. He looked dangerous and I guess I must have looked the same. Seemed to me we were lucky to be offered the ride and the money, but it never does to look too grateful.

'You mentioned the pay,' I said.

'Two dollars each if we finish the run, one if we don't.'

Springfield ambled to the back of the truck, lifted the tarpaulin and took a look at the cargo. He spat in the dust and strolled back. 'Plus a jug each at the end of the job,' he said.

'You got a deal. Ride up here with me, gents. My name is Abner Wynn. Who do I have the honour of employing?'

'Springfield.'

'And Browning,' I said. We looked at each other and laughed when we heard the names teamed up like that. Wynn smiled uneasily as he held the truck cab door open.

'I guess Abner here ain't no veteran,' I said, swinging my bag up and climbing aboard.

'I got a family,' Wynn said.

'So've I,' said Springfield.

. . .

Wynn drove his truck slowly and carefully the way he should, given the goods he was carrying. We stopped at roadhouses, and family stores and a poolroom, and unloaded the jugs. They were stoneware, big and heavy and there were a lot of them. Wynn hadn't mentioned loading on the empties but that was part of the job too. There was red wine and muscatel and we tried to persuade Wynn to open a jug to give us a little nourishment along the way.

'No deal. You get your jug after the last stop and not a drop before. Drunk men drop jugs.'

They can cut that on your tombstone,' Springfield said savagely as he hauled a jug in each hand towards a flight of steps. Every delivery point seemed to have steps up to it.

'They'll be cuttin' yours long before mine if I'm any judge,' Wynn replied.

'I'll have more fun along the way.'

'Don't know about that. I've wore out two wives and you should see my present one – eighteen she is, and a peach.'

It was no use trying to get the better of Wynn, he had an answer for everything.

The last stop was made on the outskirts of Fresno and Wynn paid up like a man. Two dollars for each of us and a jug – Springfield took muscatel and I, one-time salesman for Robespierre and Co., Importers of French Wines & Spirits, took a gallon of dry red. Springfield uncorked his jug and sniffed.

'Is it good stuff, Abner?'

'I wouldn't know. I'm teetotal, totally. Have been since January one, nineteen hundred. Took the pledge.' He pulled off his straw hat and stuck his face close to mine. 'How old d'you think I am, limey?'

'I'm not English,' I said. 'Australian.'

'Could've fooled me. How old?'

He'd hefted his share of the jugs full and empty, climbed up and down from the truck and done all the driving. I noticed how straight he stood and the absence of belly sag. I looked closely at him; he was bald but his face was scarcely lined and he seemed to have a full set of teeth. There were wrinkles on his neck but more evidence around there of firm muscle and sinew. 'Sixty,' I said, 'give or take a year or two.'

'You hedge your bets, son. I'm seventy-five and goin' strong. Don't drink, don't smoke, don't eat no red meat.'

Springfield had taken a pull on his jug. He grinned and wiped his mouth. 'You're really twenty-one, Abner,' he said. 'It's just all that self-denial makes it *feel* like seventy-five.' This was the first time I heard anyone crack that joke – I wish I had a dollar for every time I've heard it since.

'Goodbye, boys, and good luck.' The truck roared off, kicking up dust and leaving Springfield and me standing in the road with our bags, a little more tired, with a little more money and the wherewithal to get drunk. Not a bad result for a day.

I crooked my fingers through the handle in the neck of the jug, lifted my bag and took a step towards the south. The sun was just sinking towards the trees in the west – fig trees, stretching for what looked like a mile.

'Well, Springfield,' I said lightly. 'I'm sorry, I don't know your rank . . .'

'Major.'

'I reckon you'd boost it by one pip at least. Well, Captain Springfield, where now?'

'Have you got anything on you to eat, Sergeant?'

'No, sir!'

'Neither have I. But we've got these.' He swung his jug. 'There's a hobo jungle near here and with these as our calling cards we'll eat like kings. There's just one thing though.'

'Yes?'

'Put that two dollars in your ear or up your ass or wherever you reckon no one's going to reach it.'

CHAPTER FIVE

Dwight Springfield told me that his family had picked fruit and grapes in the San Joaquin valley when he was a boy and that was how he knew so much about the area. This was before a rich uncle had taken him under his wing, educated him and sent him to military academy. The latter bit was probably all lies; I never saw much evidence of education in Springfield and his military knowledge seemed to be more practical than theoretical. But he knew this bit of California sure enough. We tramped south for a while, took a turn west down a narrow, bumpy road, crossed a sluggish, reedy creek by means of a decrepit bridge and there we were, in the hobo jungle.

It was like and unlike an Aboriginal riverbank camp in Australia. There was the same use of sheet iron in the shelters, the same sort of cooking fires and washing lines for clothes, but there were important differences. No women here, of course, and there was none of that feeling of being permanent that the blacks' camps had. For these men, maybe twenty of them, this wasn't the end of the line. Some of them were going up, some were going on to another place just like this, and some were going down – although God knows, down couldn't have been very far.

I had a camera in my bag but this was no place for taking pictures. Eyes ready to be hostile turned on us as Springfield and I ambled up, tired enough not to look too sassy, and with coats slung so as to conceal the jugs. Note I don't say *pairs* of eyes – one of the men wore an eye patch which gave him a dangerous look, and one young fellow gazed blankly ahead of him. He was blind, I found, and in the constant care of one of the others.

'Howdy, gents,' Springfield says.

'Howdy.' The speaker was stretched out on the ground near one of the several fires that were burning. He was long and spare with wild hair and eyes that looked as red as the coals in the fire. One look at him and I felt like stepping back and heading into town to spend the two dollars on a bed and some food on a table.

'Okay if we set?' Springfield asked the question of the five or six men nearest the fire, although he managed to make it sound as if he'd be most interested in the views of the man with the red eyes.

There was a murmur of 'Sure' and 'He'p y'self and Springfield gestured for me to follow his example. We moved away from the fire a little, put down our bags and lowered the coat-covered jugs carefully to prevent the sound of liquid sloshing or stoneware clinking. Apparently etiquette dictated that we should keep ourselves to ourselves for a while and this we did, lighting cigarettes and leaning back against a tree.

'We should've gone to town,' I whispered. 'These guys'll cut our throats while we sleep.'

'The hell they will. Which one you distrust the most?'

I inclined my head at the group by the fire. 'That one, with the patch.'

Springfield sighed. 'You've got a lot to learn, Sergeant. Have a look at what's stickin' up out of the bib of his coverall.'

I squinted and saw an oblong object I couldn't identify.

'Harmonica,' Springfield said. 'Music man, probably the most harmless of the bunch.'

'What're we doing here, anyway? When we finished that job I was too tired to ask.'

'You want to get south, don't you?'

'Yes.'

'An' arrive with a dollar in your jeans?'

'Yes.'

'Same here. Only way to do that's to grab a freight. And the only *safe* way to do that is to pick up all the information we need in a place like this here.'

'And what information's that?'

I didn't get an answer because Red Eye had got up and was mooching over towards us.

'Smoke-sharing time,' said Springfield. He was right. Red Eye introduced himself as Buff Clayton and graciously accepted one of Springfield's Fatimas. He broke it in two and passed the other half to a stocky blonde man who lounged across and volunteered a match.

'Thanks Jeff,' Clayton said. 'You two fellers look like you done some workin' an' walkin'.'

'Enough of both for a while,' Springfield said.

'Where you headed?'

'South,' said Springfield. I nodded.

'He ever talk?' Clayton blew smoke over my shoulder.

'South,' I said.

'Ah, a limey.'

'Australian.'

'That right? Now you can tell me about them kingaroos, I guess.'

'Kangaroos.'

'What's the difference?'

'Well . . .'

'We can skip the nature lesson for now, Buff,' Springfield said. 'My belly's growling. You boys got anything to eat?'

'You come right out with it, don't you?' Clayton drew on his cigarette and pinched out the butt which he tucked into his shirt pocket. 'Now there ain't a man here hasn't been on the road longer than you two can remember. Take a look at the boot leather you don't believe me.'

I looked around; the fires had had been added to and were burning brightly. The men had sorted themselves into two groups and had drawn in closer for the warmth. Suddenly, all eighteen of them (I had time to do a count) were looking at us.

'I believe you,' Springfield said quietly.

'An' you come panhandlin' to *us*?'

I could feel the fingers of fear creeping up my spine; the bearded, half-bearded and bristly faces seemed to draw closer and Clayton's eyes burned like brothel lamps. My leg cramped the way it always does when physical danger looms in front of me.

'I wouldn't do that,' Springfield said. He reached back and whipped the coats free of the jugs. 'We're hungry but we weren't planning on being thirsty.'

Clayton made an odd movement of his hand, like a Catholic crossing himself. Maybe that's what he *was* doing. He blinked a few times and the glow in his eyes dimmed. 'Why didn't you say so? How does beans and rabbit stew sound?'

'Fine,' said Springfield.

'Fine,' I said.

. . .

They cooked the beans and stew over the fire, flavoured it with roadside herbs and some of the dago red and it was delicious. It was a sort of loaves and fishes situation. Everyone brought something out from somewhere – bread, onions, coffee. The wine jugs went round and there was plenty for everyone because two of the hoboes didn't drink and Springfield drank very sparingly. I had my share and his I guess, and I was feeling fine by the time the fires had died down and we were all relaxed, smoking and just sipping on the jugs.

The man with the eye patch played his harmonica over by one of the shelters, almost out of hearing. I caught the strains of 'Oh Susannah', played slow, and other tunes I didn't recognise. There'd been a lot of 'Thankee's' as we'd passed the jugs and there was no hostility towards Springfield and me in the camp now. As is the way with men on the move, and I should know because I've been down on my luck and doing the gypsy more times than I care to recall, hostility was replaced by curiosity. Jeff and the blind man wanted to know about Australia; one of the others was a seaman and wanted to hear about the *Sternwood* and Honolulu; Clayton turned out to be more interested in our futures than our pasts, or in kangaroos.

'I was to Mexico once,' he said, after Springfield had outlined his plan. 'Prospectin' for gold.'

'Find any?' Springfield asked.

'Found it an' lost it.'

'How so?'

'Long story, mister. I was down there with two other guys, good guys but, you know, the loneliness and all, and no women – those things play hell with a man.'

'I thought there were plenty of women in Mexico,' I said.

'Not where we were. Just work and dirt and sand, plus Mexican bandits and Indians.'

'And gold,' Springfield said.

'And greed, and wind,'[13] Clayton said. 'How about you from Down Under? My pappy dug for gold down there. You ever do any prospectin'?'

'No.'

'Say, you ever see Less Darcy fight?'

'Lez,' I said. 'It's pronounced Lez. Yes, I saw him.'

'Wisht I had, must've been good. Well, you're in the land of the free now, what're your plans?'

I don't know what it was; I was drunk so maybe his red eyes weren't really glowing again and maybe there was nothing unusual in the way he was eyeing my bag, I just thought Mr Clayton might need keeping in line. Springfield shot me a glance that suggested he had the same idea.

'Well,' I said. 'I might take a look at Mexico too, but I've a mind to continue the sort of work I did in the moving pictures back in Australia.'

'And what was that?'

I'd started breaking Springfield's cigarettes in two as well. I plucked the stub from behind my ear, leaned down to the fire for a stick and lit it. 'Stunt work,' I said, 'riding and shooting. Particularly shooting.'

Springfield passed the muscatel jug across and Clayton took a sip. 'Best of luck,' he said.

'But first we've got travelling to do, Buff,' says Springfield. 'Now you'd be the man to tell us about the freights – when they come, where they slow for the grades and how to dodge the bulls.'

'That's so,' Clayton said. 'I'm the man for that all right. Would you have another smoke on you?'

I was sleepy and could hardly follow the discussion of boxcars and freights and wagons, and I had no idea of where Snake Pass and the Rocky River ford might be. The second last thing I remember after I crammed my head down onto my bag and draped my coat over myself was hatred in Buff Clayton's voice as he spoke a name.

'Broken-nose Flanagan,' Clayton said.

The last thing I remember was Springfield's response. 'Oh, fuck, no,' he said.

. . .

Soon after daylight the following morning I was crouched in the wet grass at the bottom of a railway embankment. My head ached from the rough wine of the night before and my body ached from the unaccustomed work we'd done and the hard ground I'd slept on. I was feeling depressed and anxious. Springfield was chirpy. He'd strapped his coat to his back and got me to do the same. We had long rope loops on our bags so we could sling them too when we needed our hands free. It was cold, my teeth were chattering and I hadn't had any coffee.

'Never jumped a freight before, Dick?' Springfield asked. At least he'd dropped the 'Sergeant' nonsense.

I shook my head.

'Nothing to it. We'll hear her a mile off. She'll come up the grade there, real slow. We run alongside, pick a car and jump in. Sometimes you have to slide open a door or cling on for a while until you can get up and over. That's harder.'

'Up and over?'

'Over the top. Over a locked car until you can get down to an open one.'

'What if there isn't an open one?'

'Always is. The boys in the yards leave 'em open. They're on our side.'

'Don't the bulls close them?'

He looked at me through narrowed eyes. 'You were listening last night, huh?'

'Some,' I said. 'Who's Broken-nose Flanagan?'

'Meanest bull on the Southern Pacific.'

'Is he likely to be on this Pullman Deluxe we're going to board?'

'Can't tell. Hope not. Hey, I think I hear it.'

I heard a long, lonely whistle note. It sounded like a dog baying over its dead partner and I shivered some more.

'Come on.' Springfield climbed the bank and I went after him. My boots felt heavy and my legs were stiff and leaden. There was a pile of sleepers stacked a yard or so from the track and we crouched down beside them as the train approached.

'Sling your bag.' I put my arms through the loops. 'Check your bootlaces and your belt and pull that cap down. You don't want anything flapping when the time comes.'

I looked down the track; the train seemed to be coming on at an impossible speed, but then it started on the upgrade and slowed.

'Stay here long's we can, then hustle. Just follow me.'

I wanted to roll back down the embankment and I should have, but Springfield was in charge of the situation and that seemed to rob me of the power to make my own decisions. It's always been a grievous fault of mine – following madmen.

The train came up the slope and it didn't seem so hard all of a sudden. The boxcars seemed to be moving past slowly and Springfield and I jogged along beside them easily, stepping on the ends of the sleepers.

'Next one coming up,' Springfield said, 'door's open. It's jump an' roll. Watch it, she's picking up speed.'

We jogged a bit faster and I gathered myself to jump and roll. Springfield jumped through the opening. I took another step to get on my right foot for the jump.

'Jesus, no! It's Flanagan!' Springfield moaned.

I looked behind and saw a man lumbering towards me, going faster than the train and faster than me. He was tall and wide and his broad features were spread flat as if he was pressing his huge red face against glass.

'Jump, Dick!'

I was still moving but felt as if I was frozen solid. Only the accompanying motion of the train carried me on.

'Jump!'

Flanagan came on; he was moving faster and so was the train. So was I. *Jesus, we're going fucking down!* I thought. I jumped and scrambled for a hold; out of the corner of my eye I saw Flanagan's arm swing up and something flew at me like an attacking bird. Noise and light filled my skull and I was falling, floating, drowning . . .

CHAPTER SIX

When I regained my senses I was lying on the ground under the scrawniest-looking tree I had ever seen in my life. The sun was beating down fiercely out of a deep blue sky and this tree was just barely shading my eyes. The rest of my face was hot and I could feel rivers of sweat running over my body. Springfield was sitting next to me in the dirt. He had a long-barrelled pistol on his knee and was taking a swig of a clear liquid from a bottle with a coloured label.

'Water,' I gasped. My mouth and throat felt ready to be rented out for sand mining.

'Dick, you son of a gun. Welcome back. Can't give you no water here, boy. Take a swig of this, but take it slow.'

I lifted my head which felt heavy and sloppy like an over-ripe watermelon, and let him put the bottle to my mouth. A trickle of the liquid went in and down and I bucked and let out a roar.

'Jesus Christ, what is that?'

Springfield didn't answer. He was sweaty and dirty with a longer growth of beard around his moustache. I raised a trembling hand and felt the lengthening stubble on my own face.

'How long since . . .?'

'Since Flanagan got you with his shillelagh? Three days.'

I grabbed his hand and forced the bottle down again. After this sip I snorted and gasped. Drinking that stuff was like sucking in the sun. 'What is this?'

'Tequila,' Springfield said. 'Made from cactus.'

'Where are we?'

'San Ricardo.'

'Where's that? Southern California?'

'Mexico.'

I eased myself slowly up into a sitting position. Everything hurt, as if all my joints and limbs had rusted stiff. I worked my arms around in the sockets and flexed my fingers. Springfield looked at me calmly.

'I was going to Hollywood.'

He jerked his tobacco stained right thumb back over his shoulder. 'Passed it. It's back thataway.'

'You bastard, Springfield. *Private* Springfield, I'll bet.'

'You know how to hurt a man, Dick. But I'm tough-skinned. Here, have another drink.'

I drank some more of the liquid sun. This time it made me feel better as the warmth rushed through me. Now I was hot inside as well as out. 'Hurt a man! Christ, what've you done to me!' I looked around; the tree was the only patch of shade at a crossroads – white, dusty roads stretching off in four directions to nowhere. I could see a line of blue hills in the far distance. There were eight or ten buildings in sight – drab, mud brick affairs with flat roofs and shutters instead of windows. Some flies were buzzing around a horse trough and a couple of chickens were picking in the dust over by one of the buildings.

Springfield looked too. Then he spat in the white dust. 'Saved your miserable life is what I did.'

I had another drink and thought about it. I had to admit I couldn't remember getting a good clean jump onto the train. 'Tell me about it. Have you got a cigarette?'

We lit up and both had a little more tequila. I wriggled to get a fraction more shade on my face. 'Why aren't we over there – inside?'

'Man said to meet him here.'

'What man?'

'What d'you want to hear about first, Dick? How I saved your life or how I'm going to make you rich?'

I shut up, smoked my cigarette which actually seemed to cool my throat, and let him tell it. It appeared that Flanagan's club had landed solidly on the back of my head but that I'd got a little protection from my wool cap. I was unconscious when Springfield hauled me aboard. Flanagan had left his run a bit too late; he'd stumbled after hitting me, lost his footing and fallen down the embankment. The train went on.

'On to where?' I said.

'Ain't you going to thank me?'

'Thank you. On to where?'

'South, then west.'

'It's the west I want to hear about.'

'Branched off way south of Bakersfield. Good run, only had to change couple of times to get here.'

'I jumped on and off trains?'

'Nope. You walked and sat like a gentleman. 'Course, you didn't say much and what you did say didn't make no sense.'

'You could have dropped me off close to Los Angeles.'

'Now how could I do that? You were like a child. Besides, there was the money.'

'What money?'

'Your money. How d'you think I bought tickets?'

I turned out my pockets, including the shirt pocket where I'd buttoned in a couple of dollars and reached across for my bag. Springfield passed the bottle.

'I used the money, Dick, all of it. So I had to bring you along with me, didn't I? Otherwise it'd be stealing.'

I sighed. 'Across the border and everything?'

'Sure. At Yuma. You was moving a bit strange but no one looked twice at you. Have to admit I was worried there.'

'Why?'

'Thought you might be on the run from the law. You look like a desperate character, Dick. But I guess not.'

Desperate is right, I thought. Desperate to get away from this lunatic. I had no idea where San Ricardo was but I knew the Mexican border wasn't so far from Los Angeles. Perhaps I was close to Hollywood after all. Then I recalled the word 'Yuma' which didn't sound so good. 'Where's this Yuma, Dwight?'

'South-west of LA, like I said.'

'How far south-west?'

'Oh, about two hundred miles.'

'Jesus. And San Ricardo, where's that?'

'South-west again.'

I looked at him. He took another pull on the tequila and held out the bottle. I shook my head, staring at him. He fiddled with the gun.

'Well?' I said.

'"Bout another two hundred.'

'And we've got no money?'

He shook his head.

'Who's this man we're meeting?'

Springfield sighted the pistol at a chicken; he moved the gun slowly as the chicken picked and scratched at the ground. 'He's a Mexican general, Dick. He's got some oil wells hereabouts and he figures he should run the whole country. We're here to help him.'

I should have snatched the gun from Springfield, brained him and pawned the pistol for the price of a ticket to Yuma. Or I could have held up the cantina and got some money that way. Or I could have forced the priest (it was a fair bet that one of the miserable buildings was a church) to give me sanctuary. I should have done almost anything but what I did do, which was to lie back and let Springfield tell me how we were going to make our fortunes out of General Pablo Domingo.

'I heard about this from an oilman back in Oklahoma. He'd worked for him. This Domingo found out there was oil in certain parts and he made sure he did his fightin' around there when the revolution was on. One way and another he got control of the acres, found the oil and now he don't want to go shares with anyone.'

'Enterprising,' I said.

'Some time back he'd have been all right. Long's he gave to the church and the right government men, he could do what he liked with the oil.'

'But now . . .?'

'New government now under this General Obregon – one-armed bastard, dresses himself up like a *peon* and talks about giving the land back to the people.'

'What about the oil?'

'You control the land, you control the oil. That's how Domingo sees it. Now, the government's sent lawyers and like that to talk to him and he won't talk to nobody much, 'cept to certain folks in the USA who want to talk oil.'

'And money.'

'You bet your ass, money. That's what he's already got a lot of. He reckons the government's goin' to send some troops against him soon. Not too many on account of he's still a popular revolutionary general and they don't want a fuss. But some.'

'You've volunteered to fight against government troops?'

'Not exactly. Domingo's got his own army. Some of them loyal to him from the revolution days, some he's bought with the Yankee dollar. They want training. They want arms drill. They need to know about tactics.'

'No,' I said.

'Dick, it's a lead pipe cinch. We give 'em some training, run 'em around, you know how it is, an' we get top pay while we're doing it.'

'Then there's a fight and they all get killed. We get killed too, or caught and hanged.'

'No chance.' He looked around as if a spy might be hiding behind a blade of grass, except that there weren't any blades of grass. 'Afore it gets to that we slip away and report all we know to the government. We're law-abiding men.'

'Then we have to fight on the government side and we get killed that way. No thanks.'

Springfield removed his greasy, wide-brimmed hat and fanned himself with it. A little of the breeze stirred across my face too and was welcome. He looked calm and confident. 'You know how many big, well-set-up fellows like you hit Hollywood every month, Dick? Let me tell you – hundreds. And do you know what happens to them?'

I shook my head.

'They go home broke. That what you want? Of course it isn't. Now the difference is this – man who arrives there with the right clothes and the right car, and can afford to stay in the right hotel, he's got a chance. First off, he can get an agent to do the spadework for him. Money talks in Hollywood, boy. You must know that.'

I listened because it made sense. Those three words 'go home broke' cooled me a lot more than any hat-fanning.

'You think it'd be easy work here?' I said.

'Piece of cake.' He squinted at me. 'That is, providing you're going to be all right and not suffer dizzy spells or like that. How d'you feel?'

I stretched and moved my shoulders. 'Fine ... I guess.'

'To hear you talk in your sleep, you're one hell of a good shot. That right?'

Suddenly I *was* feeling fine. Visions of swimming pools and everything that goes with them – girls in bathing costumes, martinis, silk shirts and white suits danced in my head. I grabbed the pistol, cocked it, sighted and blew the head clean off the nearest dirt-scratching chicken. The gun made an almighty crack and the other chickens squawked and clucked and scattered.

'You crazy bastard!' Springfield took the gun from me and got to his feet as men ran from one of the buildings. They wore grubby white shirts and pants and were as dark as Aborigines. They screamed and waved their arms. I staggered up and stood close to Springfield. A woman ran from the building, looked at the dead fowl and let out a screech. She ran at me with her fingers hooked into claws. Before she got to me she tripped and sprawled in the dust.

More men came blinking and shouting out into the sunlight. A stone sailed past my shoulder and hit the tree.

'There's another gun in my bag! Grab it!' Springfield was levelling the pistol at the advancing men. I saw the sun flash on a raised metal blade. I scrabbled for the gun.

'Tell them I'm sorry,' I babbled. 'Jesus – merci, I mean, pardon, pardonnay, oh, Christ . . .'

Dust swirled around their dirty bare feet as the men paused when the second pistol was pointed at them. I cocked it but I was shaking so hard I probably couldn't have hit the cantina.

A tall man in the middle gave a wild yell and rushed forward. Springfield swung the pistol on him and then there was the sound of a shot. But it was too far away to be the pistol and it was followed by several other shots. Loud reports, heavy calibre. Rifles.

My eyes were full of dust but I heard the roar of an engine, more shots and the squawk of the chickens again.

'Thank Christ,' Springfield said. 'It's the General!'

But I only half-heard him. The pistol felt as heavy as a blacksmith's hammer and my eyes were suddenly sweeping across miles of blue sky. I tasted the tequila in my mouth, retched and started to slide into a dead faint.

CHAPTER SEVEN

Springfield caught me as I fell, slapped me hard and scraped his boot down my shin. I blacked out only for a second, then I was standing with him trying to look enraged. My face would have been pale and my trembling might have helped the impression of anger. I discovered I was still holding the gun and I imitated Springfield by bringing it up and resting the long barrel across my crooked arm – manly, at-the-ready but not provocative, you see.

Two men got down from the big, black Hispano Suiza tourer and the village folk scattered in front of them. One was slow and got a cuff over the ear. They were nasty-looking chaps, these two – big, dark, wearing light blue uniforms with all the trim. Their boots were highly polished indicating that they never walked, only rode. One of them carried a rifle and looked as if he knew how to use it in more serious ways than firing into the air to scare away peasants. He stood back while the other did the talking.

'Which of you gringos is Springfield?' A wave of pepper and garlic came from him and, in my weakened state, nearly knocked me over.

Springfield touched the brim of his hat and didn't say anything.

'Why did you kill the *pollo?*'

Now I never like to be left out of a conversation; it gives the wrong impression and can get you stuck with the bill or the dirty jobs. 'I was hungry,' I said.

The Mexican burst into laughter. 'Hongry! You hear that, Luis? The gringo was hongry.'

Luis worked the bolt of his rifle, ejected a shell and caught it neatly. He grinned, showing broken, stained teeth. 'He looks hongry, Fidel. He is a skinny as *el pollo.*'

That was probably true. Springfield hadn't mentioned me eating in the three days I'd been wandering about like a sleepwalker and I suddenly felt famished. The smell coming from Fidel worked against that feeling however.

Springfield looked at Luis. 'I will enjoy teaching you how to shoot with that rifle, amigo.'

A man had climbed out of the car and moved towards us as this banter was going on. Luis' face darkened still further and he swung the rifle towards Springfield. He stopped when he heard the chuckle behind him.

'Two jokes in such a short space of time. Very good.'

'*Si, General.*' Luis swung the rifle away as the speaker stepped between him and his pal. He was a small man, five feet three or four but built wide and solid. He wore a spotlessly white uniform with polished belts and buckles and some gold braid here and there. A big moustache covered a good deal of his swarthy face; his uniform cap was pulled low and under it were eyes that gleamed like a pair of black pearls.

'I am Pablo Jose y Mendez Domingo.'

Springfield pulled off his hat. 'Dwight Springfield and Richard Browning, at your service, General. I got your telegram in Yuma and here I am.'

'Yes. How is he – the one who told you of my needs?'

'Rich, General. He struck it rich in Oklahoma.'

'Rich, eh? That is good. It is a good for a man to be rich. Is it not so, Senor Browning?'

I pulled my knit cap off and felt my hair tangle around my ears. With the beard and the sweat and dirt I knew I must have looked anything but rich. I wondered if the General was going to hand out those nice pale blue uniforms. 'Yes, General,' I said, 'it must be nice to be rich. I'm looking forward to it.'

The General showed even white teeth. 'And you, Senor Springfield. Are you looking forward to being rich?'

Springfield drew himself up and tapped the pistol. 'I'm a soldier of fortune, General. I like the soldiering and if the fortune comes too, well, that'll be just fine with me.'

'Come, we will talk.' He turned abruptly and Luis had to step lively to get out of his way. 'Torres, the bags.'

Fidel Torres looked as if he'd like to turn the job over to Luis but he bent and picked up Springfield's bag and mine. Springfield gestured for him to open his bag and he put the pistols inside. He didn't take the bag and Torres carried them over to the car. I had the feeling that Springfield had made an enemy.

'Torres, you and Luis can stay here. You will warn everyone to remain silent about the gringos.' He grinned. 'You can eat the evidence.'

'General?' Luis said.

'*El pollo, idiota!*'

We climbed into the back seat after Domingo. Torres closed the door, gently. He stepped back. The General spoke to the driver who turned the key, pressed the starter button and took off smoothly. I looked back at the two men standing in their clean uniforms and polished boots in the dust, under the sun, and I wondered how they were going to get home. I wondered where home was. I wondered about what I'd been babbling to Springfield over the past three days. I wondered what the hell I was doing there.

...

General Domingo had a nice little place a few miles out of town, over towards those blue hills I'd spotted in the distance. That is to say, his *fence* started a few miles out and the ranch land extended for some miles after that. The Hispano Suiza cruised along the rough dusty road riding over the bumps and holding nicely in places where sand and gravel covered the surface. Having been a professional driver myself, I knew that the man at the wheel was talented and knew his car. It was a car worth knowing, with genuine leather upholstery in a delicate cream colour. The wood panelling and polished brass fittings were well maintained as were, to judge by the quiet purr, the vital working parts. The gun rack mounted low behind the front seat, carrying two carbines and a double-barrelled shotgun, was a nice sporting touch.

Springfield and the General muttered about military matters while I gazed out at the countryside. It was dryish land, although off in the distance a long line of trees indicated a river or creek. There was enough grass and low scrub around to make it viable as cattle country, just. But cattle were evidently a back number with the General; I saw a few scrawny cows that looked as if they knew they were unimportant. The oil wells were what mattered. They were well back from the road, down hard-baked, rutted tracks. I could see the derricks framed against the clear blue sky and the constant movement of the drills, up and down like slowly nodding heads. The field extended for about a mile along one perimeter and God knows how far back. Any grass that had been around had turned black; any water lying on the ground was a shiny, dark ooze.

Domingo saw me looking out at the blackened landscape. He waved his hand and I noticed for the first time that he wore tight white gloves.

'What do you think, Mr Browning?'

I thought I should say something appropriate to the role Springfield had cast me in. I leaned forward to examine one of the carbines in the gun rack. 'Damned hard to defend,' I grunted.

Springfield nodded as if to say, take damn good men to do it – lucky you've got 'em. The General looked impressed. He seemed to mull things over for a bit and then he turned to Springfield and flashed those sensational teeth.

'If they are hard to defend, means they are easy to attack, no?'

'Follows,' said Springfield.

'Good.' Domingo reached into a compartment below the gun rack and pulled out a box of cigars. 'You will defend mine and we will attack others.' Springfield and I accepted cigars, good rich Havanas, and all three of us lit up.

'Attack is the best means of defence,' Springfield said.

'I like that.' Domingo puffed luxuriously. 'Who said that?'

'Napoleon,' I said.

'Nelson,' said Springfield.

The General nodded, happy with the company. 'Both great men.'

And both about your size, I thought, and both mad and dead fairly young if memory served me right, along with a lot of the crazy bastards who followed them.

The car swept around a bend and entered an avenue of orange trees that led up to a white building that gleamed in the sun like a mirage.

'My home,' Domingo said proudly. 'Also my headquarters.'

Springfield and I nodded respectfully. I suppose I should have been relieved he didn't say, 'My palace.'

The home and HQ was a hundred yards of two-storeyed facade with higher and lower bits at the back. There was something like a turret over a massive door at the top of an impressive set of steps. The windows were at regular intervals and barred. The orange trees stopped short of the building and gave way to lawn and flower beds. The road curved around in front of the house. There were two light cannon mounted at the base of the steps and a green, white and red flag flew from a mast on the turret.

'You will live in my house, you will train my men and you will help me to win my war. I will deal directly with the Americans.'

'Yes, sir!' said Springfield.

'Do you know my family . . . what is it, motto?'

'No, sir!' I said.

'*Orgullo y libertad.*'

'Sounds good,' I said. 'What does it mean, General?'

'Pride and freedom.'

A servant came rushing from the house, opened the car door and looked willing to bend over in the dust to be used as a footstool if Domingo so wished. The General stepped down and didn't even look at him. Springfield and I peeled ourselves off the leather seats. The servant reached for our bags, spoke quickly to the driver and scuttled ahead of us towards the house. The Hispano Suiza cruised off with whispering tyres and the motor giving a barely audible tick.

'What d'you think of this place, Dick?' Springfield whispered as we approached the steps.

'Worth fighting for – if it's yours.'

'Maybe a few more around here just like it. One for you an' one for me.'

'You're dreaming.'

'That's right. I'm dreamin' big dreams.'

'I'm leaving, first chance I get.'

He gripped my arm; his long, dirty fingers were strong and there was desperation as well as muscle in the grip. 'You're staying, boy. He likes you. I can tell.'

'I don't care if he wants to dance with me. This is crazy.'

Domingo had mounted some of the steps; he turned and looked back at us, arguing at the bottom.

'Senors, what is the trouble?'

'My compadre wants to talk about money,' Springfield said. 'I'm telling him to be patient.'

The servant had the door open now. 'We will talk about money tonight,' the General said. He disappeared into the house.

Springfield and I climbed the rest of the steps. 'You like money, don't you, Dick?'

'Yes, when I'm sure I'm going to be alive to enjoy it.'

'Trust me.'

'No.'

We were bowed into the house by the servant. The lobby was large, dark and cool. It had a smooth, polished floor and a ceiling so high it was shadowed in the corners. We followed our bags up a wide staircase, through some tall carved doors and along an open balcony which ran towards the back of the house around a flagstonedcourt-yard. There was a garden in the courtyard and pot plants along the balcony. Everything was clean, dry and light; I felt too dirty and damp to touch anything. I was tired and parched and my head ached; I wanted to eat and drink and sleep but I think if anyone had offered me a donkey, a canteen and the way to the border I'd have accepted. The place smelled of danger.

We walked around two sides of the balcony and the servant stopped at a door. He planted Springfield's bag in front of it.

'Your room, Senor,' he said.

Springfield nodded, picked up the bag, opened the door and strode in.

'Your room is here, Senor.' He ushered me to the next door, opened it and handed me my bag.

I mimed drinking. 'Something to drink, please.'

'Si,' he said. 'Si.' He jabbed his finger at the door.

'Fair enough.' I opened the door and stepped in. The room had a stone floor covered with a coarse mat. There was some kind of cloth hanging on two of the walls; a fan turned slowly in the ceiling and soft light filtered in through a shuttered window. There was a big, low bed and a series of hooks along one wall for clothes. I dropped my bag and walked to the window which ran from floor to ceiling. I opened the shutters and stepped out onto a balcony.

'Greetings, Senor.' A woman was tipping water from a bucket into a hip bath which had a shoulder high wicker screen around it. She wore a long, patterned skirt and a white blouse that exposed smooth dark shoulders. White teeth flashed in a face as dark as chocolate. She touched herself between the breasts, pressing the cotton in and outlining her full, rounded shape.

'Maria,' she said. 'Your servant. No English.'

I took off my cap and unbuttoned my jacket. 'Hello, Maria,' I said. 'Don't worry, I don't feel much like talking.'

CHAPTER EIGHT

I blame Maria for a lot of the misery that followed. If she hadn't been around I might very well have got together a few provisions and sneaked off that night or the next. As it was, after she'd soaped me all over and rinsed me off and rubbed me dry, it seemed like the natural thing to just go on rubbing.

If I hadn't built up a head of steam from long deprivation, her idea of lovemaking would've seemed a trifle too demanding. We tore the bed apart as we went about it; she was a tiger, thrashing and bucking and moaning and putting her feet on the floor and the walls and getting me to do the same. Eventually I fell into a sweat-drenched, exhausted sleep. When I woke up Maria was towelling me down. Her hair, which had come loose during our romp, was tied back again. Her blouse was unwrinkled, her eyes were demure and she smelled of soap as if she'd just dropped by between her morning wash and her sewing class. Hanging over a chair was a neatly pressed blue uniform. She tapped my chin; I lifted my head and she began to shave me.

'Careful of the moustache,' I said.

After the shave and a bit of expert work with the scissors, she helped me to get dressed. The clothes fitted as if they'd been tailored for me; the boots were a trifle loose though. There was a full-length glass on a stand in the corner of the room (I'd caught a glimpse of us in it while we were performing one of our contortions earlier and I resolved to bring it closer to the bed next time). In it I saw a fine figure of a man – topping six feet, very lean with curling dark hair and a heart-breakingly handsome moustache.

'My soldier,' Maria said. I should say at this point that I picked up a fair bit of Spanish from Maria and others over the next few weeks. She had next to no English, but after a short time I was able to understand a good deal of what she said. None of it was complicated, being mainly about sex, food and drink, but, by a quirk of the mind, I remember it now as if she'd spoken in English. It's an odd thing, that. Whatever little bits of foreign languages spoken by women I've been able to understand, I remember as if it was English. Doesn't apply with men – I can still hear von Stroheim bellowing in his beastly German, for example, even though I know he was calling us fools, idiots, sodomites and worse.

Anyway, Maria saw me as her soldier and all I could think of was what a convincing figure I'd cut before the cameras. She gave me to understand that she'd be available for the night if I wanted her. I patted her bottom, loaded up with a few cigars from the box in the room, and went off in search of dinner and Springfield in that order. I was standing in the courtyard having a smoke as the last of the daylight faded when Springfield appeared. He was togged up the same as me in a clean blue uniform with shining brass and boots. Like me he'd been barbered and I couldn't help wondering if he'd had the full treatment. He accepted a cigar after I'd given him a mock salute. He lit up. 'What are you leering like that for?'

'I was wondering what you've been doing.'

'Getting cleaned up, then studying some maps of the territory.'

'Any women about?'

'One. I sent her packing. Have to concentrate on the job.'

I blew a plume of smoke at a bush covered with red flowers that gave off a strong, sweet scent. 'Quite,' I said.

He glanced at me sharply. 'We're going to have to be good to earn the money and grab our chance when it comes.'

'We, eh? I thought I was going to be Private to your General. Your batman, maybe?'

'That'd be crazy. I'm calling myself Major, you can be whatever you like.'

'Captain, then.'

A servant padded into the garden and summoned us to join the General for dinner. I ground out my cigar in a bird bath and set off after him. Springfield grabbed my arm.

'Let me do the talking.'

'Do you speak Spanish?'

'A bit.'

'Then you can do the talking *and* the listening. I'm just along for the dinner. Oh, and if it looks like going on too long I'll have to slip away. I've got an appointment for later.'

'Just be careful what you say to her.'

'Why?'

'Because she's sure to be a spy, you fool.'

. . .

I got drunk pretty quickly at the dinner, so I don't have a very clear memory of it. They were serving that bloody tequila for starters and throughout and the stuff has always boiled my brains. What with that and wine, and brandy with the pudding, it's no wonder that I'm a bit vague about the proceedings. And they were talking in Spanish a good deal of the time too, which left Dick little to do except eat everything that was put in front of him and drink likewise.

The dining room was a big, wood-panelled affair with a stone floor on which the barefooted servants made no sound as they trotted in the bowls of this and that. I couldn't identify much of it – there were various meats and lots of rice and vegetables, all as hot as hell and needing a lot of washing down. Domingo was there, of course, wearing a red sash over his uniform now and there were eight or ten other men as well as Springfield and myself. Some of these were in blue like us, the rest wore dark suits with white collars that looked as if they'd been unwrapped from the cellophane an hour before. Sitting to one side of Domingo was a priest – a huge, fat creature with thick lips and tiny piggy eyes. He ate enough for three and drank enough for six. I didn't hear him say anything all evening.

The General did most of the talking but the other officers and some of the civilians had their say. I heard names – Don this and Don that – and places – San something and Los something else – and none of it made any sense to me. Springfield wasn't chatty but he spoke up when required and I gathered he had a high opinion of me as an arms instructor, horseman and disciplinarian. Himself he modestly declared to be a tactician without equal as well as an expert in all the higher branches of soldiery.

Domingo kept them all pretty much in order but, as the level of the tequila in the bottles and the wine in the stone jars went down, it became apparent that one of the boys in blue, a thin, dark-faced character with slanted Indian eyes, had no time for gringos, although he spoke good English.

Major Springfield,' he challenged. 'Have you ever commanded cavalry?'

'I have, sir.'

'And infantry?'

'Yes.'

'Can you use a sabre, Major Springfield?'

'Yes.'

The General held out his glass for more wine. 'Enough, Porfirio,' he murmured. 'You must excuse Captain Calderon, Major Springfield. His family is notoriously hot-tempered.'

'One last question, General, by your leave,' Calderon said smoothly. 'If you were going to fight *me*, Major Springfield, what weapon would you use?'

The room suddenly went quiet. The murmuring voices stopped, the noise of eating and drinking stopped. No one belched or dropped a fork. Calderon was sitting opposite Springfield; he was wearing a blue uniform with a lot of extras, braid and such. He was a dandy with a high collar which he adjusted from time to time, and slightly frilled shirt cuffs that protruded half an inch from the sleeves of his uniform jacket. As he spoke he reached to pluck at his cuff.

Springfield moved faster than I'd ever seen a man move before, unless it was myself ducking for cover in the trenches of France. He stood, lifted his boot and his hand was a blur as it went down, came up and scythed through the air. I was sitting two places from Calderon on his side of the table and I leaned forward to see what had happened.

The Mexican had gone pale around the mouth and was sitting as still as stone. The fingertips of his right hand were resting on a handle of a knife which he'd just managed to ease out of a sheath strapped to the underside of his left forearm. His left sleeve, about two inches above the cuff, was pinned to the table by the knife Springfield had drawn and thrown.

'I'd chose knives, sir,' Springfield said softly. 'Against you, knives every time.'

. . .

A dinner party is not enhanced, in my opinion, by having sharp steel flying through the air. My reaction was to thump the brandy so that when I finally stumbled back to my room (leaving the mad, bloodthirsty bastards to discuss land mines and howitzers), there wasn't much chance of me revealing any secrets to Maria. Not much chance of doing anything else probably – I really don't recall.

The next day my second spell of military life began. I can't say I enjoyed it much more than my first – which had lasted from my enlistment in 1916 in the 1st AIF to my desertion in France two years later. Of course being an officer helped, but it was still necessary to do a lot of the marching and horseback-riding and rifle stripping and saluting. Looking back, the main benefit of officer status was being provided with a clean uniform and boots every morning. Maria offered other comforts as well but an ordinary sergeant can get those if he's stationed in the right place.

The heat was one of the problems. Out on those dusty roads it threatened to dry up your spit and piss and all other fluids. The Mexicans were willing enough, I'll say that for them. But they were too excitable to make good marksmen. Show them a target and they'd blaze away at it until their guns were empty. That was their style although there were one or two exceptions. On horseback they were even worse; a lot of them were peasant types who felt they'd arrived in heaven when they got up on a horse. A couple did make it to heaven (or became eligible) when they attempted impossible jumps or insisted on charging downhill at full steam. Of course, there were probably some malingerers who fell off deliberately. If so, some of them got more than they bargained for because they ended up with that peculiar tilt to the head which results from breaking the neck by falling from a horse.

Week after week I was out there licking this rabble into shape. My health suffered; it was probably the food because I didn't drink much water, but I had dreadful bowel trouble which became embarrassing. I caught a couple of the footsloggers holding their noses one time. (They got a doubling round the parade ground in full kit at midday for their pains. Springfield was right about that – I was a natural disciplinarian.) Although I'm dark complected I got a bad sunburn at first which Maria treated with a cream that contained cactus juice. Turned me dark as a nigger. She also took out one bad tooth after anaesthetising me with tequila (the cactus juice again) and massaged me for sprains and dislocations. If this sounds like a series of complaints, well, that's military life in my experience.

Springfield thrived on it of course. He became very pally with Calderon the way these blood-letters will if they survive their initial confrontation. Calderon could see that I was a horse of a different feather, although I'd demonstrated my abilities with a rifle and pistol convincingly enough for him not to take too many liberties. Still, he liked to rag me.

'I am told you fainted after shooting a chicken,' he said to me one day. He'd got this from Torres who disliked me only slightly less than he disliked Springfield. He wasn't in my training troop thank God, but Springfield had had a little trouble with him.

'Touch of the sun,' I said.

'That Maria is a wildcat, no?'

You see the sort of thing I mean, letting me know he had the goods on me. There wasn't much I could do but grin and bear it but I promised myself I'd score a few points if I ever got him in the right spot. Meantime, the training went on and after a few months my sixty or so illiterates knew which end of a rifle was which and could get on a horse from the right side. Springfield's troop was larger and better drilled and, after spending a little time as observers of the master, Calderon and Torres both assumed command of teams of fifty raw recruits. The brutality of their basic training methods would sicken you.

Duties got lighter once the roughness was off the rookies. Domingo presided at parades once a week and exhibited occasional interest in the training, but seemed to spend most of his time locked up with. Americans who wore big hats and arrived in big cars. Two things kept me from being bored – Maria and the pay. Maria was an inventive and energetic lover who taught me quite a few new tricks beside the mirror, on and off the bed. I kept Springfield's warning that she was a spy in mind, but when your verbal exchanges are limited to, 'This way?' and 'Harder!' and such things, it's difficult to fish for or betray any secrets.

Domingo handed out the gold as if he had a hill of it. I was salting away the stuff most satisfactorily. Everything was free of course – it was like being comped at Vegas[14], with slightly rougher living quarters. It had to end, of course. One evening, after I'd just finished a session with Maria and was having a recuperative smoke on the balcony, Springfield barged in.

'It's on, Dick.'

'What's on?'

He sat on the balcony, accepted a cigar and spat the end down into the courtyard. Bellicose, you see. 'Domingo's had word that the government plans to occupy his oilfield.'

'He won't like that.'

'In a way he does. He's got big plans to deal with it. Would you believe he's got a couple airplanes?'

I'd seen some planes in the sky off to the east while we'd been drilling but I hadn't thought anything of them. 'Might not need chaps on the ground, then,' I said.

'Don't you believe it. He plans to wipe them out and counter attack.'

'Attack what?'

'Don Pasquale's oilfield. We could be in for a long campaign.' He blew smoke, stuck the cigar dead centre in his mouth and rubbed his hands contentedly.

'Time to go then, is it?'

'No chance.'

'How come?'

'Campaign pay is double.'

'The danger goes up about a hundred times, or more.'

'If I know you, you'll protect your ass.' He flipped his cigar out into the dark, velvety night and stood up. 'I'm in fine fettle. Think I might rustle up that little gal was here the first day. I see you're still doing all right for yourself there. Goodnight, Dick.'

I nodded to him and hurried to get to the brandy. Maria was standing by and the mirror was in position. She looked sleek and glossy and she'd murmured about trying something new a short time before. Maria looked her very best in the evening glow, but, somehow, I didn't feel a bit like it that night.

CHAPTER NINE

It was sheer hell from start to finish. I would never have survived if I hadn't been half full of brandy most of the time, an expert at taking cover, and if I hadn't trained my troops specifically in techniques of protecting yours truly. As it was, my survival was frequently a near thing.

The day following my conservation with Springfield was spent in the house, looking over maps, checking on equipment and preparing for the defence of the oilfield. By evening we were in position waiting for the attack. Domingo had a spy in the enemy camp who'd named the date but not the time or the direction of the attack. The planes couldn't operate effectively at night, so that little piece of advantage was lost, which was worrying. I was on a perimeter of the oilfield with twenty men preparing to repel attackers from the hills which were riddled with arroyo beds (gullies, we'd have called them in Australia). Raiders could move along the arroyos almost to within pistol shot of the oil derricks without being seen. Spring-field was stationed on the main road, heading a heavily armed strike-back team and in charge of the flares which would be sent up according to pre-arranged signals. Blue was for 'advance right', red 'advance left', green for 'diversionary action forward' and so on.

'Nothing for retreat,' I'd whispered to Springfield during the pow-wow in the house.

'That's right,' he said.

'What does your *compadre* want to know, Dwight?' Calderon asked.

'He wants to know whether we should take prisoners.'

'No,' said Domingo.

I nodded. 'Quite right. Thoroughly good show.'

Calderon looked at me as I rubbed my already cramping leg. I reached out and took his arm to look at the repair job on his sleeve where Springfield's knife had cut the cloth. The stitches were a little uneven.

'You should have asked me and I would have got Maria to do that for you, Senor. First class at everything, that woman.'

Calderon scowled and turned away. *Points to me,* I thought, but it was little consolation. The next words I heard from him were 'sacrifice' and 'reckless courage' and I had to rub hard to stop my calf from knotting.

Well, I wasn't feeling sacrificial or courageous as I crouched there with those damned drills going up and down and the knowledge that several hundred men were about to start hurling lead and steel at each other. My gallant twenty were armed to the teeth with Mannlicher rifles, Colt .45 automatic pistols and knives to the individuals' tastes. I've been in the situation many times and my reaction has always been the same. I've wanted to get everyone to sit down over a smoke and a bottle, talk it over and go home in one piece. Never happens of course; I think some chaps must *like* fighting and the rest are stupid enough to follow them.

I'd had a few good pulls on the brandy bottle before we boarded the trucks that took us to the oilfield and I had two flasks with me for emergencies. I wasn't carrying a knife as I've never had much fancy for the cold steel encounter, but I had my share of other weapons and ammunition. A tin hat would have been welcome but Domingo's quartermaster didn't run to such things. It occurred to me that I hadn't seen any morphine or bandages and that, as far as I knew, the only medical knowledge available in the whole unit was of the veterinary variety.

As luck would have it, the attack came first in my sector. I'd sent out a scout and he came scuttling back to say that a file of men was approaching a bit to the left. He pointed out the dark smudge on the hillside that indicated their likely entrance. There was some moonlight, enough to fix on the spot and see anything that moved there. I adjusted the sights on my Mannlicher and when a man appeared out of the darkness and threw back his hand so that the light fell on his upturned face, I shot him through the neck. He jerked and the hand came down and there was an explosion at his feet – flame shot into the air and in its light I could see men running from the arroyo.

'Fire!' I shouted and my men poured it into them.

I got down flat and fired an occasional shot but the rest of my team was shooting from the crouch or even standing up. A few shots came from the attackers and a man near me threw his rifle away and screamed.

'Down! Down!' I yelled. I scurred off to the left where there was better cover and picked off one or two more by firing at the rifle flashes. Shooting started over on our right flank and I heard the rattle of the potato digger[15] we'd mounted to protect a water pump that serviced the whole field. The attackers must have had their spies too.

Things went quiet for a minute and then there was an explosion on the far side of the field. A sheet of flame wrapped itself around one of the derricks and illuminated the area. I saw men advancing in a column along the road and going down like scythed wheat to Springfield's Maxim guns. There were figures darting around on the oilfield but we'd stationed men by every derrick and they stood up at the right times and cut the attackers down with pistol fire and machetes.

I mustered my men. We'd lost two or three, through their own stupidity of course, but that was no matter. It always looks well to have a few casualties as a sign that the unit has been in the thick of things. I established myself behind a boulder with a good supply of ammunition and pointed to a tree near the spot where the first grenade thrower had emerged.

'Fire that tree,' I said to the keenest of my followers.

He went forward, stripped the jacket off a dead man, lit it and threw it into the tree. The dry foliage caught and crackled.

'I will kill any who come from the arroyos,' I said. I waved my hand behind me. 'We will guard this place. Understand ?'

Most of them nodded; the one who looked most anxious to get on with the fighting I sent with a message to Springfield that there was heavy fighting in this area but that we were holding them off.

Don't think it wasn't dangerous. Bullets whizzed overhead from time to time as the battle raged for an hour or more. Domingo's men had trouble getting the one big fire out and the attackers made several brave attempts to launch assaults from the road. Springfield's flares went up and the manoeuvres must have worked because the attacks were repelled. A grenade went off uncomfortably close to my rock and one of my men got tired of safety and took a stray bullet in the head when he set off in search of action. I fired three times at the gully – twice just for show but once at a poor devil who staggered forward with a stick grenade in each hand. I got him through the chest. Almost as soon as the sound of that shot of mine died away the battle ceased.

I waited until I was sure and then marched my depleted troup up to the road. We even had a couple of wounded, scratches really, but, again, that makes the right impression. There were celebrations going on all over the place. Springfield pumped my hand and told me that they'd killed two hundred of the enemy for minimal losses.

'What about the fire I said.

'No problem. They've got a guy here who's a genius with oil fires.'

'Good,' I said. I transferred some of the grime and grease from my hands to my face with a weary, war-is-hell gesture. 'Got a drink, Dwight. Hot work.'

Calderon appeared by my elbow with a flask. 'I did not see you in the fighting, Captain Browning.'

I took a swig. 'I killed the first man, I believe,' I said coolly.

'Y el ultimo.' Speaking up was one of my men who'd stayed beside me the whole time. I had hardly noticed him before but now he had a big smile on his dirty bearded face and he was looking at me as if I was Pancho Villa himself. Such admiration has to be rewarded. This was NCO material if ever I saw it but his Spanish was much too quick for me. I handed him Calderon's flask.

'What did he say,' I said.

Springfield slapped my back hard enough to break the spine. 'He said you killed the first man *and* the last. You son of a gun, Dick!'

...

That was more than enough action for me, especially as I could tell that in the minds of Springfield and Calderon it was just for openers. Domingo took off his still spotlessly white gloves and made a short speech in which he praised everyone for winning a great victory. That drew a few cheers. When he promised tequila – one bottle between three men – the cheers were loud enough to drown out the groans of the wounded men. In the truck on the way back to the camp (the men were billeted in prefabricated huts some distance from the house), I was aware of the eyes of the bearded man who'd spoken up for me. He watched me, his black eyes fixed and staring, but I would have sworn there was a question in the brain behind them.

I jumped from the truck when it stopped for me near the house and was surprised to see the man who'd been watching me jump down as well.

'Drill in the morning . . .'

'No, wait, Captain Browning. A word, if you please.'

He didn't sound like the other Mexicans who spoke a sort of cantina English not unlike the dialogue in *Zorro* on TV.

'Well?' I started for the house and he walked along with me. He was slight and small and seemed to be weighed down by his Mannlicher and other armaments.

'My name is Pedro Cortez,' he said.

'You're Sergeant Cortez from tomorrow.'

'Thank you, Senor. But I do not wish to be a sergeant.'

'What do you wish to be?'

'A civilian.'

'Ah.'

'You are not a brave man, Captain Browning.'

I stopped in my tracks, furious. I'd done the job, hadn't I. 'You damned impertinent .... Forget the promotion.'

'I have already forgotten it. I would rather be a civilian, cleaning *las esusados*[16], than a general in an army. I do not like being shot at. Neither do you.'

I lit a cigar and walked on. 'Well, I'm not foolhardy . . .'

'You trained us to protect you, Senor. To group around you, provide diversionary fire. I admired that greatly.'

He was sharp all right. That was exactly what I'd done. Still, I wondered what was coming; some form of blackmail no doubt. A threat to report to Porfirio Calderon on my training tactics? A request for a letter from Domingo to release him so he could nurse his sick mother? I looked down at his lean, eager face and saw that he was a little older than the average, late twenties perhaps. 'Well, what do you want?'

He looked longingly at my glowing cigar. I gave him one and lit it with the tip of mine. 'Thank you.' He blew smoke, closed his eyes and looked soothed. I knew the feeling. 'In my village I was a teacher. The revolution reduced my village to a heap of stones and I became a wandering teacher. Then I became a wandering teacher who stole to live. That brought me here. It is better than being dead but not by very much.'

I nodded. It was nice to find a kindred soul. 'And getting dead is very much on the cards.'

He smiled. 'Or *in* the cards, you might say – if you were superstitious.'

I laughed and realised that it was a good long time since I'd heard a joke. Maria didn't go in for them and I've never met a soldier with a proper sense of humour yet. 'What did you say your name was?'

'Pedro Cortez.'

Something came back to me from the hours of boredom spent in the classrooms at Dudleigh Grammar. 'You're not very stout,' I said.

His teeth flashed in the dark night. 'Nor am I silent. Nor is this shitheap Darien. Keats, "On first looking into Chapman's Homer".'

'That's it exactly!'

'I told you I was a teacher.'

We were close to the steps at the front of the house now. I could feel the tension in him and I had a sense myself that something big was afoot. That feeling has to be attended to – never go to bed with that feeling around, you're sure to regret it.

'I'll ask you again, Cortez. What d'you want of me?'

'I want to escape with you. To the United States.'

I looked around. I doubted there was anyone hidden in the cannon. 'We must talk about this.'

'No, we must do it.'

'Yes, quite. A plan . . .'

'I have one.'

'Oh.'

'You hate Porfirio Calderon and he hates you.'

'True.'

'My plan involves him.'

'He wouldn't tell me the time.'

'We can use him to escape. He can be our passport and our shield.'

I dropped my cigar butt and put my boot on it. I was tired and feeling like a drink and bed. All this talk of Calderon had taken the edge off me.

'Oh yes,' I said. 'Well, as I say. Let's talk. Tomorrow perhaps . . .'

'No!' he said fiercely. 'Let us act. Tonight!'

Suddenly the tiredness was gone and the edge was back. 'Tonight ?'

'Yes. They have had their victory, now let us have ours!'

He threw his cigar away and a shower of sparks arced through the air and died on the grass. 'There is only one essential item in my plan I am not sure about. If this can be managed, we can proceed and we are sure of success.'

'What the hell are you talking about?'

'Senor Browning, can you drive a Hispano Suiza automobile?'

I let out my breath in a long hiss. 'Cortez, old chum, I can drive anything.'

CHAPTER TEN

Pedro's plan had the merit of simplicity and the virtue of good timing. We would grab Porfirio Calderon and through him commandeer the General's car. Then it was a matter of Calderon saying the right things to the guards as we drove out and heigh-ho for the US border. The only tricky bit was getting hold of Porfirio.

'He's a careful man,' I said, 'and a moderate one.'

'Less so tonight,' says Pedro. 'They will celebrate and Calderon has a notoriously weak head. That is why he drinks little. Tonight he will take a glass or two more.'

'He won't be easy to scare.'

'He was second-in-command of the soldiers who turned my village into rubble. I will scare him. Make ready, Senor Browning. Bring money, a gun, anything else you need. Papers. And say nothing to that woman.'

'Maria?'

'She sleeps with Porfirio Calderon when she is not sleeping with you.'

'How do you know?'

'Everybody knows.'

I bit my lip at that. *Definitely time to be going, old son,* I thought. But suddenly I felt cautious. What if this was a trap? Perhaps laid by Calderon himself? I hesitated.

'You do not trust me,' Pedro said.

'I'm not sure.'

'I know Keats, I also know your namesake.'

'Eh?'

'."I sprang to the stirrup, and Horace and he;

I galloped, Dick galloped, we galloped all three."[17] 'This is Browning, Senor. A great English poet.'

'Great stuff,' says I. 'D'you know any more?'

'Reams, Senor.'

I was aware that I still had a good deal of brandy in the bloodstream. I felt it bubbling up now, lending courage. 'Righto, Pedro. Lead on. Anyway, I've always wanted to drive a Hispano Suiza.'

We arranged to meet in an hour in a sheltered garden at the side of the house. Pedro had been planning his escape for so long that he could walk around the house and immediate environs blindfolded and tell you where he was from the ground underfoot and the scents on the air. I went up to my room and collected my belongings. The gold I'd accumulated was a hefty weight. Reason was, there'd been no one congenial to play cards with. I got rid of the Mannlicher and its ammunition but checked over the Colt thoroughly. Seven cartridges in the magazine, one in the chamber. Slide working easily, hammer smooth. I packed a few clothes, shaving tackle, a bottle of brandy and all the cigars and cigarettes I could find, into the bag I'd arrived with and crept down the stairs.

No sign of Maria. Probably with the conquering hero. I wondered how Pedro planned to proceed if Porfirio and Maria were doing the bedsprings polka. Springfield's room was quiet; I was tempted to leave him a note but I didn't. Never been a great one for notes; I've been left a few in my time but they've seldom told me anything I didn't know already.

I was early at the appointed place and spent the time pacing up and down and smoking cigarettes. I was getting more nervous by the minute and the sounds coming from the house didn't help. There seemed to be a couple of parties in progress and a good deal of activity on the terraces and balconies. Good in some ways – the guards were bound to be drunk; bad in others – there's always some busybody around who's alert when everyone else is getting blotto. After a while the noise subsided, lights went out and the house settled down.

I was on my sixth waiting cigarette when Pedro appeared. He had Calderon with him but it wasn't the Porfirio of old. He looked as if he'd been locked in a freezer for a few hours. He was pale around the mouth, stiff and shivering. He smelt of brandy and tobacco and fear.

'What did you do to him?' I said.

'I talked to him,' Pedro said quietly. 'He will do whatever we ask.'

'Why?'

Pedro shrugged. 'It is an old trick. I have put a thorn into his . . . near the *cojones?*'

'Scrotum.'

'*Escroto, si.* If he moves very quietly all will be well, if he moves suddenly or is unlucky enough to suffer a blow in the . . .?'

'Balls.'

'Balls. He will be a eunuch. Porfirio Calderon does not want to be a eunuch. He has no sons, only daughters.'

'Can he talk?'

'Of course he can talk. I would not advise him to shout, but he can say things like "I want you to fuel the General's car and provide us with some extra fuel" or "I have an important message from the General to Don Morales". You could say that, couldn't you, *bastardo?*'

'Yes,' said Calderon softly.

'How did you, you know . . . manage to ... ah ... ?'

'Easy. He was naked and tired after finishing with *la puta.* Very tired. But he does not want that to have been his last love-making. Do you, *perro?*'[18]

No.'

'What about the woman?'

Pedro produced a knife. He pricked the ball of his thumb and grinned at me.

'You didn't!'

His grin widened. 'No, Senor Browning. She is wrapped up like a . . . how the Egyptians prepare the dead.'

'A mummy.'

'Si, a mummy. A fine word. I hope to learn much from you. Let us go. We will leave the bags, Senor Browning, further along the road and collect them as we drive past. Bags might make the guard suspicious.'

'Won't they be suspicious anyway?'

'Perhaps, but Don Porfirio must persuade them, convince them, or he knows what will happen. We will see.'

I took my bag and Pedro's down the driveway and left them behind a tree. Back in the garden, Calderon was standing as stiff as a board and it occurred to me that if he didn't stop clenching his teeth like that he was going to have a very sore jaw to match the other part. We moved around to the back of the house and our boots rang on the flagstoned area in front of the garage. The guard, standing in the archway at the front of the garage, threw up his rifle and challenged us.

'*Alto!*'

Pedro nudged Calderon forward. He was dressed in full uniform – white jacket and trousers with Sam Browne belt – and looked an impressive sight in the moonlight; his lean face was drawn tight by stress. You'd have sworn he was on a mission from God. He spoke in rapid-fire, parade-ground Spanish to the guard who practically fell at his feet. The guard was sober but the soft strains of celebration had reached him. He was a little languid in his movements which gave Calderon the chance to abuse him. I caught the words *borracho* and *castigo*[19] in his tirade. An immediate snag was that the guard knew nothing about cars, didn't have the key and didn't know where the fuel was kept. Calderon, still standing as if to bend an inch would cripple him, ranted at the guard and Pedro to look lively and do the best they could.

I scouted around in the garage and found the fuel drums. Pedro set to work siphoning out the gas into a couple of jerry cans while I lifted the bonnet of the Hispano Suiza and investigated the wiring. Back in London (God, what I wouldn't have given to have been there then, despite the weather), I'd driven for Green's Hire Cars & Limousines long enough to learn to cope with flat batteries, dead starter motors and a hundred other automotive frustrations. The wiring on the Hispano Suiza was a snap; I knew I could have it ticking over in seconds and I told Pedro in English.

'The guard is suspicious,' he said. 'He wonders why we have not brought the chauffeur. Look at him, he wants to challenge Calderon.'

I glanced across. The guard was fidgeting nervously, dancing his rifle butt on the garage floor. Pedro shut off the siphon and screwed down the cap. 'Enough,' he said. 'We cannot take any more time.' He lugged the two cans across to the car, lifted one and heaved it into the back seat. The guard's eyes rolled but Calderon's authority held him still. Pedro slung the second can into the car.

'No!' the guard yelled. '*La piel!*'[20] He launched himself forward and Calderon screamed as he stepped aside. Pedro moved as fast as Dempsey at Toledo; he slid across the flagstones and slipped his knife in between the lower ribs of the guard as if he was eyeing potatoes. The blood welled, then spurted out over Calderon's white uniform. More screaming.

'Start it!' Pedro yelled. I bridged the terminals with some wire I found on a bench in the garage and shoved the crank handle home, feeling it click into place.

'*Pronto!*'

I cranked hard and the engine caught and roared.

'In, in!'

I leapt in behind the wheel. Pedro had his knife under Calderon's chin and guided him across to the car by its point. Calderon shuffled and seemed to take an age. The engine ticked over smoothly. Pedro opened the back door and helped Calderon climb up. Then he went to the archway and dragged the body out of sight. He came back to the car carrying the guard's rifle and got in the back with Calderon.

'If you say the wrong thing,' he said. 'The rifle butt will speak for me. You understand?'

Calderon nodded.

'*Vamos*!'

I backed the car out, turned and took off down the drive. It was a clear night and I easily spotted the tree where I'd left the bags. I had a feeling that Pedro might get above himself if given the chance, so this seemed like the right time to restore the balance.

'You'd better get the bags, Pedro,' I said. 'I have to keep this engine running. They're down there behind the tree.'

Pedro recovered the bags, slung them in and took his seat next to Calderon. I heard the bolt slide home as he cocked the rifle. 'This could be more difficult. You have a gun, Senor Browning?'

'Yes.'

'Good. I hope we do not have to use them because Don Porfirio will die without sons if we do.'

'Sit straight and act your part, then,' Calderon grated. 'You are a *guardia*, nothing more.'

I hadn't driven a car for some months but the skill never leaves you. The big Hispano Suiza handled superbly; I ran through the gears and experimented with the steering. By the time the guard post at the main gate came in sight, I was confident that I could've driven it to Canada. My instinct was to put the headlights on full beam and roar on through but Pedro tapped the back of the seat.

'Slow and stop, but be ready to go fast. You can do this?'

'Yes.'

I rolled to a stop at the gate and one of the guards came out of the small mud-brick watchhouse. There were usually two or three of them at all times. This one was yawning but he had the flap on his pistol holder unbuttoned and he was still close-shaved, meaning he hadn't been on duty very long. I engaged first gear and waited with my foot on the clutch – left leg, luckily, the one that doesn't cramp when I'm windy.

The guard saluted briskly. *'Commandante.'*

Calderon told him that he was on business for Domingo.

Pedro looked straight ahead; I tried to look relaxed at the wheel. I lit a cigarette, offered the pack to the guard but he stiffened and shook his head.

'A donde van ustedes,[21] *Commandante?'* He w0061ved his hand and another guard appeared in the door of the watchhouse. I saw Pedro's mouth tighten.

'Hermosillo.'

I was watching the guard and I saw what he saw and what he was thinking just as it happened. I didn't need a translation of 'gasolina' either. He'd spotted the cans of petrol in the back and must have known that the place Calderon had named wasn't far enough away to need extra fuel. His hand went down to his holster but Pedro proved again that he was the fastest ex-schoolteacher in Mexico. A colt .45 appeared in his left hand; it boomed and the guard's face collapsed. I had the clutch out and was revving when Pedro's rifle cracked and bullets spattered the wall and windows of the watchhouse.

I don't know the statistics on acceleration from a standing start of the Hispano Suiza but they must be pretty good. The big car seemed to leap forward like, well, a Jaguar, and we were rocketing down the road with headlights blazing. I ducked my head and fought the wheel on the rough, rutted road. A couple of bullets zinged into the bodywork of the car, others whined overhead and kicked up little puffs of dust on the road ahead. Pedro let go a few rounds in return. I waited for a tyre to blow or to feel the thud in the body which I'd been told means you are shot. Nothing happened. The engine screamed and I changed gear about two hundred yards and thirty miles an hour later than the manufacturers would recommend.

'Turn right at the junction,' Pedro said, 'away from the oilifield.'

I strained my eyes to pick up the crossroad, saw it, changed down and flung the big car around. The road was marginally better and I settled into a steady seventy mph and slowly eased myself up to a proper driving position.

'What do you think, Senor Browning, of this *serpiente?*'

'*Por favor!*' Calderon said softly.

'He did his best,' I grunted. 'Let's not worry about him. How far again to the border?'

'A thousand kilometres.'

It sounded a long way but we had the car to do it. 'Do you know back roads, Pedro? A way they can't follow?'

'Yes. But how can they follow? This is the best car, surely?'

I tried to remember what else was in the garage or around the estate. A T-model Ford, a Buick, certainly nothing to touch this machine. I nodded. 'That's right, this is the best.' I looked ahead; the road was straight and white and the sky was just beginning to lighten in the east. The day would be hot, like every day.

'Have we got any water, Pedro?'

'*Si,* the car is equipped. I checked.'

'Good. We should be all right then. Farewell, General Domingo.'

The sky got lighter and I hear Calderon chuckle. He tried to suppress the sound, probably worried about the effect it might have on his manhood, but he couldn't. He laughed.

'*Callate la boca!*'[22] Pedro snapped. 'Why is he laughing?'

I looked up at the sky; it was lightening fast, the pale blue spreading across as if it was being brushed on. An eagle soared in the air; it flapped, built up speed and then dropped in a sideways sliding dive. It was a beautiful sight but it suddenly produced an image of horror in my mind. I knew why Calderon was laughing. 'Jesus!' I said. 'The planes!'

CHAPTER ELEVEN

I was so alarmed when the thought of the planes hit me that I let go of the steering wheel; the Hispano Suiza hit a bump, swayed wildly and almost tipped over. Calderon screamed and Pedro swore. The shock of nearly rolling the car wiped out the fear of the planes. I fought the wheel and regained control.

'They would not send airplanes,' Pedro said shakily. 'Not for us.'

'You have killed two men, perhaps three,' Calderon said.

Pedro laughed but the sound was forced and unconvincing. 'They lost ten times that number at the oilfield.'

'This car is the General's . . . *orgullo*', Calderon said.

I gripped the wheel, feeling the need for alcohol and tobacco. 'What's that?'

'Pride,' Pedro said. 'Yes, he would not worry about the men but he might send the planes for the car.'

'He'd send them anyway,' I said. 'Pedro, will you light me a cigarette? He'll send them because he'll think we're spies.'

Pedro passed me a lit cigarette and I drew on it deeply. 'Springfield and I had plans to sell the General out to the other side when the time was right. Springfield will think I've just picked my own time.

'*Traidor!*' Calderon hissed. Pedro hit him in the ribs with his rifle.

'It gets worse as I think about it,' I said. 'Springfield will want me dead for sure, so I can't tell anyone else what I've just told you. Dig out the brandy, Pedro. I need a drink.'

'Not while you are driving.'

'Bugger you! Get it out or I'll stop driving and we'll sit here and wait for the planes to come.'

I got my brandy. Pedro and Calderon had some too. I drove on as it got towards dawn. We stopped to open the gate on the other side of a small bridge that marked the limit of Domingo's property in this direction. We were in undulating country now; the land was much eroded, with deep gullies running between the low hills. The tree cover was sparse on the slopes, thicker on the flats where some water collected.

'We could hide the car in the trees,' I said. 'Go on foot.'

Pedro snorted. 'We would die on foot in this country. The nearest town is more than a hundred kilometres away.'

'Just a suggestion. I wonder why the planes aren't up already.'

'The pilots are all drunkards,' Calderon said. 'American scum like you, some of them. British too. It will take time to rouse them.'

'I'm Australian scum, actually,' I said.

'We have a chance then,' Pedro said. 'General Domingo is the biggest man in this province, but in the next province, not so big. He would not risk using his airplanes too far from his base.'

'How far is too far?'

'Drive like hell, Senor Browning, and we will see.'

So it became a sort of time and distance trial with me not knowing the course or where the opposition was or what the rules were. The course was the first problem. The road deteriorated after a few miles and stretches of it were half-covered by drifting sand which made traction bad. There were big potholes too, and corrugated sections where even the fine suspension of the Hispano Suiza couldn't counter the feeling that nuts and bolts were loosening along with our teeth. I remember thinking that it must be doing terrible things to Porfirio's anatomy.

We were on a straight stretch, headed towards a bright horizon on which I saw some grey smudges. There were light flashes too, as if the sun was glinting on glass or metal.

'What's that up ahead?' I pointed.

'San Cristo,' Pedro said. 'It must be. We will be safe there. Domingo would not send his men there or his planes.'

'General Hernandez is the *caudillo,* the Mayor' Calderon snarled. 'He has threatened to put out the eyes of Pablo Domingo. This is the curse of Mexico, this *disputa.'*

'Such things make the world go round,' I said. 'You mean if we get to this, what is it, Pedro, a town?'

'*Si.'*

'We'll be safe?'

'From General Domingo, not from Hernandez,' said Calderon.

'Jesus, what a country.' Just then I heard the buzzing. 'Christ,' I said, 'it's the planes.'

The two biplanes came skimming across the hilltops behind us and then sailed up high to buzz and circle overhead.

'Faster!' Pedro yelled.

I floored the accelerator and the Hispano Suiza shuddered as it responded with a mighty surge of power. The air was rushing past so fast it felt like a slipstream (something I hadn't experienced then but did later when I worked with Hughes, the craziest of the crazies, on *Hell's Angels).*[23] The smudges and glints on the horizon gave way to shapes; I could see trees and what looked like a church spire. The road was dead flat, a straight run to the town, with saltpans on either side – no chance for evasive action. We were two miles away, maybe less, and if the planes came in shooting we were like apples in a barrel. I heard the buzzing get louder and I ducked my head instinctively. The car swerved and bucked.

'Drive straight!' I screwed my head around and saw Pedro half-kneeling on the seat and sighting at a diving plane with his Mannlicher. The rifle cracked three times and I'd swear the undercarriage of the plane brushed Porfirio's *en brosse*. He was sitting bolt upright, staring ahead. The second plane dived in from the left; its machine guns chattered, sending stones and puffs of dust spurting up in a line fifty yards ahead.

'They've got us!' I screamed. 'Next time they'll cut us in half. What can we do?'

'Drive!' Pedro yelled.

My foot was welded to the accelerator and I held the wheel although it was dancing and jumping like a divining rod over water. I looked up and saw the planes circling, not far above, and with nothing, apparently, to stop them strafing us from back axle to radiator. I'd seen it done in France. The hum of their motors changed pitch and they came in. I could feel the tears jumping in my eyes and I was genuinely sorry for every mean thing I'd ever done as the sound increased to a roar, blotting out feeling.

The planes skimmed over us, sailed up into the bright blue sky, peeled off and headed away to the west. We were still half a mile short of San Cristo. I looked up, expecting another pass, but the planes were noiseless specks.

I eased up on the accelerator. 'Why?' I said.

Calderon was giggling.

'They didn't want to kill you?' I said.

His giggling changed to belly laughter. 'No,' he gasped. 'No. They must have been ordered not to damage the car. Oh, Mexico!' He laughed like a hyena. The car was in first gear now, just barely rolling. I turned around. The tears were running down Calderon's lean cheeks and he looked ten years older than he had back at Domingo's when he'd challenged Springfield across the table. I almost liked him. I laughed too.

'Stop the car,' Pedro said.

'Why? Let's get into town.'

'Stop the car!'

Something in his tone made me do it. I eased the car to a stop. We were a few hundred yards from the first of the adobe buildings that marked the outskirts of San Cristo. The road was white and dusty; the saltpans stretched away on both sides like blank sheets of paper.

'*Descenda*!'

Calderon opened the door and slowly and stiffly eased himself down onto the road. Pedro followed him. He held the rifle at port arms and moved purposefully, like a hunter stalking. He spoke rapidly in Spanish and Calderon shuffled forward in the dirt. I saw Pedro set himself, swing his leg back and deliver a thundering kick into Calderon's bum. He screamed, threw up his arms like a man shot through the chest, and collapsed into the white dust. Pedro laughed gaily and hopped back into the car.

'On, Senor Browning! Drive through San Cristo and kill as many *pollos* as you please.'

'You bloody brute! What did you do that for? He played square with us.'

'Drive,' he laughed.

I got the car moving and took a look in the rear vision mirror. Calderon had got to his feet and was standing shakily by the side of the road. He unbuckled his belt and dropped his pants. I watched until the dust we were making obscured him. Pedro was still laughing. He lit two cigarettes and passed me one. I took it although I didn't want to. I needed it.

I slowed down as we entered the main street of San Cristo. It was a fair-sized place with a big church and a few other civic buildings. The white stone gleamed in the early morning sun; the shopkeepers were laying the dust outside their establishments with buckets of water and a few of the older citizens were grouped under some fig trees around a well beside a crossroads. I could almost smell their cigars and taste their coffee. All in all, it was just the sort of place you'd stop in for breakfast if you were on a leisurely tour.

But we were not. I was still appalled at Pedro's behaviour and the talk of yet another bloodthirsty general made me anxious to get out of Mexico. I concentrated on my driving; there were horse-drawn drays and a few donkey carts on the road, no other cars. I turned as Pedro directed me and jumped like a startled deer when I heard him swear.

'What?' I said.

'*Policia* – drive on!'

A man wearing an unbuttoned khaki jacket with breeches to match strolled out of a three-storey building and stretched his arms up in an almighty yawn. His holstered pistol rode up as he stretched. He saw the car and squinted through the thin curtain of dust. By the time his yawn was finished and his arms were where they could be useful we were past.

'Go faster,' Pedro hissed. 'We don't want trouble here.'

I stepped on the gas, swerved around a man leading a laden donkey and almost scraped the car against a post as I made another turn. The road ahead was wider and led out of town. I picked up speed; the car was behaving perfectly – all gauges normal and the fuel tank more than half full.

'Don't kill anyone,' Pedro said.

'Why? Would it worry you?'

'No, but these people are savages. They would dismember us.'

'You can't talk about savages.'

We were out of the town, running past a few scattered houses with large, fenced paddocks and fields of corn. The earth was a darker, richer colour than where we'd been and there was water in a ditch running beside the road.

'Better country now,' Pedro said. 'Soon we will come to where they breed bulls for the *corrida.*'

I grunted, threw the cigarette butt away and drove.

'You disapprove of bullfighting?'

'Don't know anything about it. Does the bull ever win?'

'No, the bull dies.'

'Sounds right for this place. Porfirio is probably wishing he was dead.'

There was a scrambling, rustling noise as Pedro climbed over the seat to settle down beside me. He had the brandy bottle and a packet of cigarettes with him. I accepted the bottle, swigged, and took another lighted cigarette.

'Porfirio Calderon is undamaged.'

'Eh?'

'He was affected by wine when I found him with *la puta,* just as I said.'

'I don't think she was a whore, technically.'

'Just as you wish. Your sentiments do you credit.'

'He was drunk. So you skewered him.'

'Excuse me?'

'You stuck a thorn through his balls.'

Pedro laughed. 'No, no. That is what I *told* him, and he believed me with reason, because to him it would have felt as if his *cojones* were on fire. It is an old trick, called ... I do not know the words. You understand to put the horns on?'

'Yes.'

'What is that? A man who wears the horns?'

'A cuckold.'

'Then this is called the cuckold's revenge. It is a preparation – much chilli powder, peppers, you understand, and cactus juice?'

I nodded and puffed on the dry, loose-packed Mexican cigarette.

'When swallowed or applied to the place the feeling is as if a needle has passed through the *cojones.* Tight and hot, terrible pain, worse fear. Calderon will not be unfaithful to his wife for many days, perhaps weeks, but there is no permanent damage to him. This is better?'

'Yes,' I said. I'd wanted to even the score with Calderon after his many sly insults and I figured this did it, in spades. I didn't fancy the idea of a return bout with him, though . . . [Here Browning mutters about subsequent visits to Mexico and a feeling of insecurity. The voice is not clear; he *may* be alluding to a later encounter with Porfirio Calderon – only complete transcription of the tapes will confirm this. Ed.]

Swigging judiciously on the brandy and taking an occasional sip of water, munching on bread and fiery sausage, I drove on through the steadily improving landscape. The road crossed two sizeable streams and the grey-white and drab olive of the land around the Domingo estate gave way to deeper greens and dark reds. The rickety wooden fences and dry stone walls gave way to solid uprights and tautly strung barbed wire. A pocket in the front passenger door had yielded a set of maps which Pedro studied. The sun climbed and drops of his sweat fell on the maps.

'It's hot,' I said. 'We'll have to stop soon. I'm tired.'

'Yes. I am trying to find the right place. Is the automobile functioning correctly?'

I checked the gauges. 'Yes, perfectly. It's a fine car.'

'Worth a lot of money in the United States? Yes?'

I hadn't thought about it but it was worth considering. 'Yes.'

'Fifty-fifty?'

Somehow, I thought Pedro was going to get along fine in America. 'Fifty-fifty. We'll have to re-fuel soon. Where are we making for?'

'Tijuana. You have heard of it, Senor Browning?'

'No.'

'I am told that all gringos like it.'

CHAPTER TWELVE

It wasn't a drive I care to remember. The good, rich country didn't last. We hit more semi-desert and then rough, climbing roads through a series of hills that threatened to become mountains. I re-fuelled and checked the water and oil but the Hispano Suiza handled it all as if it had been manufactured to drive on rough Mexican roads. People were more of a problem than mechanics. The car was stoned in one village and we exchanged a few shots with policemen in another. The needles on the dashboard dials held steady. But no machine is perfect: a tyre blew on what we thought was a lonely stretch of road. I set about changing the wheel and three men on horseback appeared from nowhere.

'Work fast,' Pedro hissed. I skinned my hands with the tools – wheel-changing was a more cumbersome business in those days – while Pedro got the carbine from the gun rack. He waited until the riders were about fifty yards away and then pumped four quick rounds into a tree just ahead of them. I dropped a wheel nut and tore another strip of skin from my hand retrieving it.

Pedro yelled at the riders to stop. At least that's what they did.

'What do they want?'

'Everything,' Pedro said. 'How soon?'

I worked like a demon and had the wheel on in record time. 'Now,' I said.

'Get in and drive like hell.'

I revved up and drove away. The carbine barked again and splinters flew from the tree. The riders whooped and yelled and followed us down the road. They were bearded, dirty fellows (I was much the same, come to think of it); a few shots whipped by us but if there's a man alive who can shoot accurately from a galloping horse I've yet to meet him. We were clear of them quickly and Pedro slumped down in the back seat. He administered more brandy and cigarettes from the diminishing supply.

'How far now?'

'Getting close,' he said. His face was tight with exhaustion and I realised that after fighting a battle we'd been travelling for more than fourteen hours and had had no sleep for twice that time. Tiredness crept through me as I made the calculations.

'What's our next move?'

He puffed on his cigarette and looked at me; his eyelids were drooping over red-rimmed eyes that looked out through a mudpack of sweat and dust. 'For an officer, Senor Browning, you seem to be very short on ideas.'

'I'm a survivor,' I said. 'This your bloody country and I'll rely on you for the ideas for now. Over the border, things'll be different.'

He sighed and went into stage Mexican. 'Si, Senor. I suppose they weel.'

I laughed. 'It was a good trick you played on Porfirio.'

'Yes. He will have to invent some story for the General.'

'So will Springfield.'

Pedro threw his cigarette end away and passed me the brandy bottle. 'If we are lucky they will talk to each other before they talk to the General. They should see that we are not a threat to them.'

'You'd say we're in the clear, then?'

'I am an optimist, Senor Browning.'

'So am I.'

'Then to answer your question, what we do next is take off these goddamn uniforms and get ready to spend some money in Tijuana.'

We stopped by a creek and took turns at washing and changing clothes while the other stood guard. I kept the uniform pants and boots, they were the most respectable clothes I had, but achieved a civilian touch with a white shirt and black waistcoat. Pedro had a red shirt, dark trousers and soft hide boots. We shaved in the cold water and slicked our hair down. I climbed up the creek bank to where Pedro stood with the carbine.

'How do you feel?' he said.

'I am tired.'

'Me too.'

'See how fast the water runs. We are close to the coast.' He squinted at the western sky which was a clear pale blue with a few light clouds down low. Since our flight had started I hadn't thought to consider the time. We'd been operating on things like night and day, dawn and noon. I checked my pocket watch now; it was almost two o'clock in the afternoon. 'How long to Tijuana?'

'One hour,' he said, 'maybe less.'

...

Tijuana was a border town and that's about all there was to say about it. Like all border towns, it made its living out of moving people and money. It has a racetrack and a bullring and no one stays overnight at a racetrack or a bullring; it also has a lot of hotels where people stay overnight or for a week or so but seldom longer. Their money stays longer – at the track, in the bars and brothels and in the sort of fix-it places Pedro and I were headed for.

Pedro didn't know the town; he'd have been over the border in a flash if he'd ever managed to get this close before. But he did have a cousin there and the cousin knew everything there was to know. Pedro directed me to the tacked-up apartment house where his cousin lived and left me to guard the car. I was bushed and needed to sleep. The Hispano Suiza looked pretty conspicuous in the alley along with the empty bottles and discarded racetrack newssheets. A Mexican teenager strolled over, leaned on the side of the car and looked at me. He had a pale brown skin and the beginnings of a wispy black moustache.

'You wanna girl?'

'No.'

'Wanna boy?'

I showed him the hole at the end of the barrel of a Colt.

'Hey, easy, man. I jus' wanna help.'

'All right. You sit in the front here and mind the car while I sleep in the back. If there's nothing missing when I wake up I'll give you a dollar. Deal?'

'Two dollars.'

'Depends how long I sleep. If it's over an hour, okay, two dollars.'

'Deal.'

He got in; I climbed over the back and curled up on the seat with the pistol by my hand. Our bags were in the trunk and the key was in my pocket – there was nothing for him to steal. I went to sleep as soon as my head touched the leather.

I woke up with that feeling of not knowing who or where I was or what century I was in. Pedro was shaking me; there was no sign of the Mexican kid. I sat up and rubbed my eyes.

'Where's the kid?'

'What kid?'

'The one I left guarding the car.'

Pedro looked at the car. 'At least he didn't take the wheels.'

I looked around the back seat. The gun rack was empty. 'He got the carbine and the shotgun.'

'No matter. Come on, we have somewhere to go. And we don't need the guns, just money.'

I struggled into the front seat. 'Where are we going?'

'The United States of America, *after* we get some papers for the car and some papers for me.'

We drove down a succession of dirty, dusty streets in which life seemed to be lived out in the open. Merchandise from the shops was outside; women washed clothes in tubs and hung them on lines in front of the houses; children played in the streets and horses and dogs shat in them. Pedro directed me to drive down an alley behind a fruit market and wait.

'Don't eat the fruit,' he said, 'your delicate gringo stomach couldn't take it.'

'I need a drink,' I said.

He pointed over to a stall where water was dropping from an ice chest and running across the dusty street. 'They might have some beer in bottles. Get a couple for me. I won't be long.'

I checked the Colt .45 for anyone who might be interested, shoved it in my pocket and walked over to the stall. After some mime and stammered Spanish I got six small bottles of beer. They were cool rather than cold, but the first one went down so fast it didn't matter.

I sat in the car, shooing off the occasional too-curious kid, sipping the beer and thinking about my situation. I had some Mexican gold worth maybe a thousand or so American dollars. Then there was the half share in the car. That led me to consideration of Pedro and how I felt about him as a travelling companion. Invaluable up to now of course, but over the border? From what I'd heard, Mexicans were servants in Hollywood and damn good servants too. Somehow I couldn't see Pedro in the role. It looked like the parting of the ways was close.

Pedro came out of the tin shed behind the fruit market and approached the car. For the first time since I'd met him he looked tentative. He accepted one of the beers and drank off half in a couple of gulps.

'We can get papers and licence plates for the car, that is not a problem. I can also get an envelope, stamped and posted in the United States.'

'What for?'

'To contain a letter which you can write engaging me as a servant and saying you will pick me up in Tijuana on this date. The envelope and the paper are genuine, with an American business name and address on them.'

'Sounds good,' I said. 'Let's get them. We can go to a bar and I'll write the letter.'

'The envelope and paper will cost money. Such things are very valuable. Also we need money for the men on the Mexican side of the border.'

'How much, all up?'

'All up?'

'For everything.'

He finished the beer. 'Three hundred dollars, Mexican.'

I unbuttoned my shirt and slid two fingers into a pocket on the money belt. I laid a gold coin on the seat. 'How many of these?'

Pedro breathed out slowly. 'This is how you were paid by Domingo?'

'This is how.'

He swore and shook his head. 'Six of these. Senor Browning. Have you got it?'

I extracted five more of the coins and gave them to him.

'*Gracias.*'

I waved my hand. 'That's all right, Pedro. You can pay me back out of your split on the car.'

. . .

We drove into the centre of Tijuana which was no cleaner or better-smelling than the outskirts unless you like the smell of money. I felt the need of a clean start before I tried my hand at letter-writing. We left the Hispano Suiza at a garage and Pedro extracted some more money to pay a man who would put Californian licence plates on it.

I went into the first men's outfitting shop we came to. I emerged in a white linen suit with a soft shirt and a string tie. I bought a Panama hat, silk socks and white shoes. Pedro got a fresh white shirt, a Stetson hat and some new dark trousers to replace his old shiny ones.

'I must look like a servant,' he said.

'Yeah, you should. How d'you feel about that?'

'Safe.'

I drank whisky and soda while Pedro drank beer as we composed a letter on paper headed 'Happy Valley Funeral Services, Santa Monica, Ca.' The letterhead also contained the name of the Director – Joshua P. Underhill – and what I wrote was a letter to Paco Olivares (the name on the envelope) from Underhill engaging him as a 'Happy Valley' employee at a salary to be negotiated. Richard K. Browning, Services Director of the firm, was travelling to Mexico and would give Olivares transport back to Santa Monica.

After a few rough copies on dime store paper I wrote the genuine forgery in a bold, nerveless hand. Pedro took it from me, rubbed his hand across the slightly greasy table top and folded and re-folded the paper several times.

'They might ask you where you crossed into Mexico. Where was that?'

I tried to remember and then I recalled that I had been insensible at the time. 'Place called Yuma, I think.'

'That'll do.'

'Have you got anything else to show you're Olivares?'

'Yes. That was part of the deal.'

'I haven't got anything else to connect me with the funeral place.'

'You've got the car,' Pedro said. 'You can say it is open because it is for funerals in Hollywood, so people can see the stars riding in the procession. They will believe you.'

It was late in the day when we reached the border post. I sat like a ramrod in the car while Pedro removed his hat and showed his letter to a fat, sleepy-looking official. He also passed across two envelopes into which he'd stuffed Mexican banknotes. I'm always the same at frontiers – close to panic and filled with imaginings. What if Domingo had put out an alarm on the car and a price on our heads? What if Porfirio had guessed where we'd be heading? What if Springfield had decided to play bounty hunter? The fat man glanced at the car, yawned and waved us through.

The American post was manned by an over-stuffed Texan in stiff, ironed khakis. (Texans, as I later found, seem to specialise in border guard work, God knows why.) Pedro took his hat off again and I passed across the documents – passport, papers for the car and the letter to Paco Olivares.

'Where'd y'all cross, Mist' Brownin'?'

'Yuma.'

'No stay-umps.'

'No, they didn't stamp it.'

'Lazy sons of bitches. Y'all got a California licence?'

I thought fast. 'No, I've applied for it but it hasn't come through yet. I've got an Australian one but not with me.'

'Don' matter.' He squinted at the letter in the fading light. 'What's the Mex goin' to be doin' with your outfit?'

I removed my hat and put it on my knee. 'Well, Officer, there's a lot of Mexicans in the Santa Monica area and they die, just like anyone else. We need someone who can communicate with them. It's a difficult task at a time of bereavement. They're Christian folk, sir.'

'They are? Well, ah never knew that. Welcome back to the USA, Mist' Brownin', and welcome to you too, Paco. God bless you both.'

CHAPTER THIRTEEN

The air smelled sweeter, the stars shone brighter and all that sort of thing. I'd been so tense in Tijuana that I hadn't thought to buy any liquor. A good slug of whisky would have gone down well but I could manage without it – I've always used liquor more for comfort in adversity than for celebration. Pedro seemed to feel the same; he lit two cigarettes and passed one across. Instead of a drink he contented himself with spitting fulsomely out of the car.

'No brandy left, I suppose,' I said.

'Are you crazy?'

'What d'you mean?'

'Haven't you heard of Prohibition. Strong liquor is against the law now in this country.'

'Christ, I'd forgotten.'

'Didn't you see how that fat fool looked at us. He managed to touch a few things in the car too. If we had clinked like bottles . . .' He drew his hand swiftly across his throat.

'What can a man drink here – wine?'

'Don't think so. Beer, maybe. Doesn't matter. We have freedom.'

'From what?' Seemed to be a contradiction there to me.

'Communists, anarchists, monarchists, republicans . . .'

'They have republicans in the US, I think.'

He drew on his cigarette and blew smoke luxuriously. 'Not quite the same, Senor. Where there are no monarchists, Republicans can get on with making money. Am I right?'

I shrugged. 'Never understood politics.'

'What are your plans?'

I was sure there was a sneer in his tone. I was tired, physically and also in the other way – tired of this bloody Mexican and his uppity ways. I hammered the brake; the Hispano Suiza slewed a bit on the road but came to a stop much faster than Pedro could have anticipated. He shot forward and slammed his head into the windshield. He slumped back, swearing and moaning. When he'd recovered he found that I had pulled off to the side of the road. There was nothing around but sage brush and desert. A coyote howled, long and desperately, off in the hills. Pedro shook his head and looked into the muzzle of my .45.

'Give me one good reason why I shouldn't dump you here.'

'I rescued you from Domingo and Springfield.'

'I drove the car. I rescued you from the Communists and whathave-you. We're even.'

'I can give you another reason.'

'And what's that?'

'The car is out of petrol. You wouldn't make one kilometre.'

I glanced at the dial, just quickly, but long enough for Pedro to grip my wrist and shake the Colt out of it. I don't know how a schoolmaster could get to be so strong; they weren't like that back at Dudleigh Grammar. Now it was my turn to look into the business end of the pistol.

'Very foolish, Senor Browning. You are not a man of action.'

'Maybe you're right.' I think I kept my voice pretty level because I realised I had an ace in the hole – Pedro couldn't drive, so he couldn't kill me or leave me on the road.

'I have the *pistola*, so I will do the talking.'

'Could we talk as we go?' I said. 'There's not a lot of petrol and I'm dying for a drink, even if it's only beer.'

'Yes, let us go on, but we need to talk before we sleep or I know I will wake up to find myself alone. Or you might even hand me over to the police.'

I started the car, thinking I should hear more about that idea. 'Why would I do that?'

'To save dividing the money for the car.'

'Never entered my head. I'm deeply hurt at the suggestion. Put the bloody gun down, Pedro. Let's find something to drink.'

We drove on a few miles to a roadhouse where they sold gas, beer with an alcohol content just above water and something they called 'Eats'. This turned out to be hamburgers, fried in thick grease and served with limp lettuce and watery potatoes. The place was empty apart from us; maybe it had a reputation. Pedro pushed his aside, drank off a glass of beer and lit a cigarette. I've never been a gourmet; the food was hot and I was hungry. I drank some beer to help it down.

'How can you eat it?' Pedro said.

I waved my fork at him while I chewed. 'This is just the problem,' I said when I'd cleared my mouth. 'You're so bloody superior. It's not going to work, you and me travelling together. Let's sell the car and split up, soon as we can.'

Pedro sipped his beer and puffed on his cigarette. The man in the dirty apron who'd served us the food looked surprised at Pedro's easy manner.

'Could you teach me to drive a car?'

'Of course, of course. Should be snap for a man like you – someone who can quote Shakespeare and everything.'

'I am serious. I know we cannot be equals here in the United States. I, too, see the way this *lavaplatos*[24] looks at us.'

'Right.'

'What do you plan to do now, Senor Browning. Are you returning to Australia?'

'Christ, no! I'm going to Hollywood to be a movie star.'

'That is perfect. You will need a manservant.'

'Oh, no.'

'Yes, listen, I can be very useful to you. Servants know everything about their masters. I could be your spy.'

'I won't need a spy.'

'Will you be making the movies yourself? With your money?'

'Of course not.'

'You will be working for other men? Others will hire you?'

'In a manner of speaking, yes.'

'Will there be others who will want the jobs you want?'

I thought back to the jealousy and rivalry I'd seen in Australia – the manoeuvring for even small parts in a turkey like *The Kelly Gang*. 'Yes,' I said.

'Then you will need a spy. Rich men are unpredictable, knowing their moods is everything in dealing with them.'

It was time to lay it on the line. 'You're too uppity.'

'Too uppity for a Mexican?'

'For anyone.'

'You're not a star yet, so you can't afford to have only men who say "si" around you.'

There was something in that. I couldn't take any more of the greasy food; I shoved the plate aside and swilled some beer. 'You would have to pretend to be a servant.'

'Si, I can do that – in public'

'And in private . . . ?'

I looked at him across the stained, greasy table. A neat, compact man – black beard, sharp dark eyes, the brain of a schoolteacher and the reflexes of an athlete. Only a fool would've turned down an ally like that. I held out my hand. 'In private we're friends. Hollywood, here we come!'

We shook, filled our glasses and drank a toast to ourselves. It was too much for the counterman. He banged his fist on the glass case that held some fly-blown cakes and pastries. The glass splintered and broke. He swore and sucked at a cut hand.

'You two guys git outa here, or I'll call the Sheriff. Git!'

I'd already paid for a tank of gas and some oil; I left some money on the table for the food and we got. A mile down the road the word

'Autocourt' was picked up in light bulbs. I pulled in and honked the horn. A light appeared in an office at the front of the shabby clapboard building.

'This is where it starts,' I said.

Pedro nodded. I climbed down from the car and went into the office. An old man in his pyjamas was scratching himself through the opening at the crotch. He looked past me, out to the car and to where Pedro was unloading my bag.

'I want a cabin,' I said. 'He'll sleep in the car.'

. . .

Around noon the following day we were a couple of miles from San Diego; Pedro was at the wheel having his first driving lesson and I heard the siren. I screwed around and saw the black police car gaining on us rapidly. The siren screamed in the still desert air. Pedro reacted instinctively – he floored the accelerator and the Hispano Suiza picked up instantly. He'd been an apt pupil, mastering the basics of driving very quickly, but I didn't fancy my chances with such a novice at a hundred plus miles an hour.

'Slow down,' I screamed. 'You'll kill us.'

Pedro threw the car into a bend; he was a natural driver and used the power to get around rather than the brake which would probably have rolled us. I wanted to grab the wheel but didn't.

'Pedro,' I said, fighting for calm, 'slow down. We haven't done anything wrong. I'm a licensed driver, I'm allowed to teach you.'

'The plates,' Pedro said. He accelerated early to cope with an upcoming hill.

'What d'you mean, the plates?' The air rushing passed whipped my words away. I leaned closer and shouted in his ear.

'The plates we got in Mexico,' he yelled, ' . . . stolen from a car in California . . . *policia* ... a record of the number. So they are chasing us.'

'Jesus, but we didn't steal them.' I looked back again; we'd gained a little on the police car. The road was narrow and winding and there were cars up ahead of us. I hadn't instructed Pedro in passing technique.

'No, but we *did* steal this car.'

'But that was in Mexico.'

'You think you can steal whatever you want in Mexico? Eh, Senor Browning? How in hell do you go around another car?'

The speedometer needle was flicking over ninety and we were gaining on an Oldsmobile that was crawling along at about seventy.

'Do you sound the horn?'

'Yes! No! Christ!'

Pedro honked; the Olds moved to the edge and gave Pedro room to get around. He eased the big car out without losing speed and we were confronted by another car rushing at us with its horn blaring.

'What do I do?'

I shut my eyes. The oncoming horn blasted, the siren behind wailed and I expected the next sound to be like the guns at the Somme. Instead I heard the squeal of rubber on road; stones flew up and rattled against the bodywork, there was a loud *whoosh* and we were past. Pedro hadn't touched the brake or moved the steering wheel a fraction more than he should. To the police it must have looked like demoralisingly brilliant driving. They dropped back. Pedro maintained speed as we neared a huddle of faded, white-painted adobe buildings that marked the outskirts of San Diego.

'Slow down,' I said. 'Put your foot on the brake gently. Just touch it.'

He did it as if he'd been driving for twenty years. The car slowed to seventy and it felt like walking pace.

'Have you got a cousin here too?' I said.

'Probably. Why?'

'We have to get rid of this car.'

'I am enjoying this driving.'

'Mate,' I said, 'you were closer to death then than at the oilfield or any other time in your bloody life.'

He grinned and put on the fake accent. 'I am lucky, no?'

'Yes, you are lucky. Now let's get into this town and turn a few bloody corners in case those cops still have ideas.'

...

Pedro didn't have any actual cousins in San Diego but once he'd located the *barrio* he found a dozen substitutes. The deal was similar to that in Tijuana, with no-Spanish-to-speak-of-Browning waiting in the car while he went into bars and cafes and talked, waving his arms, with other men on the street. In the end he sold the Hispano Suiza for two thousand dollars.

'It is worth more,' he said, 'but it would take time to get more. These people do not know me well enough to trust me.'

'You told them it's the General's car?'

'Hell, no. I told them you stole it in San Francisco.'

'Great.' I accepted my half of the money. That put us on the street in downtown San Diego with a bag apiece, some clothes, two .45s and a couple of thousand dollars.

'What now?' Pedro said. 'Gamble, drink, whore?'

I looked at him. He'd shaved off the beard in Tijuana but there was an ironic tilt to his moustache. 'What d'you mean?'

'I mean, are you going to be stupid or smart?'

'What would be smart in your opinion, Senor Cortez?'

He guided me along the street; we were a couple of blocks from the waterfront but the strong smells of a big seaport were in the afternoon air. Many of the buildings had a strong Spanish flavour but the place wore an air of having expanded recently. Spanish fronts had been modified and there were modern extensions to old buildings as well as brand new ones. There were more automobiles on the roads than I was used to seeing; shiny and new, a lot of them, along with some horse-drawn traffic and well-worn T-model Fords and other dusty vehicles in from the farm. It was a warm afternoon with dark clouds building up on the western horizon. Pedro wiped sweat from his face and flexed his fingers as if the driving had cramped them. 'I mentioned our plans to go to Hollywood to some people where I sold the car. I have been told about a man here who knows everything about Hollywood. It would be wise to speak with him.'

'You could be right. What's his name and where do we find him?'

'His name is Bartholomew Booth and he is living at the Hotel Columbo.'

'Well, it'll be the same deal. You'll have to find somewhere else to stay.'

'No, it is a *barrio* hotel, or almost so. Mexicans can stay there.'

'This man who knows all about Hollywood is staying at a Mexican hotel?'

Pedro shrugged. 'Perhaps he is a saint, then again, he might like Mexican whores. Let us find out.'

The Hotel Columbo was a few blocks closer to the waterfront and a few further away from the respectable part of town. The pre-dominant colour of the faces in the streets marked the boundaries – we had walked from white to brown country; black was probably on a bit further. It was an old building in the Spanish style – arched at the bottom, square-sided and flat on top. The white paint had peeled off long ago, leaving a mottled pink and grey beneath. The palm trees outside were dying of thirst.

Inside, the place was dark and smelled of sweat. The desk clerk registered us without comment and took two dollars each up front. The place must have had pretensions once; there were old, heavy furnishings and elaborate ceiling decorations ideally designed to gather dust.

'Can you tell me where to find Mr Booth?' I asked the desk man.

'In the bar.' He pointed to a narrow corridor on the left of the lobby.

'Take the bags up, Pedro,' I said. 'I'll take the room with the most light and you can draw me a bath.'

Pedro said nothing; he took the keys, shouldered the bags and moved towards the stairs. When we were out of earshot from the desk he whispered, 'I am going out. I want to do some more car driving.'

'What about my bath?'

'If you can find a bath in a place like this you will be fortunate. If there is water in pipes to it you will be very lucky. If there is a plug, God must be your best friend.'

He went up the stairs. I took the corridor to the bar which had been positioned so as to allow no natural light to enter. It was a long narrow room with a long bar, a few tables and chairs and no windows. The only light came from some heavily shaded lamps. How the barman would be able to tell the scotch from the brandy in this gloom was beyond me. There was only one customer – a heavy-set man with a white beard who was laying out cards on the table in front of him. He had a bottle and glass on the table, an ashtray and a thick, leather-bound book. I ordered a near-beer (which was all you could get legitimately) at the bar and indicated that I wanted it served at the table. The Mexican barman scowled and seemed to go looking for a dirty glass.

I walked over to the table. 'Mr Booth? Mr Bartholomew Booth?'

He didn't look up – the game of solitaire appeared to have his whole attention. 'Yes,' he said.

'I believe, sir, that you are well-informed about Hollywood and the movies.'

Still gazing at the cards, he brought his glass to his mouth and drank and took a pull on his cigar which he then laid in the ashtray. 'That is true,' he said in a deep, stagey voice. 'What do you want to know?'

'How to . . . conduct oneself there.'

'Oneself, eh?' He raised his head and showed me the most alcohol-damaged eyes in the most alcohol-damaged face I had ever seen.

It was almost enough to send you rushing off to sign the pledge. Almost. 'Don't say "oneself" for a start. If you use words like "oneself" every door will be closed against you.'

'What should one . . . you say, then?'

'A guy. What should a guy say?'

'What should a guy say?'

'A guy should say, "When's the next train out of here?" and catch it.' He laid a card, took another drink and puff. My beer arrived.

'Do you mind if I join you?'

He waved the cigar and I nodded to the barman who put the drink on the table. I sat down. 'I'm going to Hollywood, Mr Bartholomew, to be an actor. I'd be grateful for your advice.'

He raised the ravaged face again. 'How old d'you think I am?'

I shook my head. 'I don't know.'

'Forty-one. When I arrived in Hollywood in 1915 I looked something like you. More mature, of course.'

'What happened?' I blurted.

'Success, celebration, failure and ruin. Hollywood corrupted me and threw me away. I am the first of its major victims.' His voice went up a level and trembled. 'I will not be the last, mark my words. Do not go to Hollywood, young man. Go back to England. Work on the legitimate stage if you must.'

'I'm not from England. I'm Australian.'

'Even better, because even further from the pit of vice that is Hollywood.'

I was getting excited by the possibilities. 'Pit of vice?'

'Drink, drugs, women, money, corruption.'

'Really?'

The solitaire game was a bust. He put the last card down and became serious about the bottle and the glass. 'You are attracted by what I say?'

'Well, not exactly, but I feel . . .'

'You feel you have the strength of character to resist the pitfalls and ascend the heights?'

'Well, yes, I suppose so.'

'You are a fool. I made a fortune in Hollywood. I worked for Sennett and Griffith; I worked with Francis X. Bushman.[25] All of them. One slip and it was all over. No forgiveness, no compassion. Have you read this, young man?'

He pushed the book across. It was *War and Peace* by Tolstoy.

'No,' I said.

'You should. The whole world should, but since it will not, it is imperative that it be brought to the screen. That is my life's ambition, to film *War and Peace*. Only for that will I return to Hollywood.'

'Sounds like a good idea.'

'So you would think, but it is the idea that brought me down. The vision was too big, too noble . . .'

'I can't say I've seen your name . . .'

He put down an inch of whatever was on the bottle (it had no label), and poured some more, automatically adding some to my glass. 'Ah, names. Pay no attention to names, particularly if you are set on going to Hollywood. What is Theda Bara's real name, d'you know?'[26]

I shook my head and drank; the stuff in the glass bore some relation to whisky but the kinship wasn't close.

'Theodosia Goodman, of Cincinnati, Ohio.'

This came as less of a surprise to me than it might to others, since I have travelled under a few names myself. I was beginning to have doubts about the usefulness of Bartholomew Booth when he surprised me by stubbing out his cigar and taking a deep breath of air which couldn't be called fresh but wasn't two-thirds tobacco smoke. He focused his red-veined eyes on my face and blinked. 'Have you got fifty dollars?'

'Yes.'

'For fifty dollars I'll give you the advice you need to make a start in Hollywood.'

I dug into my pocket where I'd put away some of the money from the car. Without letting Booth see how much was in the roll, I detached five tens and put them on the table. He quickly covered the notes with cards. 'First, you need an agent.'

I nodded. Harry Southwell had said the same thing. 'Do you know one?'

'Yes.' He pulled out a card and a pen and wrote with a shaky hand. 'H. Elliot Silkstein is the man you want. Second, you must make an entrance.'

'An entrance?'

'Yes. Here is what you do. You wire some of your details – physical description, war service . . . you do have a service record?'

'Er, yes.'

'Good, very important. That was another count against me. I was unfit – back problem. Anyway, you send that to Silkstein and plus, oh, a hundred dollars.'

'What for?'

'To show him you're not a bum. Tell him when your train gets in and he'll do the rest.'

'Which is?'

'Press coverage. My boy, since Carl Laemmle pulled that stunt with Florence Lawrence,[27] the movie business has thrived on publicity. If you're in the papers you're alive, that's how they look at it.'

'They?'

'Sennett, Griffith, Ince, Laemmle himself. They know most of the publicity is fake but they still believe it. They believe it even when they fake it themselves. They're children. Children!'

'Would this Silkstein meet me at the station.'

'Not exactly. He'll have someone there to see what sort of impression you make. If you come through it well, nothing will be too good for you.'

'And if I don't?'

'Five hundred dollars might get you another chance. Might. It's a dog eat dog world, Mr . . .?'

'Browning. Richard Browning.'

'Browning . . .'He rolled it in his mouth as if to mellow it. 'Good, quite good. Ever been in gaol under it?'

'Not in America.'

'Keep it then. Well, get busy, young man. Here's Silkstein's address and make sure you put a San Francisco address on the cable.'

'Why?'

'My dear boy, no one goes to Hollywood from San Diego. San Diego is where you go after Hollywood has finished with you.'

He drained his glass, poured again and opened the book. I stood and looked down at the thin hair brushed carefully across his pink skull. Forty-one? Impossible. I didn't know it then, but I was to see forty-one year olds who made Bartholomew Booth look like Barrymore.

CHAPTER FOURTEEN

First stop was the telephone in the hotel lobby. The next Hollywood train left at 9 a.m. the following day. I made reservations for two. Then to the Western Union office. Composition[28] was never my strong point at school, but I did the best I could on the subject of 'Richard Browning, actor'. Scott Fitzgerald once told me that his writing was just a whole lot of lies about himself and other people. I followed the same principle, increasing my height a fraction to six foot two, claiming an acting credit on Longford's *Mutiny of the Bounty*, writing, producing and acting credits for Southwell's *The Kelly Gang* as well as close acquaintanceship with both directors. Well, it was partly true.

It *was* true that I could ride and shoot better than most and that I was a better than average runner, cricketer and tennis player. The war record was tricky; I kept it vague as to unit and rank, but tried to get the impression across that I'd been through it all from Egypt to France. I also said I'd served in the 'Mexican revolution' and concluded by authorising the collection of a hundred bucks by H. Elliot Silkstein of 501 Sunset Boulevard, Hollywood, Ca.

Back at the hotel I found Pedro had returned from a driving lesson claiming to be a hundred per cent perfect at the art.

'We'll see,' I said, 'when we get to Hollywood.'

His face fell. 'We're not driving?'

'No, we're going by train tomorrow. And you're going to have to put on a good act at bag carrying, door opening and the like. Would you like to get into practice by drawing me a bath?'

'No. I'm going to get a drink.'

Of course I went with him and naturally we tied one on. We were soldiers fresh from a trying campaign as well as refugees and car thieves on the run. I was about to perpetrate a kind of fraud and I daresay I could've thought of a few other reasons to let off steam if I needed them. In fact I didn't think; I didn't think about the Volstead Act, which made every drink we had in every low-life speakeasy (and they were way down the scale on account of Pedro not being Anglo Saxon) illegal, I just went along with Pedro, drank drink for drink with him, ate the same steaks and finished up in a whorehouse with a more or less identical girl.

'*Muy limpio,*' Pedro had insisted drunkenly as we entered. 'Very clean.'

'I'm glad to hear it,' I said, but in truth, I was beyond caring. Maria, with her wild, bucking ways, seemed so long ago it felt like another life and before her ... I tried to remember and shuddered. Elizabeth Macknight. My loving wife. I had a few glasses of tequila with the girl before we went up to the room. She was dark and wore a pretty white blouse and white cotton undergarments. I remember the undergarments and not much else – I fancy she had a pretty easy night of it.

I woke up to feel Pedro shaking my shoulder. He needed a shave but otherwise looked fine. I felt like hell; tequila hangovers are perhaps the worst of all and I've had enough of all kinds to qualify as an expert. The worst thing about them is the bells; I hear bells, like church bells, and have a sense of guilt as well as a gritty throat and eyes, sick stomach, trembling and all the rest. Sheer hell.

The desk man at the Columbo looked indifferently at Pedro and me as we came in at around 7 a.m. I went upstairs, bathed and shaved and put on a clean shirt. The linen suit was a little crumpled and there were a few stains on the panama. *What the hell,* I thought, I'm a man of action. They can't expect me to look as if I've just come from the tailor's. How wrong I was.

Pedro looked a little scruffy too; more like a bodyguard than a manservant, but I was inexperienced in such matters in those days and thought nothing of it. I paid what we owed at the hotel (I'd noticed the night before that Pedro had developed a knack of dropping back deferentially when it was time to pay), and we got a taxi to the station. Here we blended in perfectly with the other travellers who all looked as if they'd slept in cheap hotels if not whorehouses. We put my bags in the first class compartment, Pedro's in the second class carriage, and found a cafe to kill the time until the train left with coffee and tortillas. Well, perhaps there were one or two snorts from a bottle Pedro had picked up the night before, just as hairs of the dog.

It's only around a hundred and fifty miles from San Diego to Los Angeles, but there were stops along the way and trains were slower in those days. The journey took until mid-afternoon. It was comfortable enough, with negro waiters serving sandwiches and pitchers of iced drink that just begged to have some gin added, which they'd do for a consideration, and some good cigars as mementos of my Mexican adventure, but I was beginning to feel nervous. I went through to the second class carriage and took Pedro back to the observation platform for a smoke and conversation.

'Ever done any acting, amigo?' I asked him, after we'd got the cigars alight.

'But of course. A schoolteacher who cannot act is nothing.' He puffed smoke which was whipped away by the rushing air. 'Poof! Nothing!'

'And a tough audience, eh?'

'Impossible, or nearly so. The teacher must act furious, pleased, critical . . . interested. Everything.'

'How d'you go about it? I mean . . . damn it, how do you get in the mood?'

'It is an art.'

'Eh?'

'Could you always shoot so straight?'

'Well, yes, I suppose . . . practice . . .'

'Practice improved you, yes. But you could do it from the start. It is the same with acting. You can do it or you cannot.'

'Thanks a lot, Pedro. Very encouraging.'

He waved his cigar majestically. '*De nada.* It is nothing. If you will excuse me I will go back to the carriage. I am already working on your behalf. Earning my salary.'

I realised that the subject of salary hadn't been broached but I was too curious to do it now. 'How's that?'

'I am having a very interesting conversation with a man who works for a movie star. One Senor Beery – a strange name.'

'Wallace Beery?' I said.

'Just so. I have learned where we must live when we get to Hollywood.'

'Oh, and where's that?'

'Beverly Hills.'

'And what else have you learned? How come he's travelling on this train, anyway.'

'He is on his holiday. We must discuss holidays, Senor Browning. What else? Oh, yes, I know what kind of car I . . . you must drive.'

'And that is?'

'A Studebaker, with whitewall tyres. Excuse me.'

Pedro never was much of a one for boosting the confidence, unless it was his own, which never seemed to need boosting. I went back to my compartment and spent the time smoking, looking out the window and working myself into a near panic. The desert, which had seemed to run from a line of mountains to the east right down to the ocean, began to yield to orange groves and vegetable farms. The train rushed through a couple of small, one-street towns and then we were coming into the South Pacific Railroad depot at Los Angeles.

My first impressions were of the heat and the flatness. The buildings around were low-lying. We could have been in some part of Australia were it not for the palm trees and the weird red-brick Arabian look of the station. The train pulled in on Track 3; I got down and saw Pedro hurrying along the platform with his bag. I passed mine across to him, pulled myself up to my full height, straightened my suit and looked around. People rushed about; porters wheeled trunks and Mexicans carried bundles. I could hear trolley cars clanging out on the street. I moved a few steps away from the train and lit a cigarette which I hoped would add a more popular touch than a cigar. Still nothing.

Pedro pointed across the tracks. 'Look there.'

A train was shunting out and six or seven men, looking oddly alike, in dark suits and hats, trooped away from the tracks and towards the barrier. Something about their slouching bodies and alert, inquisitive heads told me they were newspapermen.

'Hey,' I said weakly. 'Hey, I'm over here.'

They couldn't hear me and kept moving. I was about to walk across the tracks when I heard a shout.

'Get back, you goddamn fool!' A hand-driven trolley whizzed past on the tracks, missing me by inches. When I'd stopped shaking I realised that I'd dropped my cigarette. I stamped it out and lit another. Across the track, a man in a checked suit put his hands up to his mouth and hollered, 'You Browning?'

I nodded. He pointed ahead to the barriers. Pedro and I walked to the gate and handed in our tickets. The checks on the suit were loud – brown on a yellowish background. He was a thin, nervous-looking man with black hair brushed straight back.

'Browning, eh?' he said.

I held out my hand but he looked up and down the station and didn't take it. 'Herbie Green. Boy, you really screwed up.'

'What d'you mean?'

'Mr Silkstein was impressed by your credentials. He had all the press boys down here to meet ya.'

'Well?'

'You said you was comin' from 'Frisco. They waited for the 'Frisco train and you ain't on it. Then I see you comin' in from Dago. Phew, just as well nobody else seen it. Nobody but a bum would come in from Dago.'

CHAPTER FIFTEEN

'Pity,' Herbie Green said. He flicked a Lucky Strike out of a packet and lit it with a petrol lighter.

'What d'you mean?' I was so stunned at my blunder that I could scarcely get the words out.

'Fairbanks 'n Dwan are castin' for *Robin Hood*. Mr Silkstein figured you might be the right type.' He turned to head towards the street.

'Wait, wait! Mr . . . Green. He's right! I could be Little John or . . . Richard the Lion-Heart . . .'

Herbie turned back and eyed me with interest. 'You're a limey, right? You knew all those guys?'

'No, of course not. They're all dead.'

'Yeah? That's tough. How'd they get it?'

'Hundreds of years ago.'

'Is that right? Well, it figures – historical pictures are very big. Especially with Doug. Yeah, it figures. Too bad, like I say.'

I grabbed his arm and held him. Herbie Green was the first of the many people I met in Hollywood who had no education and knew nothing whatever about the world except as it pertained to moving pictures. I'm an ignoramus, always have been, but at least I know the framework for all the things I'm ignorant of, if you see what I mean. Not Herbie and his kind – tell them the Crusaders brought in Prohibition and they'd scratch their heads and try to recall who played the second rum runner in the picture.

'I know all about Robin Hood,' I babbled. 'Friar Tuck, Maid Marian, Sherwood Forest . . .' This practically exhausted my knowledge but I had Herbie's attention.

'Yeah, that's it. Sherwood Forest – Doug's buildin' it out on Santa Monica, along with the castle an' ever-thin'.'

'I've been there,' I lied. 'I could tell them what it's like.'

'Yeah? Where is it?'

'Scotland, up that way.'

'Well, Doug took a trip I hear an' studied up on all that. Plus he'd have his experts for sure. Nah, Mr Silkstein had figured you for one of the Merry Men maybe, but you sure screwed up.'

There was only one answer I could think of to that. I'd learned one rule – that appearances count for almost everything in Hollywood. The second rule I stumbled on at that moment; that the only other thing that counts is money. I peeled five twenty dollar notes off my roll and held them up. Herbie's dark, shifty eyes took on a reverent look.

'Yours, for an interview with Mr Silkstein.'

He licked his lips. 'What could I say about you comin' in the wrong way?'

My mind raced. 'Tell him nothing. I'll say it was a stunt to get the press interested. I'll say it misfired. I'll say I was delayed. Just get me in to see him.'

He scratched his chin, still looking at the money. 'Probably cost you another five Cs, even if he buys your story.'

'That's all right.'

His hand snaked out and he took the money. 'Have the Mex bring the bags. Car's this way.'

. . .

Coming out of the train station I saw more automobiles in more colours and more models than I'd ever seen before. Magazine writers talk about America's love affair with the motor car. I think it must have begun in Los Angeles. Big red trolley cars rattled past crowded with people and then you'd see a long Olds or a Buick with just one man in it. As I found, the trolley and train lines ran for miles in all directions but people still drove, even if they were literally travelling from one streetcar stop to the next.

Green shepherded us towards a Ford parked under one of the lush green trees that shaded the road. The sky was a clear, pale blue and the sun was still hot. There was no breeze and a heat haze shimmered on the distant hills. But there were all these green trees. I never lost the feeling that Los Angeles was an oasis in a desert. Pedro loaded the bags and stood ready to climb aboard.

Herbie got another Lucky going from the stub of the last. 'Does the Mex drive?' he said.

I nodded. 'Sure.'

'Let's have him drive us then.' He got in the back and gestured for me to follow. Pedro grinned and climbed behind the wheel. Green handed him the keys. 'Head north and turn when I tell you,' he said.

'Si, Senor.' Pedro had that bloody accent working again, but Green appeared not to notice.

A few minutes later he was pale and shaking, the cigarette burning unnoticed between his fingers. Pedro drove like a madman, careening down the middle of the road terrorising horses and motorists, slamming on the brakes at the first few turns Green indicated and skidding around on the dusty roads. We passed trolley cars and autos, the latter slewed towards the kerb to get out of the way. Nondescript buildings rushed past; I had a sense of flat roofs and arches, palm trees and bricked courts, pale, dried-out lawns and sun-baked gardens. Children played with balls and dogs in the front yards and people dawdled along the streets.

'What's with this guy?' Green stammered.

I touched Pedro on the shoulder. 'Slow down, amigo. We've got a nervous passenger.'

'He always drive like that?'

'We just escaped from a Mexican general who was looking to kill us. I guess he's out of practice at driving any other way.'

Despite himself, Green was impressed. 'Keep him about this speed if you don't wanna open your account in Hollywood with a speeding ticket.'

'Hollywood!' I yelped. 'This is it?'

'Up. Left here . . . what's his name?'

'Who? The general?'

'Nah, the Mex here.'

'Pedro.'

'Left, Pedro. Hey, maybe there'd be some stunt driving for him, if you can just get a hearin' from Mr Silkstein.'

'How do I do that?'

'Search me, brother. I'll take you in and he'll throw you out if that's what he wants to do. Here we are, we're on Sunset. The office is on the next corner.'

Sunset Boulevard was nothing like what it was later to become; it was just a street, flanked with two and three storey buildings and higher ones here and there on the corners. The only impressive building I could see was a pink stucco affair which I later found was the Beverly Hills Hotel. Sunset Boulevard ran straight for a couple of miles before it snaked away for ten miles or so to the sea. In response to Green's command, Pedro stopped the car an inch from a plate glass window.

'Say, this guy is great,' Green crowed. 'A nacheral. Well, here it is, second floor.'

'Stay here and act natural,' I growled to Pedro.

'Si, Senor Browning. *Muchas gracias.*'

I followed Green through a door which had 'Silkstein Enterprises' etched into the glass. Below that was a list of companies indicating that H. Elliot Silkstein was involved in real estate, oil exploration, private enquiries and moneylending as well as 'artistic management'. The second floor was lavishly carpeted and the blonde receptionist sat behind a desk the size of a ping pong table. Green took off his hat and approached her respectfully.

'This is Mr Browning, Miss Dupre. Mr Silkstein's expecting him.'

'Was,' Miss Dupre said, 'since Collins from the *Globe* phoned I don't think he's expecting to see him any more. I'm not sure he's expecting to see you again, either.'

'Me?' Green yelped. 'Whadid I do?'

Miss Dupre raised a plucked eyebrow and let her cupid's bow mouth wrinkle just a fraction. It looked as if she'd said her last word on the matter. Green suddenly seemed like a frail reed to be grasping at. I stepped forward and gave her an eyeful of the manly Browning figure plus moustache and dark, appealing eye.

'Miss Dupre,' I said. 'I'm sure Mr Silkstein will . . .'

'C'mon Herbie,' she said, 'another fag limey, who needs 'em?'

Talk didn't seem to be the answer. I strode around the desk and opened the door behind it. I heard Green and Dupre protest behind me but by then I was looking into the largest, most expensively appointed office I'd ever seen. Late afternoon light seeped in around the edges of a huge picture window which was covered by a slatted blind. The light fell on a deep rich carpet, another huge desk, massive bookshelves and plump armchairs. There was also a long, low, black leather couch. On the couch a fat man with his vest unbuttoned and his trousers down around his ankles was having sexual intercourse with a semi-naked redhead.[29] One long shapely white leg was hooked over the back of the couch and she was using it for leverage to receive his thrusts and deliver some of her own.

He must have heard the door open because he turned his flushed face towards me, still moving up and down.

'Who the hell're you?'

'Browning, Mr Silkstein, I . . .'

'Get out! Sorry, honey.'

It was embarrassing but I hadn't come twelve thousand miles the hard way to be put off by witnessing some natural bodily functions. 'There was a mistake at the station. Your Mr Green mentioned the *Robin Hood* film and I feel I'd be perfect . . .'

'What good would you be? You can't even catch the right goddamn train.'

'I can explain.'

'Get out!'

'Bartholomew Booth suggested five hundred dollars might help.'

He was still moving rhythmically up and down. 'Who said what?'

'Bartholomew Booth.'

'Never heard of him. Do you know who this is?' He grabbed the redhead's jaw and yanked her head around to face in my direction. Thin lips and eyebrows, high forehead, small eyes.

'No.'

He pushed the face back to the wall. 'Maybe just as well you don't. She's gonna be the biggest thing in pictures. You think I need five hundred lousy bucks?' He moved faster.

'I'm an expert on Robin Hood.'

'Doug's got experts. He's got the Professor of the British Museum, for Chrissake. Get out, you bum!'

I backed out and closed the door. I kept backing until I ran into the desk.

'Nothin' doin', huh?' said Green.

I grinned weakly. 'I wouldn't say that.'

Miss Dupre was working on her nails. She didn't look at me.

'Well, better go,' Green said. 'Got a few things to do. Sorry, it didn't work out. I still think we could use that Mex driver. Whaddiyasay?'

I ignored him and walked out. Pedro was standing on the sidewalk with our bags at his feet. He was leaning back against the window he'd almost shattered and a cigarette was looking jaunty in his mouth. I took the cigarette and had a long drag on it.

'You are not a star yet, eh, Senor?'

'That's not funny. If I could just get in that picture. I know it'd suit me.'

'You mean Robin Hood, the outlaw of Sherwood Forest? The story comes from a number of ballads of the fifteenth century but if there really *was* such a person he must have lived much earlier . . .'

'What d'you mean – *if* there really was?'

'Scholars argue about it.'

'Bloody fools, everyone knows there was a Robin Hood. If only I could see Fairbanks.'

'Who is he?'

'You know all about Robin Hood scholars and you've never heard of Douglas Fairbanks? He's a big movie star, the biggest.'

'Where does he live?'

'How would I know?'

'I wager he lives in Beverly Hills. Among my people we have a saying – I will translate it for you. "If you would catch the eye of the Master you must stand by his fence".'

'Very poetic. So what?'

'Let us find out where this Fairbanks lives and take up residence there. Become his neighbour and catch his eye.'

I didn't have any better idea. There seemed no reason not to use Silkstein's real estate agency to carry it out. I doubted if the man I saw upstairs spent much time poring over the tenant lists. Through the glass door again and down a corridor to the office. The clerk behind the desk looked unimpressed at our entrance. My suit had wrinkled some more and I'd sweated considerably into the shirt. Our boots were dusty and Pedro, with his dark, late-in-the-afternoon stubble looked like a gunfighter again.

Hollywood, from what I'd already seen of it, didn't strike me as a subtle place. I reached into my pocket, pulled out a wad of bills and plonked them down on the desk. The clerk's eyes widened and he started to take a little more interest.

'Can I help you, sir?'

'I hope so,' I said. 'Do you know where Douglas Fairbanks lives?'

His eyes shot open and he looked nervously around the room. There were two doors behind him, both firmly closed. It was late in the day, maybe everyone else had gone home. That's what he seemed to be thinking. Pedro bit the end of a cigar and flicked it accurately across the room into a spittoon. The clerk's eyes rolled and his voice came out nervously.

'Er, yes, of course I know.'

'Well?'

'Pickfair.'

'And where's that?'

'Beverly Hills.'

Pedro hooted and slapped my back. 'See, Senor. What did I tell you?'

CHAPTER SIXTEEN

Within four days I was installed as a tenant in a house which was *not* on Summit Drive, but had ten acres of irregular-shaped land which gave it a short joint boundary with the Pickfair property. This was at some distance from the house and although I strolled down there often enough I caught no sight of Fairbanks. I also drove past Pickfair, staged a flat tyre outside the gates. Another time I sent Pedro over there to borrow a cup of sugar. No dice. I covered myself with grease changing the flat and Pedro returned without the sugar. The Fairbankses didn't have Mexican servants he learned, and what men there were around the place looked like heavyweight boxers just coming out of training.

My house had gardens, a swimming pool, a tennis court, a leafy terrace, five bedrooms, and a bar stocked with every drink I'd ever heard of. I also had a Pierce Arrow tourer (no Studebakers available from the hire company), several suits and some sports clothes. After paying a month's rent in advance and a security bond I had about three hundred dollars in the bank and would be able to keep up the front for a couple of weeks at most.

Christmas came and went. I got drunk with Pedro. They had a big New Year's Eve party at Pickfair. Cars arrived and departed for forty-eight hours and I could hear the band playing and the corks popping as I played cards on the terrace with Pedro. We both got drunk and he won some money. One day, desperate and hoping somehow to get close to Fairbanks, I followed his motorcade out to Santa Monica Boulevard where they were building the sets for the film. The castle you could see from a couple of miles away – it was a huge structure, ninety feet high, that dwarfed everything else around. There were bits of Nottingham and Palestine around, quite big sets, but the castle dominated the scene. It had a moat around it and a massive looking drawbridge.

The whole area was fenced off and guarded and I had no chance of getting close so I trained a pair of binoculars on Fairbanks as he strode around inspecting things. That man just couldn't walk, he strode. He couldn't climb over things either, he vaulted or just plain jumped. He was exhausting . . . [Browning swears at this point and mutters about getting ahead of himself. Ed.] ... to be with. He was like a small boy with a free pass to everything in the amusement park. I saw him pick up a sword and fence with one of his hired hands before doing a handstand on the steps of a gallows and walking up the steps on his hands. This was fully dressed; his minions ran around afterwards collecting the money that had fallen out of his pockets.

Feeling very low I hung around until the cars had left as well as the trucks carrying the props and the workmen. I walked along to where the trucks had been parked, trying to get a closer look at the stand of cottonwood trees which they'd converted into the out-laws' lair in Sherwood Forest. I tripped in the thick grass and bent down to pick up the obstruction. It was a long bow and a quiver of arrows. I'd seen the props men set up the jousting lists and an archery range and fire a few arrows, no doubt to gauge the effects of wind and judge the right distance. Somehow the bow and arrows must have got left behind. I took them back to the car thinking that an introduction to the properties man might be a way onto the set. I was grasping at straws and Pedro and I were down to the last of the groceries we'd bought when I'd taken the house.

This was Friday, nothing to be done until Monday. Saturday saw me out at the Pickfair boundary idly shooting arrows at a makeshift target. The arrows were the real thing, properly flighted with metal tips. I discovered that I had a talent for it which wasn't surprising, given that I was a first class rifle and pistol shot, particularly under target rather than combat conditions. I had the quiver strapped on and had plunked a few arrows pretty close to the spot I'd been aiming at when, for the first time, I saw some activity on the other side of the fence. Fairbanks and his wife were walking along together with another fashionably dressed couple (Fairbanks always looked as if his manservant had just laid down the brush). One of the heavyweights was a discreet distance behind.

Suddenly, I heard a scream. Mary Pickford had had two little poodles on a leash and now her hands were empty and she was waving them helplessly in the air and trying to scream again. The dogs had run off a short distance, probably surprised at being let free. Then I saw the reason for the scream – a big spotted lynx was moving fast down a hill in the direction of the dogs. Beverly Hills was very countrified in those days and there was plenty of wildlife in the rough country up behind the mansions. Fairbanks moved just as he did in the pictures; he held out his hand to the bodyguard who placed a pistol in it. Fairbanks aimed at the cat and fired. I was running towards the fence by this time to get a better look. I had an arrow notched. Spurts of dust kicked up around the bobcat as Fairbanks' shots missed. Mary screamed some more and Fairbanks swore. The other people were rooted to the spot as the cat gathered itself to spring at the yelping dogs. I stopped, drew, sighted and let the arrow go. It was a perfect shot; the cat jumped, exposing its chest and the arrow struck home, dead centre. Its hind legs gave out instantly and its spring turned into a tumbling collapse. It twitched and lay still.

Mary Pickford stopped screaming and Douglas Fairbanks strode towards the fence. God knows why, but I'd pulled out another arrow and had it notched when he arrived.

'You won't need that, old man,' he said. 'Damn good shot. My deepest thanks.'

I smiled weakly and un-notched the arrow. My hands were trembling and I doubt I could have drawn the bow let alone made another shot. I must have looked a ridiculous figure, standing there in plus fours with a quiver on my back and a long bow in my hand, but nobody seemed to think so. Mary had gathered up the dogs and had run across to the fence with them in her arms.

'Oh, thank you, thank you. You saved their lives.'

'Quite all right, ma'am,' I said. 'Lucky I was here and doing a spot of archery.'

'I say, are you British?' Fairbanks said.

'Australian, actually,' I said, trying to sound as near to British as I could.

'Wonderful. You must know my wife, Mary, and this is my brother, Robert and his wife. Thanks, Chuck.' He handed the pistol back to the bodyguard who drifted away to look at the corpse of the bobcat. I nodded and smiled to the nice people and put the arrow back in its quiver.

'Do you live here?' Mary said.

I nodded.

'Neighbours, eh?' said Fairbanks. 'You must come up to the house for a drink. What's your name, old man?'

'Dick Browning.'

'Dick. Splendid.' He moved along the fence a little and I moved with him. 'Mary's had a shock, I'll have to take her inside. You come over now, must have a little chat.' I nodded again. 'Thank you, I'd like that.' He lifted his hand majestically and strode off. I had caught the eye of the master.

...

I hurried back to the house and started pulling off my clothes as soon as I got in the door. I ripped my shirt from neck band to tail getting it clear of the quiver.

'What's wrong?' Pedro said.

'Nothing. I'm going next door for a drink.'

'Won't work.'

'I'm invited. Fairbanks invited me.'

That impressed him; he even helped me with my clothes after I'd cleaned up. I told him how it had happened and he whistled.

'Couldn't have happened at a better time. We're out of milk. Plenty of whisky, no milk.'

I clipped him under the jaw. 'That's Hollywood, kid.'

'Let's hope he doesn't just give you ten bucks and a box of cigars with his autographed photo.'

I pushed in a collar stud and selected a quiet tie. 'Somehow I think he's got it in mind to do more than that.'

Then minutes later and I was past the guards and at the front door of Pickfair. It wore an air of baronial splendour with a lot of white marble everywhere and fancy trimmings that must have been hell to keep clean. I wore wing-tip shoes, wide, pleated slacks, a woollen vest, shirt and tie, and a grey blazer with gold buttons. I know is sounds ghastly, but it did for high fashion, semi-casual, then. A servant answered my ring and ushered me through a series of rooms and passages to where Fairbanks and his brother were taking drinks on a patio. The women were no doubt inside, sharing the shock they'd just had. Fairbanks got up lithely and came bounding across the flagstones.

'Ah, Dick, old chap. C'mon over and have a spot. What's your poison?'

It was about eleven o'clock in the morning. I'd had a quick bracer of gin before leaving home and thought I'd better stick with that.

'Gin and tonic, if you have it, thanks.'

'Have it? Wouldn't drink anything else myself on a morning like this.'

He had hold of my arm and I was able to take my first good look at him. He wasn't as tall as he looked on film, probably under six feet. His skin was deeply tanned and his wavy hair was thick and firmly in place. His clothes I can't remember, but I felt properly dressed for the occasion so they were probably something like mine. His brother, I think, was wearing a suit. Fairbanks seemed more vivid, more alive than he needed to be, but that was his way, from morning coffee to bedtime, as I found to my cost.

Robert Fairbanks stood and shook my hand. 'Wonderful shot, ah . . . Browning. I must go. You and Robin Hood here must have things to talk about.' He nodded and walked inside. Fairbanks looked thoughtfully after him for a moment and then busied himself with the drinks. He mixed a big, generous g.'n t. for me and a small, weak one for himself. We sat down on the garden chairs and breathed clean country air while sipping the drinks. Fairbanks seemed to be studying me. I offered him a cigarette but he refused.

'Try not to,' he said. 'Bad for the wind. Need a good wind in my line of work.'

'I suppose so. Don't mind if I do?'

He shook his head and I lit up. I needed something to steady the nerves and slow the heartrate.

'Done much of that, Dick? Archery, I mean?'

'First time this morning. Extraordinarily lucky shot, don't you know.'

I thought that might be laying it on a bit thick but he was fanatically pro-British and a terrible snob. He soaked it up.

'Quite. Lucky, as you say.' He leaned forward. 'Now look here, Dick old chap. It wouldn't do for this story to get around.'

I puffed on my cigarette and began to feel a little more relaxed. It takes one to know one, and Fairbanks was firmly in the role of a man who'd let himself and others down, badly. 'Oh, why's that?' I said. 'No harm done.'

'Well,' he sipped his drink and looked off towards the hills as if seeking for an appropriate message to flash on the screen. 'Well, you see, I have a lot of people visiting here – important people some of them. Women . . . and, you know, if it were known that there were bobcats around about, well . . .' He laughed and took another sip. 'My social life would suffer frightfully. Business life too, of course.'

I smiled, puffed and sipped and thought about it. What he meant, of course, was that he didn't want the story to get around of how he'd missed three times at point blank range *and* been outshot by a bloke with a bow and arrow forty feet further away. Vanity is a terrible weakness.

'I see what you mean, Mr Fairbanks. I think.'

'Doug. Look, I *will* have one of those gaspers of yours, if you don't mind.' I lit him up and he drew in and expelled smoke gratefully. Then he leaned forward and put his lean, sun-bronzed hand on my knee. 'Mum's the word then, eh what?'

'Sure,' I said.

'Now if there's anything I can do for you, *anything* at all, just let me know.'

I finished my drink and stubbed out my cigarette in a big beaten copper ashtray. 'As a matter of fact, Doug,' I said, 'there is something you can do.'

CHAPTER SEVENTEEN

Three of Douglas Fairbanks' big gins, on top of one of my own, made me pretty tipsy by the time I got back home. Pedro was looking moody as he fished leaves out of the pool. It occurred to me that his share of the Hispano Suiza money must still be intact. Perhaps he was wondering whether he'd hitched his wagon to the wrong star. Well, I was now in a position to set him right on that score and it seemed like a good time to show him who was boss. I crept up behind him, stepped quickly forward and pushed him into the pool. He surfaced, spluttering angrily.

'Holy God! Why did you do that?'

'You're going to have to start playing your part soon, amigo. As of Monday, I'm working for Fairbanks at seven hundred and fifty dollars a week. What d'you think of that?'

He seemed to be impressed and to be considering his answer as he breaststroked to the side of the pool.

'Well?' I said. 'Hey, don't splash me!'

'No, Senor.' He reached up, grabbed my ankle, jerked me off balance and plunged me into the water, wingtips, blazer, gold buttons and all.

Later we sat by the pool drinking martinis. Pedro had spent some of his spare time learning to mix cocktails. He quickly became an expert.

'So, what will you be doing?' he asked.

'Some of this and some of that. Some acting, I understand. Also helping with production matters. Which reminds me – I'd better give them back their bow and arrow.'

'Didn't I tell you to stand by the master's fence.'

'You didn't say anything about a bow and arrow. Wouldn't have been much use to have just stood there.'

'That was your good luck. Without luck, nothing matters.'

'There's just one thing that worries me.' I sucked on the olive and flicked the pit into the bushes. The neat garden had started to become overgrown in the warm, moist climate. Maybe I could persuade Pedro to attend to it.

'What's that?' Pedro said.

'He asked me who my agent was. I told him Silkstein. Well, I didn't know any other agents and it seemed important to have one.'

'Have another drink.' Pedro emptied the pitcher into our glasses, puffed on his cigar and tossed the butt into the bushes. 'You're going to have to get a gardener – I'm damned if I'm going to cut grass like a *peon.*'

I needn't have worried about Silkstein. Robert Fairbanks had phoned him soon after his brother had hired me and Silkstein himself was on the phone to me on Sunday morning.

'Hi, how are you?' he said brightly.

'I've got a hangover.'

'Welcome to Hollywood. I knew you was the goods the minute I set eyes on you.'

'You kicked me out.'

'That was to test your mettle. You came through, boy. How about you get your ass . . . you come in here first thing Monday before you go out to the lot? We'll fix you up.'

'With what?'

'There's a lot to do, boy, you want to work in the movies.'

I had only a few drinks on Sunday and spent most of my time in the pool and on the tennis court. Pedro had never handled a racquet before, but after a few pointers he could at least return the ball and give me a bit of a workout. As a result, I was clear-headed when Pedro drove me in to Silkstein's office on Monday morning.

Miss Dupre greeted me with a bright smile and ushered me into the office. The fat man was behind his desk and a mountain of paperwork. He got up and danced around to meet me before I got my hat off.

'Richard, Richard, so glad you could make it. Sit down. Coffee?'

I sat in an armchair. 'Sure.'

Silkstein buzzed for Miss Dupre and ordered coffee. 'Well, you sure made a hit with Doug.'

I smiled. He'd made a joke and didn't know it. He shuffled some papers and looked suspicious. 'Did I say something?'

'No, no. It's nothing. What do we have to fix, Mr Silkstein ?'

'You got here, how?'

'By train, from Mexico. You know that. That was the trouble.'

He lit a cigar and waved the smoke away. 'No, no,' he said impatiently. Then he remembered who he was dealing with and why. I got the impression that he didn't like being proved wrong or being forced to change his mind. But he made an effort. 'I'm sorry, Richard. Would you like a cigar? Ah, here's the coffee.'

I felt better smoking Silkstein's cigar and drinking his coffee than I had when watching him screw the redhead on the couch. He felt worse.

'I meant,' he said after Miss Dupre had departed, 'how did you enter the USA originally?'

'I got here by ship, from Australia.'

He scribbed on a notepad. 'Ship . . . Australia. Yeah, that's good. We c'n use that for sure. We got a guy from Australia doin' okay here. Snub Pollard.[30] You know Snub? He's from Mel-born.'

'No.'

'He's doin' okay. Not great, but okay. You know Mel-born?'

'Yes, but I'm from Sydney.'

'Sidney who? Hay, hah, that's a good one. Maybe you can use it. I give it to you free. You got a passport?'

'Yes.'

'But no resident card?'

'I'm sorry.'

'You want to work here, you need a card. Never mind, just drop off the passport and I'll fix it.'

'How much will it cost?'

'What?'

'Fixing it?'

'Nothin'.'

I sipped some coffee and drew on the cigar. 'What's your fee then, generally?'

'Ten per cent.'

'Of what?'

'Of everything. Ten per cent off the top – salary, bonuses, everything.'

'That seems a lot.'

'It ain't when you consider what we do.'

'Which is?'

'Publicity, contracts, options, negotiate billing, legal services. I can divorce you faster 'n cheaper than anyone else in Hollywood. You married?'

'Er, no.'

'Good. That helps. Not queer, are you?'

'No. Does that help?'

He slurped some coffee and opened his hands like a man waiting to be thrown a football. 'Sometimes it does, sometimes it don't. All depends. Certainly helps with Doug.'

'Has he . . . ah, made it clear what he wants me to do?'

Silkstein looked at a pad on which there were some pencilled notes. 'Let's see, what did Bob say. Seven fifty a week, you got that?'

I nodded.

'From now to the end of the shoot. That's, let's say, twelve weeks – nine grand, nice piece of change.'

'I'm hoping to make a career in movies, Mr Silkstein. I have to think beyond this picture.'

'Yeah, sure. Doug wants you for stunts, archery . . . You're livin' out in Beverly I unnerstand. Must've had a bit put by to set up like that?'

'Acting, Mr Silkstein. What acting am I to do?'

'Elliot, call me Elliot. Now, Bob didn't actually mention any acting. More on the production side, he said.'

I leaned back in the armchair and drew on the cigar. Whenever I smoke a good cigar I swear I'll never smoke cigarettes again. Cigars give you confidence, cigarettes don't. I felt confident then. 'Tell you what, Mr Silk-stein . . . Elliot. You get Bob on the phone, tell him I'm here and we're talking about my movie career, publicity angles and all. You could mention that I was a sniper during the war. Dead shot. Mention that, and ask him about my acting role in the film. Meanwhile I'll just visit the toilet. Perhaps you could direct me?'

Silkstein stared at me for a long minute; he pursed his lips and his eyes went shrewd. It was as if he was weighing me by the pound, multiplying by the month and calculating what ten per cent of me might be worth. He pointed to the wall on the left. 'Got a john right here. Feel free.'

I winked at him as I got up. He pulled the phone towards him and I went through the door.

When I got back he'd swivelled his chair around and was staring out the window at the blue grey hills.

'Well?' I said.

'Bob says Saladin, maybe, or the Sheriff of . . . what is it?'

I resumed my seat, poured some more coffee and didn't answer.

'Don't matter,' Silkstein said. 'Everyone's got somethin' on someone in this town. It's the way the fuckin' place works.'

'Do you have a contract?'

'Nope. Gentleman's agreement. I can ditch you any time I like and vicey versey.'

'What guarantee do I have that you'll do a good job?'

'The best. Ten per cent of nothin' is nothin'.'

I stood up and held out my hand. We shook across the desk; his hand was soft but dry. Up to that point I never trusted a man with damp hands. From then on I learned not to trust men with dry hands either.

'Just drop in the passport willya, Dick? An' any other papers. We'll go right to work. You'll see somethin' – should be Wednesday, Thursday at the latest.'

'See something?'

'In the press, schnook. Your name in print. That's what it's all about. I'll get somethin' drafted right away. Let's see – Fairbanks signs unknown Aussie . . . no . . .'

I nodded and left the room. I gave Miss Dupre a smile in return for hers and felt pretty good on the way down to the car. Before I could open the door to the street it came back at me violently and John Gilbert sailed through.

'Hi,' he said. 'Elliot in?' I was surprised that his voice was so high and light.[31]

'Sure.'

'Thanks.' He moved along leaving a trail of bay rum behind him.

As I pushed open the door it occurred to me that if Hollywood worked by everybody having something on somebody, then Silkstein was probably busy getting something on me right then.

CHAPTER EIGHTEEN

They didn't make me Saladin or the Sheriff of Nottingham of course. I was Sir Ian of Belvedere or something such. The character was unheard of in the original Robin Hood stories and unsighted in the film because they cut me out of every scene. It was my first experience of a standard Hollywood trick, usually played by stars, directors and producers on troublesome girlfriends. 'Sure I can get you a part, honey.' But honey's part would end on the cutting room floor because the star, director or producer didn't have 'creative control'.

But that was all in the nasty future. I went happily to work on *Robin Hood,* charging around on horseback, plunking arrows at things and generally having a hell of a good time. I think it was David Niven who said somewhere that Fairbanks was like an overgrown schoolboy.[32] That almost sums it up, but not quite. David always did tend to see the good rather than the bad in people. I suppose I'm too much the other way. Fairbanks was serious about the picture and worked hard on it with Allan Dwan, the director, but he liked to mix work with play and practical jokes were his big thing. Trouble was, a movie set was the perfect place for the practical joker.

Doug got off a few good ones, like greasing the log across the stream so that Alan Hale, who was playing Little John, fell in on the first take. Hale had to be dried off and re-costumed before they could do the scene where, of course, the script called for Fairbanks to fall in. In my own case, Fairbanks played the perfect joke in that I was never able to prove that he was behind it and he made a useful point as well. There was an Englishman whose name I've forgotten who was 'archery adviser' on the picture. He was a whiz with the bow and very conceited about it. One day Fairbanks took me aside.

'I say, Dick,' he says, very matey, 'what d'you think of whatshisname as an archer.'

'Pretty good,' I said.

'Reckon you could outshoot him?'

'If I had time to practise.'

'He needs taking down a peg or two. As of now, you've got the time.'

I enjoyed archery and was getting a bit bored with the daily routine of picture-making, which basically consists of getting up early and standing around waiting for other people to be ready, so that I was quite happy to spend a few days shooting arrows. I had a knack for it, as I've said, and before long I could score bullseyes at distances between fifty and a hundred yards at will, providing that I was sober and in the mood. I showed Fairbanks how I was doing and he waxed enthusiastic.

'I'm going to set up a match. What d'you say to three shots, one at fifty, one at seventy-five and one at a hundred yards?'

'Not much of a match,' I said.

'Keep it short. Adds to the tension. Basic rule of pictures.'

It took me a long time in Hollywood and a lot of pain before I realised this, but, like a lot of movie people, Fairbanks couldn't always distinguish between picture-making and real life. This led to different kinds of disasters for some of them, Roscoe Arbuckle and James Dean, for example; with others, like Fairbanks, it amounted to a kind of eccentricity. Anyway I agreed to the match with . . . call him Williams . . . [The tape is indistinct. Browning appears to be trying to recall the name and to be getting confused with 'William Tell', the Swiss archer. The lack of background noise indicates that the recording was made very late at night or early in the morning and Browning sounds considerably the worse for liquor.

Ed.] . . . with Fairbanks officiating as umpire (which he pronounced 'um-pah').

The whole crew assembled for the archery contest, early one morning. It was one of those rare days, rare at that time in California at least, when the weather delayed filming. Usually it was clear and sunny from sunrise to sunset (or sunup to sundown, as they called it), but this day some fog rolled in from the sea. Just light stuff that would be burned off by mid-morning, but enough to hold things up. Fairbanks was running round like a madman (in his Robin Hood costume naturally – we were mostly in costume, not Williams of course), forcing people to stand closer to the line of flight than they wanted and getting the targets set up and the distances measured.

I was keen to do well. I'd had my eye on a blonde who had a small part in the film as one of the women around Richard the Lionheart's court. Ghastly costumes they'd put them in but the charms of this particular girl conquered all. Bonnie Dalton was her name and the knights, Saracens and some of the Merry Men (not all of whom were that way inclined) had their eyes on her. I'd managed to go for a short horseback ride with her but that was as close to intimacy as we'd got. A good showing against Williams would help my cause as she was a frank admirer of male athleticism.

And Fairbanks was right, Williams was insufferable. He strutted around the set advising on this and that, exceeding his brief by interfering with the horses which was more my province, and generally trying to out-Fairbanks Fairbanks by jumping over and off things. As we were getting set up, Douglas took me aside.

'I've put a few dollars on you, Dick,' he said. 'It's worth your while to show him up.'

That alarmed me a bit. I didn't see how Williams could beat me but I doubted that I could beat him. Truth was, I expected a draw and would have been content with one. Fairbanks wouldn't listen when I protested.

'Nonsense. You can beat him. I happen to know he was partying last night. I doubt his hand'll be as steady as yours.'

I gulped. I hadn't been partying but, out of nervousness, I'd probably had one or two more than I should. Williams strolled up; he was a big fellow, about my height but more heavily built. He wore his fair hair longer than was the fashion in Hollywood, and combed straight back. In shirt sleeves, tieless and with a leather glove on his right hand, he looked the part. I felt hot and foolish suddenly in my imitation chain mail.[33]

'Well, Browning,' he crowed, 'are you ready? Are you sure you wouldn't rather we used boomerangs? Haw, haw.'

'I'm ready,' I said. 'Have you left your glasses behind?'

It was pretty weak I'll admit; Fairbanks laughed but Williams sneered. Bonnie gave both of us a big smile. It must have been a bizarre sight – a crowd of people, some dressed as medieval swine-herds, others as knights, courtiers and ladies along with men in workmen's clothes and others in suits, all milling around to watch an archery contest.

The first shot was over fifty yards; we were shooting at separate targets and were expected to fire more or less together. Williams strolled up to the line, strung his bow, drew and fired in a single, smooth action.

'Inner!' the marker yelled. 'Hair off a bull.'

Williams frowned.

'There's your chance, Dick,' Fairbanks whispered.

I knew something was wrong as soon as I'd notched the arrow, but there was nothing I could do about it. I was already late getting off my shot. I drew, sighted and let go.

'Outer!'

A sigh went up from the crowd. Williams smiled. As the tar-gets were moved back I realised what had been wrong – the flights had been tampered with, they hadn't felt quite true. We'd been given three arrows each by . . . who? Fairbanks himself. I examined the flights on the other two carefully and found them true.

Williams shot first again.

'Bull!'

I shot and this time I was aware that the shaft of the arrow was slightly bent. Too late.

'Inner!'

I had one compensation; Bonnie was watching me with a very tender look on her face. Nothing for it but to see it through manfully. I could still win if I scored a bull and Williams missed the target altogether. Some chance. Williams shot.

'Bull!'

I drew and sighted, held the shot up while I made sure the arrow was straight. At least a bull at a hundred yards would save face. Just before I let go something flashed in the sun beyond the targets; I was dazzled, I flinched.

'A miss!'

There were sniggers and some outright laughter in the crowd. Williams drew himself up and saluted Fairbanks.

'Well done,' Fairbanks said with one of his gayest smiles.

'Thank you, Douglas.'

Fairbanks was still smiling when he turned to me. 'Bad luck, old chap.' He moved closer and whispered, 'Must have been luck with the bobcat, eh?'

He laughed and moved away. I realised then the value the exercise had had for him. Who would believe that a man who couldn't hit a still target at a hundred yards could bring down a moving lynx? Still, it wasn't all defeats that day. Williams made his move on Bonnie, was repulsed, and she spent the night with me – cocktails by the pool, a stroll in the grounds and a long, sheet-tearing session in the master bedroom.

We shared a cigarette afterwards; I had to hold it while she puffed because her hands were busy elsewhere.

'How come you gave Williams the brush?' I asked. 'I thought you liked winners.'

'I do. He's a coke-head, didn't you know? Has to stoke himself up to do anything now. He won't last long in this business or any other. Give me a puff.'

I put the cigarette between her full, red lips. 'I see. Have you tried it?'

'No. Burns people out. A man should be like a horse.'

That was a bit alarming; I hoped I hadn't disappointed her. 'Er, how d'you mean?'

'He should have staying power.' She stroked and rubbed me. 'You've got staying power, haven't you, Richard?'

'Well, . . . I . . .'

'Sure you have.'

. . .

Bonnie Dalton had everything it took to make it in the movies – face, figure, good moves. She could act, too. She'd graduated from Smith College in the east, had some small parts off-Broadway and caught the *Twentieth Century Ltd*[34], with one suitcase and high hopes. In Hollywood things weren't quite working out as she'd hoped. No one was interested in her New York cuttings or her acting ability. She was getting regular work but not of a kind that pleased her.

'I'm just a decoration,' she said as we lay back on the bed after the second bout.

'I wouldn't say that. Where did you learn to, ah . . . ?'

'Fuck like that? Off-Broadway, with faggots, mostly.'

'I don't follow.'

'There's faggots who can and faggots who can't. Faggots who can're able to go all night because they're not really interested. Do you see?'

'Mm.' She was naked, pale and long-limbed with large firm breasts and interesting shadowed hollows in other places. I stroked her thigh and she opened her legs and moved my hand to where she wanted it.

'Nice,' she said. 'Don't stop. What was I saying? Oh, yes. I want to *act*, damn it! Not sit around with my titties hanging out. If only there was sound as well as pictures.'

'Why?'

'Have you heard these women talk? They sound like Cape Cod seagulls most of 'em, the ones that don't sound like cows farting.'

Bonnie's voice, very New England, seemed a bit harsh to me but in any case I thought she was talking through her hat.

'Sound and pictures – that's impossible.'

'I hear there are people working on it, but by the time they get it right I'll only be good for playing grand-mothers. Well, what the hell. Richard, let's you and me have us a time!'

And that is what we did. We hit all the high spots – the Santa Monica speakeasies, the Hotel Del Coronado, and Cal-Neva Lodge over the border in Nevada, where gambling was legal (that cost me more than I care to remember), the Caliente racetrack in Tijuana (ditto). The wildest times though were at the private parties such as at Louis Gasnier's[35] place in the Hollywood Hills where the fun would last from Friday afternoon to the early hours of Monday morning. Bonnie was tireless. She could go forty-eight hours without sleep and still look good for the cameras. I struggled to stay the pace but I was often late for work and once fell asleep on my horse. I fell off and spoiled the take.

Silkstein had got me my resident's card and was faithfully taking his ten per cent out of my salary. I tried to talk to him about my next job but he always managed to fob me off. 'Don't look too eager, boy,' he said. 'Looks real bad.'

Pedro was possibly the happiest man in Hollywood. He had money in the bank, was on wages from me and was cutting a swathe through the Mexican girls who worked for the movie stars. I saw some of whom he brought home in the Pierce Arrow for a swim and they were often much more beautiful than the women who employed them.

'Is paradise, this place,' he said one night when we happened to be alone without any Bonnies or Rosalitas.

'While the money lasts,' I said. 'You're supposed to be getting the inside dope on what films are coming up and how I approach the moguls. I haven't heard too much from you on that score.'

'What does your agent say?'

'He says not to be too eager.'

'How much longer will it take to make this Robin Hood picture?'

'I don't know. Some weeks yet.'

'And then . . . ?'

'And then, nothing. No more Pierce Arrow, no more swimming pool, no more Carmen Caranzas for you.'

'And no more Bonnie for you.'

'I was counting on you to come up with something, Pedro. But apart from all these girls you've been screwing I don't get the feeling that you've been on the job. Have you or have you not made any friends in rich men's houses?'

'No. Would it help if the Robin Hood picture took longer to film than you expect?'

'Of course it'd help. Every week is seven fifty.'

'Plus the kick-backs from the extras.'

'Eh? How d'you know about that?'

'I may not know any rich men, Senor, but I do know some poor ones, some of the extras. I have heard about the system.'

'Everybody does it. It's expected.' I got up and poured myself a drink and one for Pedro. As I've said, I always use alcohol to relieve stress and Pedro had touched on a ticklish matter. *Robin Hood* used a lot of extras – crowd scenes, battle sequences in the Crusades and so on – and there were always more available than were needed. They were hired on a casual basis, sometimes a hundred or more per day. Added to that, there was strong competition to get to the front in crowd scenes or to do things that the camera would dwell on – raise a shout, take a spectacular fall, that sort of thing.

One of my jobs was to organise the extras for any scenes involving horses. We had horses covered with medieval trappings made out of blankets and barebacks for the outlaws to jump onto and off. There were horses to pull carts and slow Dobbins to carry the likes of Friar Tuck. The lot seemed to be thronged with good riders and with men who had military experience. This made them easy to organise – they could take orders and go where they were told. But there were some independent spirits among them who took controlling. As always, money talked: ambitious extras were in the habit of slipping a few bucks to the organisers in exchange for getting the choicer bits. I found the money welcome and not to accept would have queered the racket for the other organisers.

Pedro sipped his drink. 'I didn't think that you invented the system, Senor. But not everyone is happy about it.'

I suppose not. But what's this got to do with stringing out the job?'

'Have you ever heard of the Wobblies?'

'Yes ... I think so. Troublemakers.'

'That is what you need if you want the seven hundred and fifty dollars to keep coming. You need troublemakers.'

CHAPTER NINETEEN

I had heard of the Wobblies in Australia. They were under every bed according to Cameron MacKnight, my reactionary father-in-law, and equalled as a menace to society only by the Yellow Peril[36] to the north. I was surprised to learn of their activities in Hollywood – serious politics of any kind seemed so out of place there which was why the Hollywood Ten business hit like a bombshell in later years.[37] As always in Hollywood, the first approach was to joke and the members of the IWW were known as the 'I won't works'.

'There's been trouble with the Wobblies at Universal and Paramount,' Pedro said. 'Fairbanks is next.'

'What sort of trouble. What do they want?'

'They say this is the time to unionise the movie industry. Hit it while it's *flojo.*'

'What's that?'

'Not strong.'

'I suppose it isn't. Yes, I see.' This was about the time of Fatty Arbuckle's third trial and not long after they'd found William Desmond Taylor, of Famous Players, shot to death in Westlake. The studios were getting nervous about the bad publicity and the wowsers were getting ready to move in. While I'm on this, it always seemed to me to be a bad mistake to let Will Hays change things in Hollywood. The public *loved* all the scandal and we could have turned out some really hot pictures if they'd let us. Just think what Mae West could have done if she'd been given her head. Anyway, it seemed to me that the Wobblies were probably right about the movie business being vulnerable to unionism; the studio heads were scared of their own shadows. I was puzzled by Pedro's store of knowledge though.

'How come you know so much about it. I thought you wanted to avoid politics – anarchists aren't they? These Wobblies?'

'Some of them are and some are not.' Pedro got up and took a quick turn around the room. This, I'd learned was something he did when trying to make up his mind. The only thing to do was wait.

He lit a cigarette. 'This is an affair of the heart,' he said.

'You're in love with a Wobbly?'

'No, with a Wobbly's daughter and I have been . . . trying to gain their confidence. I have told them that I fought for Villa in the Mexican revolution.'

'Did you?'

'Not exactly. Frank Henry is the name of the leader of the group here. His daughter is Angelica. My God, you should see her. What a beauty! Her mother was Mexican.'

'Have I met her? Has she been here?'

'No, no! She will not come here. She is not like the others. I must . . . court her. If you wish I could arrange for you to meet Frank Henry. You could discuss the union and the Robin Hood film. I think you might find a lot to talk about.'

And it would do you some good with Angelica?'

Pedro shrugged and butted his cigarette. 'If it improves my *credito* with the father it will improve my position with her. She adores him.'

'What's he like?'

'He is an animal!'

That was disconcerting, but I couldn't see any better idea riding over the horizon. The facts were that I was behind on the rent and owed a little money here and there – some to gambling establishments which had rough collection methods. I was also about to owe some to a bootlegger who was supplying the booze for a party I'd arranged for the end of the month. Bonnie had been at me to do some entertaining. She said it would boost my career prospects if I could get the Fairbankses and Clara Bow, with whom I'd struck up a casual drinking acquaintance, and a few other big names, along. The invitations were out; I'd had a few promising acceptances, but I certainly needed another six weeks on salary at least to meet the cost and reap the benefit.

Pedro wouldn't say any more about Frank Henry. He said I would have to meet him and judge him for myself. That made two interesting meetings coming up. The other was with the bootlegger whom Bonnie had put me on to. So far we'd only talked on the telephone, but I'd arranged to meet him in two days at a roadhouse on Santa Monica Boulevard. His name was 'Tidal' Eddy.

'Eddy what?' I asked Bonnie.

'Nothing, just "Tidal" Eddy.'

'Why "Tidal"?'

'He brings the booze in from Cuba.'

'What sort of a guy is he?'

'He's an animal.'

I told Pedro about the meeting with 'Tidal' Eddy and suggested, as a joke, that I could combine the two meetings.

'I wouldn't,' Pedro said, 'Frank Henry's a teetotaller.'

I could have told him then about my teetotal father-in-law, Cameron MacKnight, and his dreadful daughter and all the woes they'd caused me, but I didn't. It was late, I had to be on the set early the next morning and I doubted that Pedro had honourable intentions towards his Angelica anyway.

...

On the appointed night Bonnie drove me to the roadhouse in her yellow Ford. I'd had a hard day; Fairbanks had been more exhuberant than ever, leaping around doing his celebrated balcony jump and sliding down the curtain, and flashing that white smile out of a brown face so often I wanted to throw a custard pie at it. So I was feeling a little testy as we pulled up in the parking lot. The Monterey Roadhouse was a long, low place with the neon light just beginning to shine out in the gathering dusk. The cicadas in the trees reminded me of home; the long black roadster parked across two slots reminded me that I was in America.

'Don't be mad,' Bonnie said as we walked towards the roadhouse.

'Mad at what?'

'Just don't be mad.'

The Monterey was one of those places that were springing up all over the countryside. People sat along a bar with coffee cups in their hands and not one of them was drinking coffee. The place served light meals and the wine came in paper cups. The rule was 'drink up and throw the cup away' if there was any sign of trouble. Bonnie walked to the end of the bar and sat down next to a man who had empty seats on both sides of him. One look at him told you why – he was big, well over six feet and wide with it. From pad to pad he looked to be about four feet across the shoulders. He wore a hat that must have been specially made for him because his head was massive. It was squarish with dark, flat features; his dark stubble was blue under the dim bar light and his neck was about the same circumference as Bonnie's waist.

Bonnie climbed onto the stool next to him. 'Hi, Eddy.'

Eddy looked at her – not directly but at her reflection in the mirror behind the bar. 'Hi, babe. This him?'

She nodded. Eddy looked at my reflection. 'Siddown, pal.'

I sat. Pals with Eddy was what I wanted to be.

Eddy held up two fingers to the man in the apron behind the bar. 'The babe give you the proposition?'

'What proposition?'

He sighed. A wave of rum fumes washed over me. 'She didn't. Okay, this is it. How'd you like to own a yacht?'

'A what?' I yelped.

'Shh,' Bonnie said. She laid her hand on mine and smiled at me as the coffee cups arrived. I took a quick gulp of the rum-laced black coffee, almost choked but felt better when I'd swallowed it. 'A yacht did you say?'

'Yeah. The babe says you're from Down Under.'

'Where?'

'Australia.'

'Yes, that's right.'

'I need a foreigner to front for me. Any foreigner would do but I don't trust niggers, dagoes or spics. You're a white man.'

Eddy himself looked like a blend of all the races he didn't trust along with the one he did, but I didn't say anything. I just nodded and got a cigarette going. I also lit one for Bonnie and gave her an enquiring look at which she shrugged.

'The thing is this,' Eddy said. 'I run the booze from Cuba. Okay, that's fine, I have to fix a few guys along the way, that's fine too . . .'

'Fix?' I said.

Eddy grinned. His teeth were almost black and he looked worse smiling than any other way. 'Nah, nah. I mean oil the palm, apply the grease – you foller me?'

'Oh, yes.'

'But landin' it's the bitch. I can't get to the coastguard guys. Tried, but no dice. You know why?'

'They're honest?'

Eddy laughed. I decided to avoid joking at all costs – he looked worst of all when laughing. 'Nah. McGill got to 'em first. Shut me out.'

'Who's McGill? I said.

'Irish bastard. Runs a few jugs.'

'He's Dutch in fact,' Bonnie said. 'His real name's Kip.'

A look of suspicion joined with the natural hostility on Eddy's face. 'Howcha know that, babe?'

'I know one of the film stars he's screwing.'

Eddy stopped looking suspicious but looked more angry. 'Dutch or Irish, what's the difference. He's late to be dead.'

I was feeling very uneasy; when lawbreaking is discussed an unnerving thing happens to me. I see the name of the relevant prison, written in foot-high letters in front of my eyes. FOLSOM, they said.

'Look,' I said, 'I just wanted a few bottles for a party. I didn't . . .'

'You don't want a yacht, all expenses paid? You don't want to clear . . . let's say, two grand a month for takin' a few sailboat rides?'

'I *love* sailing, Richard,' Bonnie said.

'She loves sailin', Dick,' said 'Tidal' Eddy.

. . .

'You've made these sorts of introductions before, haven't you?' I said to Bonnie as we were driving back to Beverly Hills.

'Sure, and not just for Eddy.'

'What d'you mean?'

'I've made introductions, as you so nicely put it, for Les McGill as well.'

'Does 'Tidal' Eddy know that?'

'I certainly haven't told him.'

'Jesus, this is dangerous, Bonnie. How did you get into it?'

'Easily, sport. I'm not getting anywhere in this business and neither are you. It's a crummy, second-rate town anyway. Money's the only thing that counts here and I'm going to take some of it back east with me. One way or another.'

'This is my first film.'

'It's my tenth.'

'So – it's your problem, Bonnie.'

'I'll ignore the lack of gallantry. Fairbanks hates you, don't you know that?'

'No.'

'Well, he does. You'll never get another job in movies unless you . . .'

'What?'

'Shift your ass, to use a Yankee expression.'

That was Bonnie – an irresistible blend of class (which, of course, she pronounced to rhyme with 'lass") and vulgarity. I pulled of the road, ran into the sage brush a short way and we made love on the front seat of the Ford.

. . .

And that was how I came to get into the bootlegging business. The following day a truckload of wine and spirits arrived with a note saying that the delivery was 'complimentary from Eddy'. Papers for the yacht arrived in the mail a couple of days later. She was a forty-foot ketch named the *Darwin* and she'd been converted below decks to carry heavy contraband. Something had been done to disguise how low she sat in the water when fully loaded and her two engines could push her along as fast as the coastguard boats. So Bonnie told me, anyway, before I made my first run two days after the papers arrived.

A voice on the telephone told me at what dock the ketch was moored, the time to be there and the procedures for clearing the harbour. Word had got around about the party; acceptances had flowed in and all the 'complimentary' booze was going to be necessary. I was committed so I obeyed instructions. Give her her due, Bonnie insisted on coming along on the run. 'For the excitement,' she said.

There wasn't any excitement; all I had to do was give an imitation of a rakish 'movie'[38] messing about in a boat. The crewmen did the work. Directed by a grim-faced Irishman named Riley, they took the *Darwin* out to sea, managed a lurching meet up with Eddy aboard what they called a 'banana boat' and trans-shipped the cargo. It was deadly dull and Bonnie said so.

'That's the way I like it, babe,' Eddy said. 'Nice an' dull. Fun is for the dry land.'

'Not so dry,' I said, eyeing the cases going below.

'Hey, I like that. You got a sense of humour, Dick.'

'What happens if the coastguard takes an interest?'

'The boys know the drill. Run, and dump the booze.'

'Can the boat outrun the coastguard?'

'Not loaded she can't.'

'And unloaded?'

Eddy shrugged his huge shoulders. There was a crash as one case of liquor went down too hard. Eddy roared and backhanded the first worker he reached. The man sprawled and Eddy kicked him. 'Be careful,' he said softly. The man nodded and made hand gestures to his mates.

You was sayin'?' Eddy said.

'Can this outrun the coastguard when it's unloaded?'

'If she can't we got three Thompsons[39] to help decide who wins the race.'

Bonnie looked interested in that. I tried to keep my mind on the money aspect. 'Er, Eddy,' I said. 'When do I . . .?'

'Get your cut? Don' worry, Dicky.' He slapped my back and almost knocked me over the rail. 'I'll fix you up at your party.'

'Party?'

'Sure. The big bash you're throwin'. Me 'n some of my pals're lookin' forward to it. I hear that Barbara La Marr'll do it with anybody.'

'Almost,' Bonnie said.

CHAPTER TWENTY

But before the party I had my meeting with Frank Henry. Things were going fairly smoothly on the *Robin Hood* shoot. There were the usual troubles – sick animals and sick people, badly built sets moving in the wind at the wrong time, complaints about the quality of the boxed lunches served to the extras. I investigated one of these lunches one day. It was hard to tell what the substance in the sandwiches actually *was,* but it tasted okay.

Looking more closely as I now was, however, you could discern minor troubles which, if they all happened at once or were co-ordinated, could bring work to a full stop. Some of the workmen – guys who had to clean up after water was spilt or sprayed, painters, ditch-diggers and ditch fillers-in – worked at half pace or less. They staged fights between themselves and deliberately provoked the lot organisers in order to waste time and put them in line for overtime payments and special rates. As I've said, one of my jobs was to hire people for horse work and other jobs. Like everyone else, I accepted the highest bidders. One day I accepted four bucks from a big guy who said he could carry a sandbag on each shoulder and one under each arm (we were diverting water for a scene where knights had to fight in the middle of a stream). I no sooner had the money in my pocket than one of the older hands tapped me on the shoulder. I spun around, thinking that he might want a cut and prepared to argue.

'You hire that guy, Dick?' he said.

'Sure. Look at him. He'll divert that creek single-handed.'

He nodded. He was a tired-looking character who chewed tobacco and spat it with minute accuracy. 'He'll divert it all right, the wrong way most likely.'

'What d'you mean?'

He spat into a fire bucket fifteen feet away. 'He's a trouble-maker. His speciality's turnin' one job into two. That's why he's known as "Two Job" Jones. He'll screw up down at the crik, then he'll be the only guy can put it right. Take him a while, like into tomorrow, but he'll get it right in the end. What'd he slip you?'

'Two dollars.'

He nodded and spat again. 'He'll make two, three times that on time alone. Then there'll be materials to do the job right. He'll take a cut o' that. You made his day, Dick, or his week, more like.'

This sort of thing was going on all the time and with some of the slackers and grifters it was political. They were IWW men with a cause and it didn't matter two hoots to them whether Douglas Fairbanks got the girl or landed in the moat on his fanny. Their big problem was getting hired. Some of the hirers knew them and looked the other way. Others didn't give a damn but the IWW men couldn't usually do much in the way of a kick-back. I was fairly sure I could be useful to Frank Henry.

...

'San Gabriel canyon,' Pedro said.

I was shaving and nearly cut my throat. 'What! That's miles away. There's probably Apaches out there, or Comanches or something.'

'There's nothing out there. That's why he wants it for the meeting. You don't seem to understand, Senor Dick, this is a wanted man.'

That 'Senor Dick' was Pedro's latest impertinence. He had many of them and they brought us close to blows sometimes. In the movies and in novels (so I'm told), a pair like Pedro and me are kept from each other's throats by their senses of humour. They snarl and hurl apparently unforgivable insults then fall to arm wrestling and laughing. Not so with us; Pedro could be amusing enough but the real peacekeeper was the knife he wore strapped to the inside of his forearm.

'Wanted by who?' I said.

'Whom.'(Another impertinence – you see what I mean.)

I flicked lather off and skirted the moustache. I was only twenty-four[40] or thereabouts, but I sometimes fancied I could see a trace of grey in my moustache. Just the fall of the light probably. 'Okay, whom?'

'The Pinkertons mostly. They're on a retainer from the studios to control the Wobblies. There're a few Federal offences Henry could be troubled by if anyone could arrest him.'

'Like?'

'Arson, kidnapping, murder – organised and carried out across state lines, you see. Also mail fraud.'

'Jesus. Don't tell me any more. I'm supposed to meet this criminal in a canyon? I don't like it.'

'You met "Tidal Eddy" Horner on a boat. I'd call that ten times more dangerous. Do you know how many people that *pistolero* has fed to the sharks? How do you think he got that name?'

'I thought . . . never mind. I see your point. Okay, when do we meet?'

'Tonight. Ten o'clock. I'll drive you. Don't be late and don't be drunk.'

It was Lewis Carroll, wasn't it, who said something about 'Who's master and who's man'[41]? Well, that was the way of it between Pedro and me. I never felt I had the upper hand. I spent most of that day in a brown study, walking through my work on the lot, getting things wrong and taking out my ill-humour on others. I practically bit Bonnie's head off when she suggested going for a drink after work finished.

'I'm tired,' I said, 'of everything.'

'If that includes me, thanks for the hint.'

'Why didn't you tell me how "Tidal Eddy" got his nick-name ?'

'I did.'

'Pedro says it comes from his habit of dropping people into the sea in such a way that they can't swim.'

'Mexicans exaggerate.'

'And Yankees lie.'

She slapped my face and strode off. I went drinking with Wallace Beery instead – it was a terrific preparation for my meet-ing with 'Red Rag' Henry. (It was a great time for nicknames. I picked up this one of Frank Henry's some time after I met him. Few answered to their nicknames and, frequently, people didn't know the monikers that attached to them. I learned later that I was known as 'Beverly Hills' Browning. This was because I'd had a card printed and on it, by accident, the words BEVERLY HILLS in the address appeared larger than any other words including my name. That was the sort of silly thing Hollywood thrived on.) [One of these cards was found among Browning's papers. Yellowed and creased, it is as he describes it with 'Beverly Hills' printed at least twice as large as anything else. Ed.]

'I told you to be sober,' Pedro said when I arrived home about nine o'clock.

'Shut up and make some coffee. I'll be okay. I can't wait to give that Fairbanks the razz.'

Pedro started to brew the coffee Mexican style – boiling water and grounds, mixed fast. 'What did he do today?'

'What didn't he do? I had to take a tumble in the lists and I had to do a fencing scene with him.'

'He's good, hey?'

'He's flashy.'

'Where did he strike you?'

I was standing up by the bar, wondering whether another drink was possible. I'd stood up most of the day since the fencing scene. Pedro poured some coffee and carried it across to me. He looked at me standing up when there were chairs to sit on and he understood.

'Laugh and I'll throw this in your face,' I said.

'Flashy,' Pedro said. 'Drink your coffee, Senor Dick. I'll get the car.'

...

I sobered up somewhat on the drive out to San Gabriel Canyon. The sweet smells of the sage brush and desert flowers helped and I probably could have been more sober still if I'd filled my lungs with that rather than tobacco smoke, but I was nervous. The highway climbed. When the lights of Hollywood and Beverly Hills were far below and behind, Pedro pulled the Pierce Arrow off the main road, ran down a dirt track for a short distance and stopped in a spot where the canyon wall loomed up above as if it was about to fall and obliterate everything.

'Where is he?' I said.

'He's here,' Pedro said. 'Just wait.'

The man who came walking towards the car, keeping out of the direct beam of the headlights, was small and delicate-looking. White hair waved around his head and his shoulders were about the width of two slices of toast. I had never seen a more physically unimpressive man in my life. I let out a breath and opened the door.

'Sit the fuck where you are!' The voice cut the air like one of Fairbanks' sword flourishes. I sank back against the rich leather and prepared to be told what to do and how and why to do it all over again.

Frank Henry was wearing an open necked shirt and slacks, espadrilles on his feet. His hair was a mass of thin, grey tendrils and his face was weatherbeaten and lined. He looked old, tired but full of fight.

'Senor Henry, this is Richard Browning. We fought together in Mexico.'

I was grateful to Pedro for getting that in quickly. Henry's pale grey eyes bored into me as I sat stupidly with the door held open.

'Get out, bud, and let's take a look at you.'

I climbed out and stood, towering over Henry but feeling like a schoolboy.

'Shake.'

We shook hands and I got another surprise; his palm was soft and his grip wasn't strong. The most dangerous men are those who can surprise you. I judged Henry to be very dangerous. 'C'mon down to the shack 'n we'll talk. What did you think of Villa?'

I'd been primed on that by Pedro. 'Great man,' I said as I ambled along the dirt road beside Henry, 'great man, but undisciplined.' Pedro had told me that Henry was a great one for discipline.

'That's so. Angelica's in the shack, Pedro. Why don't you go on up an' see her? Leave me and Mister Browning to talk.'

'Yes, sir.' Pedro loped on up ahead. *Angelica must really be something,* I thought, if she's got Pedro calling chaps 'sir'.

The shack was a clapboard building, box-like with a couple of small windows and set well back from the road. In the moonlight it looked grey, like Henry, and had probably got that way for the same reasons – age and weathering. He walked with spring in his step and his stride was unimpeded by the pistol he wore strapped to his belt round near his spine. He squatted down on a log without the usual creaks and groans of the over 40s and I sat too. I offered him a Fatima.

'Shit,' he said, 'I shouldn't. One lung's shot.'

'You can't live forever.'

That's the truth. Okay, thanks.'

I lit us up and we puffed smoke into the cool canyon air. I heard a guitar strike up in the shack and a woman's laughter.

Henry cocked his head at the sound and smiled. 'Never had a son,' he said. 'Just as well probably – he'd most likely be a drunk like my old man or a hard ass like me. You got any kids, Browning?'

I shook my head.

'Good. Makes you less vulnerable. Well, let's get to it. You probably know from Pedro what my politics are.'

'I gather they're practical.'

He smiled at that. 'They surely are. I want to throw a fuckin' wrench in those movie works'll bring the whole thing to a full stop.'

'What then?'

'If they'll accept unions, they can go back to making pictures.'

'What sort of pictures?'

'You're not as dumb as you look. Well, that'd be something'd have to be worked out. Thing is now to apply the pressure. I understand you're willing to help.'

'To slow down *Robin Hood*, yes.'

'Why?'

I puffed on my cigarette and tried to think of an answer. As usual, I was flying by the seat of my pants – nothing prepared, nothing thought out. It's called 'living on your wits' and it's bloody exhausting. Exhilarating though, when things go right as they did now. 'Ah . . . wouldn't you need an inside man when the unions get going? Sort of a . . . (I knew better than to say commissar) . . . commissioner?'

'Could be,' Henry said.

I flicked ash and gave him one of my hard, direct looks. I have to confess that I'd picked the technique up from Fairbanks. 'Attractive post,' I drawled.

Henry drew deep, coughed and stubbed out the cigarette. 'I get it. You're ambitious. You want to swim with the tide of history?'

And *that* was the first sign I'd had that he was a fanatic. The slogan. *A weakness,* I thought.

'Something like that. Look, if you get the IWW men to give me some sort of sign I can hire them on. I can protect them up to a point, too.'

For an answer, Henry reached around behind him and pulled out the .44 pistol. He cocked it and held it up to my ear. 'Do you realise what you're sayin', boy?'

The guitar strummed and I could hear dancing feet beating on the wooden floor of the shack. At that moment I thought they might be the last sounds I would ever hear. 'N ... no,' I stammered.

'You're asking to be able to *identify* the men of the Movement. D'you know what the Pinkertons would give for information like that?'

'I didn't think of it. I just ...'

He released the slide on the pistol and uncocked it. 'I know you "just", son. No spy would have the nerve to ask for somethin' like what you just asked for. I guess you must be on the straight.'

'I am.'

'You better be. You figure we're just sittin' here alone in the dark, chewin' the fat?'

'Well, I don't ...'

'Gimme your lighter.' I handed the lighter over; he flicked it and let the wick burn. At least a dozen answering lights came from the shadows around where we sat. 'You see? I'm never alone and neither will you be. I'll work somethin' out on the hirin' an' identif-cation matter an' let you know.'

I nodded and watched him put the pistol away. The cold sweat was drying on me but I had just enough composure to stay in my role. 'And do we have a deal ... about the job ... later?'

'We'll see,' Frank Henry said. 'Offhand, I can't think of a better man than you for the job. Let's go on up to the shack and see if we can persuade them lovebirds to make us a cup of coffee.'

I lit another cigarette without offering him one and let him stand up first. I was petrified by the whole thing but the trick is not to show it. 'Okay, Frank,' I said.

He looked amused. 'Richard Browning – I know you movie folks, that your real name?'

'Yes. Is Frank Henry yours?'

'Yep, leastways, in recent times it is.'[42]

CHAPTER TWENTY-ONE

This expression 'between a rock and a hard place' seems to have crept into the language sometime in the 1970s. God knows where it came from. The first person I heard use it was Jack Nicholson when he was telling a bunch of us about the spot Angelica Huston had got herself into over the Polanski affair.[43] But wherever it came from, it accurately describes the sorts of situations I've been in for most of my life. Here I was, an alien, helping to run booze into Los Angeles, working on a film and helping to sabotage the film at the same time. All to gain time to make my mark in Hollywood. If I stopped running the booze, Eddy would pass the word and I'd be up on a Volstead charge before I turned around. If I didn't help the Wobblies, Fairbanks' blackballing would finish me in Hollywood. If I got caught helping them, some studio security man would probably take me into a canyon and lose me until next winter.

On the domestic front things weren't any better. I'd patched things up a bit with Bonnie but she was at me to go into things with 'Tidal' Eddy a bit deeper (if that's not an unfortunate choice of words). She was helping to supply some of the wetter female stars and their boyfriends and even talking of opening a speakeasy of her own.

'Admit it,' she said to me one night after *we'd* made love on the diving board of my swimming pool. Bonnie had a fancy to roll off into the water as soon as we finished and that's what we did. I can't say I recommend it; the shock to the system immediately postcoital is pretty violent. 'Admit it, Dick. You've always wanted to work in a saloon.'

'Wrong,' I said. 'I never wanted to work anywhere. Maybe in a brothel.'

'That's it! Combine the two – booze and broads. Call it "Bonnie's".'

'You're crazy. You're a respectable New England girl. You've been to Bryn Mawr.'

'Smith,' she said. 'Never mind that crap. What about it? We could talk to Eddy about capital. He'd stake us.'

'Stake us is right. Through the heart when it pleased him. Forget it, Bonnie. Let's go in and screw on a bed. You've got marks all down your back from the matting on the board. What'll they say tomorrow?'

She got up, moved away and lit a cigarette. She was naked; it's a very erotic thing to see a naked woman smoking in case you don't know. 'Makes no difference to me. I've finished. Last scene was today. I haven't got anything else coming up.'

That was why she was so restless and reckless. Tricky for me.

Pedro was acting strangely too. He still wasn't getting anywhere with Angelica, despite having won her father's respect. I suspected that he was spying for Frank Henry. Spying on me! It came out in little ways.

'How went it at the lot today?' he'd ask, all innocence while he poured the martinis.

'Okay.'

Then he'd chat a bit about what he'd picked up about some star or other – Alma Rubens say, deliberately falling down some stairs so she could get morphine shots for the pain. Then he'd slip in the sly question. 'What did you get – lame horses, broken windows, what?'

I'd have had my first drink by then and be well into my second. 'Remarkable thing,' I might say. 'This enormous chap hired on. Well, I'd had the tip, you know?'

Pedro would nod and pour some more.

'He actually organised a lay-down strike – painters, carpenters, the lot. Of course it didn't last once some money got spread around. But d'you know what? No one could find him by afternoon.'

'Trouble for you? For hiring him?'

'No. They were going to use him in the scene where they lift the dray out of the mud. Robin and Little John do. This chap was going to be pushing up from underneath. Out of sight, you see? Looked perfect.'

'What happened?'

I shrugged and took a drink. 'Dray got stuck even deeper. Needed a winch. Winch broke too.'

It was only later that I realised that Pedro had got a detailed eye witness account of a successful IWW operation. At the time, I was too caught up by plans for the party. The acceptance list was long – word had got around among the confirmed boozers that the supply would be good – but I was light on for real celebrities. I'd landed a few – Adolph Zukor of Paramount and Mary Miles Minter, for example – but, a week from the event, Fairbanks and Pickford hadn't answered and Clara Bow had given me a verbal acceptance only.

'You need a stunt, Senor Dick,' Pedro said, 'to make your party something no one will want to be away from.'

'You could be right there,' I said. 'That sounds like Hollywood.'

'Any ideas?'

Whenever anyone asks me if I have any ideas I freeze. I've had some hellish moments like that in story conferences, I can tell you. It happened now. Nothing. Blank. 'No,' I said, 'have you?'

'Why not make it a tennis party?'

'It's at night, you fool.'

'This is Hollywood. You can set up lights.'

The more I thought about it the better it sounded. It was technically feasible and utterly new. I'd never heard of a night time tennis party before and the possibilities would occur to anyone with a bit of imagination. Mixed doubles, changing rooms – you see what I mean. Then Pedro delivered the clincher. He topped up the drinks and handed me a folded copy of the *Los Angeles Examiner*. 'Did you see this?' he said. 'Bill Tilden's in town – maybe you could get him to the party.'

The item said that Tilden, who had won the Wimbledon and American singles titles the previous year and had teamed with Bill Johnson to give the United States a 5-0 win in the Davis Cup, was in Hollywood with Gerald Patterson. An Australian, Patterson had won Wimbledon in 1919 and lost to Tilden in the 1920 final. One Jacob Kramer had an idea to make a film in which a play-off between Tilden and Patterson would be the finale, and the tennis players were in town 'at Mr Kramer's expense' to talk to him.

'That's a brilliant idea, Pedro,' I said. He'd really taken to tennis recently; we played often and he was improving fast. Like a lot of players then he kept his long sleeves buttoned. I was a roll'em up man myself, but then you have to remember that Pedro had a knife strapped to his forearm.

He smirked. 'It's just an idea. What about this Patterson? He's an Australian. Do you know him?'

'There's a couple of million people down there, you know. I don't know him but I don't see why we can't get together. I have seen him play.'

This was at White City in Sydney. Patterson was built like a bull and he gave the ball a terrible thump, especially with his overhead. The day I saw him he seemed less intent on winning than on getting the balls he smashed to bounce over the hessian walls at the back of the court and rocket into the crowd. He won anyway. After the war there was a good deal about him in the papers. He was a hero, Military Medal or some such gong. One of my ne'er-do-well acquaintances in Sydney had met Patterson and told me he liked

163

a drink. A fellow countryman throwing a Hollywood party, how could he resist?

I attacked the party preparations with new vigour. I got the lighting from a company at Burbank that hired cinema equipment out to independents. It cost a bundle and so did the glasses and the food and the waiters and maids. It was mostly done on credit of course, and I reflected that I'd probably have to make quite a few runs in the *Darwin* to pay for it.

I got Silkstein to phone Kramer and get my invitation out to Tilden and Patterson. Silkstein rang me a day later.

'Hey,' he aid. 'I did a great job for you.'

'What d'you mean?'

'They both accepted – Tilden and what's-his-name.'

'Patterson. That's fine but I can't see it as a great job on your part. They probably want to meet Fairbanks.'

'Yeah. They asked if they should bring their tennis stuff.'

'What did you say?'

'I said yeah. Should I do likewise?'

'You play tennis, Elliot?'

'Nah, but I got all the stuff. Listen, boy, this is a great idea of ours, this party, great!'

'What d'you mean, "ours"? Are you helping with the bill?'

'I'll be there, won't I? Talkin' you up. Gettin' to the right people.'

'Speaking of which, anything yet on another film?'

'Patience, boy. See you at the party. You fixed the cops?'

I had, or rather, 'Tidal' Eddy had. He didn't tell me what it had cost but he said it would come out of my 'end'. I had an uneasy feeling that I owed Eddy more than I could ever repay.

The party was set for Friday. On the Monday Doug and Mary and Mary's brother Jack accepted. Clara Bow phoned (I don't think she knew how to write); Nazimova said yes; Charlie Chaplin was in Mexico but his brother Syd accepted along with Chester Conklin, Betty Compson and a lot of others.

Fairbanks, of course, fancied himself as a tennis player and the thought of getting on the grass with Tilden must have overcome his growing hostility to me. Quite what that was based on puzzled me. He resented the bobcat incident and the use I'd made of it, naturally, but he should have been big enough to rise above that. I was sure he didn't know that I was holding up the *Robin Hood* shoot. I racked my brains over the question because I didn't want to make an enemy of him if I could help it. *Does he have eyes for Bonnie?* I thought. But no, he seemed to be devoted to Mary. Had I ever looked the wrong way at America's sweetheart? No, of course not; Fairbanks was a noted boxer and I've always made it a point to imagine to myself that the wives of pugilists have bad breath and underarm odour.

Eventually, Robert Fairbanks put me in the picture. He rang me to say that he couldn't come to the party because he had to go East for a business meeting.

'Sorry about that, Bob,' I said. 'Look, I'll be blunt. What's Douglas got against me? I hear I'm not his favourite Australian actor.'

A pause and then Bob spoke slowly. 'You know that Doug's backing this picture with his own money?'

'Sure.'

'The papers're saying it's the most expensive picture ever made.'

'Think big,' I said.

'Yeah, well, Doug's anxious about it, and when he's anxious he needs someone to take it out on.'

'Is that right?'

'Yeah, and I should know. I'm his brother. Hope it's a great party, Dick.'

At least my unpopularity didn't extend far beyond Fairbanks himself, not yet. The tennis idea intrigued everyone; Tilden was a national hero and the stars were as anxious to see him as he was to meet them. It was a winning formula for a party. It should have been a big success.

CHAPTER TWENTY-TWO

Friday was hellish in Nottingham and Palestine. Props fell over, a man was seriously wounded in a sword fight and a dust cloud, kicked up somewhere off in the hills (man-made, I suspected), carried down and ruined a couple of sequences. Fairbanks was in a foul temper and Dwan spent more time calming him down than directing.

Home seemed like an oasis of peace. Pedro had supervised the staff I'd hired like the schoolteacher he had been. The tennis court was properly marked up and had a new net. The tables were ready for the food and drink which was packed in ice in the kitchen. There was a marquee and a portable dance floor. When it was dark enough we hit the lights and the court was as bright as day. I took my first drink outside and strolled around. I tossed a new ball up and it seemed to me that a very high lob might be tricky, otherwise playing on the court wouldn't be a problem. The jazz band arrived – the Dixieland Five or maybe it was Six – and they set up near the dance floor after making detailed arrangements for a supply of the right booze – gin for the trumpet man, bourbon for the bassist and so on.

The lights around the swimming pool were dimmed, making it a dark and mysterious place. Unless I missed my guess there'd be some trysting done down there and probably some falling-in which seemed to be almost compulsory at Hollywood parties. Strangely enough, I never saw anyone it happened to come up laughing the way they do in the movies.

Bonnie arrived early in a silk full-length dress and feather boa which I complimented her on. I was wearing a cream double-breasted suit that had cost a mint but I didn't get a compliment. We had a quick drink while she reviewed the arrangements. Then the cars started pouring in. The less important people came first, then the tennis players, then the stars. As always in Hollywood, there was a mixture of clothing styles. Some people had come casual, others wore dinner clothes. No one cared. Tilden and Patterson wore flannels and blazers. Silkstein made the introductions. I told the Australian I'd seen him at White City.

'Like playing there,' he said, 'show you New South Welshmen what a Victorian can do. Is that whisky I see over there?'

'Yes,' I said. 'I'll get the waiter.'

'Don't bother,' Patterson clapped me on the right shoulder; it hurt so much I wondered if it was a trick he used to cripple his opponents. 'I'll help myself.'

Tilden lit a cigarette. His fingers were stained dark by nicotine and he was thin and nervous-looking. 'Idea is for Gerry and me to have a few hits and then play a few sets with Fairbanks. That right, Browning?'

I didn't like his tone or manner. 'And others. Might have a hit myself.'

'Any chance of a bet?'

'What about your amateur status?'

'Shh.' Silkstein winked at Tilden as he moved me away. 'Go have a look at the field, Bill. When Doug arrives we'll bring him over.'

Tilden nodded coolly and strolled away. 'You shouldna said that about the amatcher status, Dick.'

'Why?'

'Bit of a problem with Kramer there. Movie's out, I think.'

'That's tough. See you around Elliot, I've got to play host. Don't forget to talk to the right people. Who did you bring tonight?'

Silkstein puffed on his cigar and looked around. 'I don't see her. I forget her name. Yeah, see you, kid. Be careful you don't beat Doug at tennis or . . .'

'Or what?'

'Anythin' else.'

I said hello to the arrivals I knew which was fewer than one in four of them. I danced with Bonnie, and with Clara Bow who already needed more support than guidance, and I had a few drinks. The music was good and everyone seemed to be having a good time. I was anxious about 'Tidal Eddy' though and with good reason. He arrived in a long, black Dodge with another similar car following. It was before the era of gangster pictures, but the scene was just like hundreds they filmed later. Eddy got down from the car wearing his tuxedo and a white silk scarf. He glanced around him, made gestures to his minions with his thumbs and came across to me with both hands held out.

'Dick. Great to see you. Some party, where is she?'

'Er, who, Eddy?'

'La Marr. You promised me.' He glared around at the dancers and the people gathering near the tennis court where Tilden and Patterson were hitting up.

'She's not here yet.'

'She betta come.'

It didn't seem like the moment to ask him for my share of the profits from the booze run. I had another quick drink and found Bonnie at the bar.

'Come and watch the tennis,' I said.

'Why?'

I shrugged. 'For fun. People seem to like it. Look at Clara.' Clara Bow had taken her high-heeled shoes off and was getting ready to chase balls. 'Ball girl,' I said.

Bonnie laughed nastily. 'That's right!'

'What's wrong with you?'

'I hate it. Come in the house and let's screw.'

'I can't.'

She tossed her boa over her shoulder and picked up a glass. 'I can.' She sauntered off towards the house. I could hear occasional guitar chords from the house when the band took a break. Pedro was having a party of his own. It was that sort of an affair. Everyone seemed to be having their own party.

I watched Patterson and Tilden play a few games. Tilden clowned, let Patterson take him to deuce on his service and then played like a demon when he was advantage down. Patterson had a whisky bottle set up at each end of the court and he refreshed himself between games. Tilden played a game or two with a cigarette in his mouth. The crowd loved it; they cheered and clapped, usually at the wrong things. Suddenly, Douglas Fairbanks was standing beside me.

'Evening, Dick, he said – very cool and clipped.

I looked him over. He was wearing a tweed suit and a soft-collared shirt. All the stress of the day seemed to have dropped away. He was freshly shaved, his hair was immaculately brushed and he smelled just faintly of gin. 'Good evening, Douglas. Good of you to come.'

'Mm. Mary couldn't make it. Apologies and all that. They say Tilden's got a weak backhand, what d'you think?'

'It's not as good as his forehand, same with Patterson. Pretty good though.'

'How many points would you need to win a game. They tell me you're pretty good.' He laughed unpleasantly. 'No, *you* told me you're pretty good.'

I watched a few exchanges critically. 'I don't know; might hold serve if I started at thirty-love. Might take Patterson's from love-thirty down – especially if he has a few more drinks. What're you thinking of?'

'You and me versus them.'

'Jesus, I don't know, Doug.'

'I hear Tilden likes a bet.'

'Yes, he hinted at it earlier.'

'That's it then! We'll play them for a thousand.'

'They probably don't have it.'

'We'll get Kramer to stake them. Okay? I'll set it up. I'd really like to beat them, Dick. It'd give me a big lift. Be very grateful for your help.' He strode away with bounce in his step.

Oh, Jesus, I thought. I've played about four games of social tennis in two years. Now I'm playing in the Davis Cup.

...

Fairbanks set it all up, God damn him, so it was all his fault. He had a quick conference with Kramer who agreed, reluctantly, to stake the players. Then he inveigled Allan Hale into acting as umpire – quite a complicated job, given the scoring system, but Hale knew tennis and had a strong head, so he was up to it. We changed into our flannels and there I was, standing on the brightly lit court with Fairbanks (who was bouncing balls with the edge of his racquet), and Tilden and Patterson, who were smoking and drinking respectively.

I'm not a shy chap in the general run of things as you'll have gathered, but I own I felt more than little nervous out there. It was a sort of stage after all, or more like a film set, and I was on with some of the greatest performers in the world. The audience was a tough one, too. I scanned the sea of faces looking for Bonnie but I couldn't spot her. Plenty of other familiar ones, though – Conklin with his great moustaches; Clara Bow, barefoot and with her dress pulled up; Zukor, looking dapper and amused. A few of them were drunk and ready to deliver the wittiest lines they could think of.

Someone yelled, 'Make it a smash, Doug!' and everyone groaned but the wit didn't get much better. The band was still playing although there were only one or two people on the floor. From the court, peering into the gloom and shading my eyes against the light, I could just see some activity over by the diving board. Maybe Bonnie was playing her trick on the diving board.

'He's lookin' for a lost ball!' someone yelled.

'Mind on the game, Dick,' Fairbanks snapped.

'Messrs Tilden and Patterson won the toss,' Hale called. 'Mr Tilden to serve at love-thirty.'

Oddly enough, it didn't go too badly at first. I received Tilden in the forehand court (Fairbanks was proud of his backhand). The first serve was long, I hardly saw it; the second was a slower kicker. My mishit turned into a perfect lob which Patterson lost in the lights. Love-forty. Then Tilden double-faulted and we had the first game.

Fairbanks served at thirty-love. His first serve was a hard top-spinner that took Tilden by surprise. He netted it. Forty-love. Patterson hit his forehand straight at me and I ducked. Forty fif-teen. I heard Fairbanks' hiss of annoyance and his next serve was a fault. Tilden clipped the slower second serve low over the net to Fairbanks' forehand. He was coming in to volley but was caught in no-man's land and flubbed it. Forty-thirty. The hard accurate first serve again; Patterson lobbed, I went back and smashed. It seemed to me that my shot was out by an inch.

'Game!' Hale called. 'Fairbanks and Browning lead two games to love.'

'Love!' Clara Bow shrieked from the sidelines. There were claps and roars of laughter. Clara had given up chasing balls and was now drinking champagne from the bottle. A young extra who'd come with the Wallace Beery party took over the job.

Patterson won his serve by putting four thunderbolts in – two down the middle and two on the lines. Then it was my turn to serve at thirty-love. For some reason Tilden was standing well back. I made as if to deliver a hard one and then lollied it over the net and caught him flat-footed. Forty-love. Patterson put my good-ish first serve down the centre of the court and I missed my swing at it completely. Forty-fifteen. Tilden moved in. I served hard to his backhand and hit the line. The ball kicked a bit; Tilden's return was just a fraction mis-timed and Fairbanks moved across and volleyed it away into the corner.

'Game! Fairbanks and Browning lead three games to one.'

'Well done, Dick,' Fairbanks said.

They were the last happy words he ever spoke to me. From then on it was a massacre. Tilden and Patterson won their serves easily. I dropped mine with equal ease. Fairbanks fought like a lion and held a serve virtually single-handed. At four-five down he was serving and I could see he was desperate not to drop serve. But Tilden passed me at the net and Patterson hit a clean winner. Tilden lobbed over me. Fairbanks produced a topswing kicker which caused a surprised and by now none-too-sober Patterson to net. Deuce. The next two serves were faults but the second one was close and Hale called it in. It would have been interesting to have heard the little pow-wow between Doug and Hale before the match. Advantage Fairbanks.

Douglas Fairbanks then sent down one of the best serves I have ever seen; it barely cleared the net, landed just inside the service line and broke out wide to Patterson's backhand. He barely reached it, just tipped it and the ball floated towards me shoulder high. I heard Fairbanks' grunt of satisfaction at the serve and I seemed to have all the time in the world to make my volley. Too much time; I took my eye off the ball, lost the rhythm and volleyed into the net. Fairbanks groaned. Tilden smiled for the first time in the game. Concentrating, Tilden and Patterson disposed of the next two points with ridiculous ease.

'Game and set, six games to four. Messrs Tilden and . . .'

Before Hale could finish, three piercing screams rose above the now soft and mellow jazz. Another scream was cut off by the harsh rattle of a machine gun. I heard glass break and more screaming. The four of us were clustered near the net to shake hands.

'Stone the crows,' Patterson roared. 'What's that?'

Tilden and Fairbanks were glowering at each other. Most of the spectators had begun to run towards the house.

'Sorry, Doug, I . . .'

'For God's sake go and see what's happened. I'm leaving. You owe me five hundred, Browning.' He marched away and I was left with Tilden who stuck out his hand.

'Thanks for the game,' he said. 'And the money.'

We shook hands; his grip was dry and very firm. He was a manly sort of chap – you'd never have guessed.[44]

Patterson had joined the rush to the house and I followed. My first thought was of all the money I'd paid as a bond on the house; then I thought of Bonnie and maybe of Pedro. Some of the members of the Dixieland band were heading housewards too. The trumpeter ran, stumbled, raised his horn and blew a long, blue note. I shoved people aside to get to the swimming pool. Someone had turned on the lights. Barbara La Marr was lying on a cane lounge with her silver sequinned dress torn from neckline to waist. She was shaking and trying to drink brandy and scream at the same time. Broken glass lay everywhere and there was a trail of blood leading to the pool. People clustered around Barbara and a young, fair man who was sitting with his feet in the pool. Blood dripped from his arm into the water.

'What happened?' I said.

'He tried to rape me!' Barbara yelled. She took a gulp of brandy and yelled it again, louder. The trumpeter blew the same note again.

'Shut up!' I screamed. 'Who? Who tried to rape . . .?'

A car engine started with a roar, then another and a hail of gravel sputtered over the pool as the tyres spun.

'Eddy,' Bonnie said quietly. 'Eddy got a little out of hand. Lover boy here stepped in and one of Eddy's boys . . .'

'Opened up on him with a tommy gun,' the trumpeter said. 'Jesus.'

'He's only nicked,' Bonnie said. 'I know a doctor. Dick, tell everyone to go back to having fun . . .'

Wailing police sirens, distant but getting closer, cut her off. The trumpeter blew an answering note. Hollywood party-goers were attuned to police sirens, they scattered instinctively towards their cars. I saw Pedro burst from the changing room dragging a woman with him. He bundled her into the Pierce Arrow and headed off towards the back gate. Tilden and Patterson were nowhere to be seen. Silkstein had vanished. I closed my eyes and leaned against the diving board steps.

When I opened them La Marr and her boyfriend had gone and only Bonnie and a few people too drunk to move were still there.

'At least Fairbanks got away,' I said.

'Did Eddy?' Bonnie said. 'That's your big problem.'

CHAPTER TWENTY-THREE

There was a strict protocol for this sort of thing in Hollywood in the twenties and I daresay it hasn't changed much. The ranking cop on the scene made a series of phone calls to discover how far the fix was in. Depending on what he learned, others present at the party/orgy/murder were allowed to leave, taken downtown, booked and let go, or thrown in the slammer.

The cop in question introduced himself as Sergeant Rourke. He had four men with him, two in his squad car and two in another, who got out of the cars and gaped at the tennis court. Rourke wasn't impressed. He ignored me for a few minutes while he strolled around the swimming pool. He bent to examine the blood and the cloudiness in the water. He straightened up and snapped his fingers.

'You,' he shouted to the nearest cop, 'round up everyone you c'n find and put some bottles in a box for evidence. See if you c'n find any dope.'

'Dope?' I said.

He was still shouting. 'Weed, cocaine, morphine, needles, take a good look!'

'This is a tennis party,' I said.

'I don't see no players. All I see is blood. The squeal said there was shooting. What happened here?'

Bonnie pointed to the flagstones. 'Someone cut himself. See all the glass.'

'How'd the glass get broke?'

She shrugged. 'I don't know.'

'You don't know,' Rourke said. 'Maybe somebody else knows. Maybe one of these guys.' Two policemen were escorting five or six of my guests towards the swimming pool. Two, a man and a woman, were bit players in *Robin Hood,* the others I didn't know. A couple of drinks waiters and a woman who'd helped with the food were also roped in.

'There's a couple passed out in the house, Sarge,' one of the cops said. 'Plus a guy looks like a horn player over by the band-stand. Drunk as a skunk. No dope but the joint is swimming in booze.'

'Keep your hands off it,' Rourke snapped. 'Well, it seems we got a situation here, Mr Browning. Where's your phone? I gotta make a few calls.

. . .

I got the intermediate treatment – taken downtown, booked for creating a public nuisance and released on my own recognisance. Eddy's cars had got clear before the cops arrived and his fix had been far in enough. The police confiscated all the liquor but they didn't charge any of the stragglers at the party. Rourke looked me in the eye before he let me go.

'We'll be watching you, Mr Browning.'

I tried to joke. 'Yes, I'm in *Robin Hood.* I play . . . damned if I can remember his name.'

'That's not what I meant, pally. You got off this time and both of us know why. Don't think you're covered for ever 'n a day. We'll be watching you an' your girlfriend. You got a resident alien card?'

'I believe so, yes.'

'You believe so. You don't seem to have a helluva lotta respect for the laws of this country.'

'I wouldn't say that.'

'I would! I'll check you with the immigration boys. I hope your nose is clean.' He spun a paper around on the desk and showed me where to sign. 'Because as of now, your sheet ain't!'

It was a depressing early hours of the morning cab ride back to the rancho. The hired help had cleaned up the grounds and the parts of the house the party had flowed over. The outdoor lights had been turned off. The dance floor had been dismantled and the marquee rolled up. My head was buzzing with booze, fatigue and alarm over what had happened between me and Fairbanks and over how 'Tidal' Eddy would react to his disappointment. I'd smoked too much throughout the police ordeal and my throat was raw. Now I had police trouble to add to the others. Bonnie wasn't at home, nor was Pedro; so I had woman, friend and servant trouble as well. Maybe worst of all, there was nothing to drink in the house. I took some aspirin and went to bed.

I dreamed I was on the tennis court with Fairbanks, Tilden and Patterson but it was broad daylight and we were playing in front of a vast crowd. I floundered all over the court, swiping at balls, missing and falling flat on my face. The crowd hooted and jeered and the harder I tried the worse I got. I served a whole game of double faults. I ran into Fairbanks as I went back for a smash. I was aced three times in a row. At last I ran headlong into the net, tripped and fell over it onto the other side. The crowd screamed its derision and I woke up. The crowd noise turned into the ringing of the telephone.

I clawed the instrument towards me and said 'Yes' dopily into the earpiece.

I heard Pedro's voice, as if it was coming from a long way off. 'Frank Henry wants to see you, Senor Dick. He says you have a problem.'

'That doesn't surprise me,' I said. 'Why should he be any different?'

'What?'

'Never mind. When does he want to see me?'

'Tonight, same place.'

'Do you think you might possibly get my car back by then?'

'Sure.' His voice went soft. 'Angelica, she found it all very exciting last night.'

'Is that right?'

'Yes, very exciting. I am a happy man.'

'Maybe some of your luck will rub off on me. Did you see who Bonnie was screwing last night?'

'Si.'

'Who?'

'I am not a spy, Senor Dick.'

'The hell you're not. Never mind, I'll ask her. She'll tell me.'

'You will not be happy.'

'I'm not happy now. I'll never be happy again. Be here with the car so we can go visit your future father-in-law, okay?'

'Okay.' He rang off but there was something in that final word, just a note, that suggested some uncertainty in Pedro about the status of son-in-law.

I got a few cautious phone calls through the day: 'Hi, Dick? How'd it all work out, you old son of a gun? Great party. Say, we gotta get together for a game of tennis some time. That serve of yours is really something', etc. etc. Nothing from Fairbanks. Nothing from Eddy. Nothing from La Marr. No news was good news.

...

Uneasy is too weak a word for what I felt on the drive out to the San Gabriel canyon. Shit-scared would be closer with a touch of foreboding thrown in. Pedro's cheerfulness didn't help. God help him, he whistled Mexican dancing songs as he drove. I stood it for as long as I could.

'If you don't stop that noise I'll put you out of the car and you can walk back. Also I won't let you drive the car any more.'

He stopped whistling to talk. 'How long you reckon we're gonna have this car?'

'What d'you mean?'

'We Latins are *muy sensitivo,* Senor. I feel that our time in Hollywood could be coming to an end.'

'But you're in line to get married.'

'That is what I mean.'

I grunted at that and he lit a cigarette and drove with it in his mouth. Maybe he could've whistled like that but he didn't. My worries were many, as I've said, but I had two in particular just then. Frank Henry hadn't contacted me at all since our one meeting. Conclusion: it must be something serious bringing about this meeting. Reaction: serious equals bad. Plus, Sergeant Rourke had said that the LA police would be watching me. What if they were watching me now? How would driving out into the bush to meet an arch-radical who happened also to be Public Enemy No. 3 look in Hollywood?

I turned my head to look for a tail so often I had a crick in it by the time we reached the canyon. Pedro drove towards the shack until a man with a shotgun stepped out of the bushes and motioned him to stop. He told Pedro to wait in the car and marched me to the cabin. No Angelica this time, no guitar and no coffee. This was business.

Frank Henry was sitting by a fireplace that looked as if it hadn't held a fire this century. His narrow shoulders were hunched down to nothing. He didn't get up or shake hands, just pointed to the chair nearest his.

'Got one 'a those cigarettes?'

I gave him a Fatima and lit it. He blew the smoke into the fireplace where it wafted for a second before being sucked up the chimney.

'Something wrong, Mr Henry?' I've been hiring the men on and they've . . .'

'I know, I know.' He waved the cigarette impatiently, drew on it and coughed. 'Fuckin' coffin nails. 'Scuse me.' He spat on the bricks. 'You've been doin' good, Browning. Boys've had a lot of fun but it's got past fun now.'

I took in a lot of smoke; I needed the comfort. 'How's that?'

'Pinkertons nailed a couple of guys at one of the lots. Security men took care of two more. They're in the hospital. There's an informer somewhere.'

'I hope you don't think I . . .'

'No, no. It ain't you. You don't fit the bill. Point is, the men're losing confidence. Losin' faith, you understand. We need somethin' big to happen. That's where you come in.'

'Something . . . big?'

He puffed again and stubbed out the long butt. '*I* want you to help us close down *Robin Hood.*'

I almost choked on my next drag. 'Close it? You must be crazy!'

'That's not a very smart thing for a man in your position to say.'

'Yeah, yeah, I'm sorry. I didn't mean that. It's just . . . what d'you mean — my position?'

'You do as I say or I'll have the word passed and these Jew studio heads will have you lynched. Probably tar 'n feather you first, and I wouldn't be surprised if they didn't do a few more things. You circumcised, Browning?'

'Christ!' I yelped. 'All right. Whatever you say. What do you want me to do?'

'Well, I don't know shit about the picture business. I'll just have to leave it up to you. Could be a fire, could be you might break Douglas Fairbanks' nice clean neck. I don't know. I just want that picture lot all quiet by Tuesday.'

I suddenly felt very cold and lonely in that cabin. I tried to steady myself with the cigarette but what I really needed was a stiff drink and that was the last thing Frank Henry would have around. 'I'll do my best,' I said.

'You'll do it, period. Is Pedro in the car with you?'

'Yes.'

'Send him in. We got things to talk about.'

...

Pedro and I were a very subdued pair on the drive back to Beverly Hills. Neither of us revealed anything or probed. That's the way it is, I've found, with real personal problems – they blot out interest in anything and anybody else. I felt that we were much of the same mind when we arrived home. I got down and looked over the tennis court and the still murky swimming pool and the garden that had grown ragged around the edges. I had a pile of unpaid bills inside, sitting on one of the empty liquor cabinets. As I stood there I heard a sharp grinding of metal on stone and an angry final roar from the motor of the Pierce Arrow.

Pedro came towards me stripping off his driving gloves and looking defiant. He lit a cigarette and flipped the match into the swimming pool. I did the same, except that his landed in the water and mine landed in one of the poolside bloodstains. 'A small accident,' he said.

I shrugged.

'Is Bonnie coming over? There is nothing to eat or drink.'

I shrugged again.

'What are you going to do tomorrow?'

'Find something to drink. Find a lot to drink.'

'*Bueno.* And on Monday?'

'Go to work. For the last time I think.'

'*Muy bueno,*' Pedro said.

CHAPTER TWENTY-FOUR

Reporting to work on the Monday morning was one of the hardest things I'd done to that date and not many things since have been harder. (Some of course – such as trying to keep the booze away from Burton on *Cleopatra* – but not many.) The hangover didn't help; Bonnie had called early on Sunday morning and she came around with enough champagne and whisky in the yellow Ford to keep the whole LA police force happy. We made a fearsome dint in it all through the day with some help from Pedro.

I left Bonnie still blotto in bed when I staggered out in the morning to drink coffee and face the choice between closing down a multi-million dollar picture and risking terminal mutilation. They talk about Hollywood not being the 'real' world – that sort of decision-making should be real enough for anyone. I had to drive myself because Pedro was in the same state as Bonnie.

Then, as now, movies weren't shot in sequence but according to a continuity schedule worked out by people who knew about these things, taking account of the weather, the availability of actors, the most efficient use of sets and props and so on. As it happened, the scene where Fairbanks was to leap off a balcony and come sliding down a heavy drape was to be shot that day. Now various authorities had given the height of the drop as forty feet or eighty feet. I never measured it, but it looked like about sixty feet to me – a hell of a long way down. What Fairbanks apparently did was jump off the balcony, hang onto the drapes with one hand while flourishing his sword in the other, slide to the ground and escape. This would have been an impossibility because of the severity of the drop. The friction burn to the hand holding on would have been terrific too.

What *actually* happened was that he jumped into a slide Dwan had placed behind the drapes and under some heavy burlap. He waved his sword and flashed his teeth and down he came, easy as pie. Just the same, it must have taken some nerve to have made the jump and I wouldn't have cared to try it.

I was going about my business, looking after horses, making sure the wind machine that set the pennants and bunting afluttering was working and such, when one of the bit players told me that Fairbanks was doing a rehearsal of the stunt before lunch.

'Say, Dick,' he said. 'Those cops were pretty rough.'

I recognised him as a party straggler. 'Oh, I'm sorry.'

'Yeah? Well, they took my name. Can you do anything about it?'

'I wouldn't worry about it if I were you.'

He was one of the first generation of blonde, good-looking but empty-headed boys who'd gone west for gold. In the years that followed his type bred with the waitresses with stunning figures who also hadn't made it, to produce the gorgeous, dumb . . . [Browning has begun to ramble at this point. He mentions Nathaniel West and Bud Schulberg, possibly meaning that one of these or both was the source of this information, and then a gunshot sounds followed by the noise of breaking glass. The tape runs emptily for a full minute after which Browning resumes in an unsteady voice but without explanation. Ed.] . . . dumb boys and girls we see today. By the forties, when I did a stint as a private eye in LA, a lot of these twenties hopefuls were wino wrecks, but then this example was still full of hope and ambition.

'You'll fix it, will you?'

'There's nothing to fix.'

He pursed his lips doubtfully. I wasn't too important to offend, and maybe he'd caught some of the Fairbanks backwash. 'Yeah, sure. Okay. I'm goin' over to see Doug do his stuff. See you.'

The scene would be shot when everyone was nice and relaxed with something in their bellies. I wandered over to watch the rehearsal which went smoothly enough. Fairbanks jumped and slid. He landed lightly with his knees slightly bent and everyone cheered. I was standing there with a spanner in my hand – the wind machine had needed adjusting – when the idea came to me. Frank Henry had suggested breaking Fairbanks' neck. That was way out of my league; but what about breaking his leg? Wouldn't that close down the picture? Couldn't the unionists make some mileage out of the lack of safety on movie sets if the star could be injured? Couldn't they make a stink about danger money? I liked it.

I hung around while the cast and crew drifted off to the lunch tent and the extras were settled down with their boxes. When the coast was clear I climbed up the scaffolding behind the drapes and examined the mechanism. It was a clever device: the slide was in two sections and held in place by a couple of bolts. There was some light scaffolding behind it. From the look of the drapes it appeared that Fairbanks made some use of them to steady him on his way down. The landing was a boarded platform, slightly springy, but painted to look like flagstones.

Although I was in no condition for the work, with a throbbing head and a throat that was crying for a cold beer, I climbed the scaffolding, undid the bolts on the lower section of the side and moved it to make the descent a bit sharper. I also made a slit in the curtain material so that it would rip if any pressure came on it in the last twenty feet.

. . .

It was a warm day, almost any day in the year can be warm in Southern California, and lunch seemed to take a long time. It probably didn't take longer than usual but I was like a boxer waiting to go into the ring. Dempsey, Harry Grebb and some of the other big ones have told me that the last five minutes of that wait can seem longer than a fifteen rounder. Grebb, of course, found congenial ways of passing the time.[45]

Eventually the time came for the sequence to be filmed. It was a long one but in those days, when off-stage sound didn't matter and no one bothered too much about stray shadows or if the third serving maid from the right had changed her shoes since the last scene, they filmed in longer takes than now. It was harder, more concentrated work in some ways, but the shoots for most movies were over sooner so there was a pay-off. Fairbanks was pursued up a flight of steps by half a dozen other swordsmen who did their best to keep him busy while not tripping over each other. Stairs were a piece of cake to Fairbanks; he was nimble, that's the only word for it. He made it look easy. I forgot what was coming in the sheer pleasure of watching him.

As a screen swordsman he had no equal from that day to this. His blade flicked between those of his attackers and he actually made *them* look good with his artistry. All this with his head thrown back and the rest of his body doing plenty of work – dancing, almost. He gave way up the stairs, lunged on the top step and dealt a mortal wound. The villain came tumbling down the stairs in a nice, tucked-up, rib-and-head-protecting roll. Knowledgeable ones among the crowd applauded the stunt man.

'Shuddup!' Dwan roared. 'Okay, Doug – back and up on balcony. Smooth and easy now.'

Fairbanks danced back, sword still flicking, contemptuous smile still in place until a few more men in burlap chain mail arrived and the smile gave way to a look of concern. His sword whistled and actually made a sound like that one you hear in the ad on TV for the razor blades.

'A . . .n . . .d jump!' Dwan shouted.

Fairbanks jumped backwards, three feet at least, up onto the balcony which was perhaps two feet wide. Without losing rhythm, he fenced, forward and back, retreating by inches. Smiling again, he let his eyes flick across to the drapes; he almost stumbled (deliberately), and recovered. He tied a Sheriff's man, who had foolishly joined him on the balcony, in knots with his blade and pitched him over the drop. The stunt man fell sixty feet to the net and the off-camera crowd murmured appreciatively.

'Qu-i-e-t!' Dwan roared. 'Okay, Douglas, this is it. One . . .' (Fairbanks thrust forward)' . . . two . . .' (Fairbanks parried) ' . . . three!'

Fairbanks sprang to his right, waved his sword and grabbed the curtain. The cheers died in people's throats as they saw the descent and the effect on Fairbanks. His eyes opened in alarm as the smooth, stately glide to the bottom didn't happen. He dropped his sword. His tights wrinkled as his legs kicked out wildly, looking for support. He slid the last twenty-five feet fast like a kid down the greasy pole at the county fair. Women shrieked in horror. Men laughed.

I don't know how long it takes to slide twenty-five feet down a slope like that. Not long, but long enough for a superb athlete like Douglas Fairbanks to collect himself. He must have realised instantly that the device was taking him down faster than usual. At just the right moment he let go of the ripping curtain and braced himself. He landed dead centre on the sprung boards with his knees bent and his weight almost perfectly distributed. He pitched forward and sprawled, that was inevitable, but he clearly hadn't broken any bones.

Dwan bellowed something through a megaphone and people rushed to help Fairbanks up. He smiled and dusted himself off. He enjoyed the consternation, clasping his hands above his head like a victorious boxer. I stood rooted to the spot.

'What the hell happened?' Dwan shouted.

'The slide's been shifted,' Fairbanks said.

Like everyone else I shook my head and looked shocked. Then I saw the bit player, the one who'd been at my party and had told me that the stunt was about to be rehearsed, rush forward and whisper in Fairbanks' ear. He mimed the action of using a spanner. Fairbanks stared at me, three rows deep in the crowd but taller than everyone around me. He beckoned majestically. One of the security men stepped up and Fairbanks spoke quickly to him. Then he flashed the famous smile and made a deep bow.

'Let's take it again, children,' he said. 'From the top!'

I pushed people aside and tried to duck down out of sight behind the props but they were on to me and no mistake. A foot shot out of nowhere and tripped me and then a hand like a dragline bucket took me by the neck. I looked up into the face of one of Fairbanks' ex-boxers who doubled as a bodyguard and lot security man. He kicked me in the ribs and lifted me like a rag doll.

'You're fired, Browning,' he said.

'Okay.'

'There's just one thing Mr Fairbanks will want to know.'

'What's that?' I gasped.

He punched me in the ribs on the other side. 'Why'd you do it?'

I almost smiled. Simple question, tricky answer. 'Practical joke,' I said. 'Doug loves practical jokes.'

He hit me again, this time on the right eye. Thump. 'His jokes,' he said. Thump, thump – body shots. 'Not yours. Savvy?'

He hit me a few more times and dragged me across to the administration shed where I was officially struck off the payroll. The clerk hardly looked at me and he probably wouldn't have thought anything of it if he had. My body was a mass of bruises but my face was undamaged apart from the eye which was starting to close. I could hardly stand but he was probably used to seeing actors in that condition. 'Bonuses?' the clerk said.

The bodyguard shook his head.

'He has six hundred some dollars coming.'

'You keep it or give it to your mother. Mr Browning doesn't want it. Do you, Mr Browning?'

'No.'

'That's it then,' the clerk said. 'We'll get in touch with your agent about credits and such.'

'I don't think so,' the bodyguard said. 'Time to go, Mr Browning.' He did a beautiful job of escorting me off the lot without attracting any attention. He even handed me my hat as I leaned on the Pierce Arrow rubbing my sore ribs.

Somehow I got the car started and drove home without killing myself or anyone else. I remembered to check for the police tail but didn't see one. It was getting hard to see out of the damaged eye so I may have missed it. I hardly cared. I'd put myself in line for the wrath of the Wobblies and had finished myself in Hollywood if the story of what I'd done got around. (It didn't as it happened; Fairbanks was embarrassed by the undignified fall and I heard later that the film that had recorded it went missing. Fairbanks swore everyone on the set to secrecy and the lid stayed on.) I felt unprotected and vulnerable as I drove the damaged car through the gates. And I was pretty badly damaged myself, don't forget.

I pulled up outside the house, half-expecting one of Henry's shotgun men, or a cop or a Fairbanks minion come to see if there was anything else needed breaking, but the only person around was Pedro. Bonnie had already surfaced, had a hair-of-the-dog and left. Pedro was sitting in the shallow end of the swimming pool in his underwear lapping water up over his head. He looked at me, closing one eye against the bright sun.

'What happened to you?'

I told him what had happened and what it meant. He nodded sadly and lapped some more water.

'You don't look so good yourself,' I said. 'What . . .?'

'Angelica's pregnant.'

'She can't be. It was just the night before last.'

'She says she is. With Frank Henry, that's the same thing.'

'Uh huh. Well, I'd better get a steak for this eye.'

'No steak,' Pedro said. 'Try beans.'

I went into the house, made up an ice pack and sat down in the kitchen. The pool water sparkled outside; the green-brown tennis court looked smart with its lines still clearly marked; the sky was a rich California blue and I felt like shit. The phone rang.

'Browning.'

'I'm callin' for Willy. You unnerstand?'

'Yes.' What he meant was: 'I'm calling for Eddy.'

'Willy likes number 3 in the sixth at Caliente on the tenth.'

'Got it.' This was a signal to take the boat out at six o'clock on a certain bearing.

'Good luck.'

I hung up and looked at the pad on which I'd written the numbers. They meant nothing to me but they would to the crew of the *Darwin*. The pile of unpaid bills was on the table beside the phone. I had nothing to speak of in the bank and less than a hundred dollars in cash around the house. I wondered if Pedro and I could sail the boat on our own. I wondered if I had any choice.

Pedro walked into the house dripping wet. He usually wore crisp, starched cotton trousers and shirts and was impeccably barbered. I'd never seen him looking so woebegone, but appearances can be deceptive.

'Pedro,' I said, 'have you got any money?'

He shook his head.

'Well, there goes that plan.'

'What plan?'

'No money, no plan.'

'This is an expensive place to live and you pay lousy wages. I've loaned money to the Wobblies .... I've got a couple of hundred dollars.'

'How would you like to go to Cuba?'

'Anywhere, Senor Dick. Anywhere.'

...

We dashed around the house collecting things. I threw some clothes into the same old bag I'd brought from Australia and tossed in shaving gear and personal documents. The camera went in too, along with a few folders of snapshots I'd taken in Hollywood. [Some of Browning's photographs, apparently from this period, have survived. One is presumably of the Beverly Hills house; the building, with ill-matched arches and colonnades, is a monument to bad taste. It was destroyed in one of the fires that ravaged the Hollywood hills in the 1960s. There is a photograph of the Pierce Arrow with Pedro Cortez at the wheel and several of a woman in the company of celebrities of the day, such as Chaplin and (unwillingly to judge from her expression) Clara Bow. This woman presumably is Bonnie Dalton, although further research among the papers and photographs will be required before this can be confirmed. Ed.]

I tried to phone Bonnie but got no reply. I guessed she'd taken her phone off the hook and was deep asleep under her mud mask and eye pads. She'd taken most of the booze away with her along with the cigarettes, so Pedro and I were short on essential supplies when we set off some time after four o'clock.

Half way to the harbour the traffic slowed and then stopped. I panicked, stood up in the car and saw the police cars ahead.

'Quick, Pedro, turn around. It's a road block! Let's get out of here!' I had visions of Sergeant Rourke getting a warrant and preparing a rock-solid rum-running case against me. Maybe they'd planted some cocaine in the car. After the traumas of the Fairbanks injury fiasco, it seemed that any disaster was possible.

Pedro kept his head. 'Shut up. It's moving.'

It was, too. The cars ahead crept forward and the traffic started to move in the other direction too. I sank back into the seat and lit a cigarette with shaking hands. My nerves were jangled; I imagined Wobblies in the jalopies and gangsters in the limousines. We came up to where the obstruction originated. One of the big red trolley cars had collided with a sleek roadster. The car was cut almost in two; there was glass across the road and firemen were throwing sand on spilt gasoline. Its smell flooded over me and made me feel sick.

'Look!' Pedro said.

I glanced across at the sandy edge of the road. A man, or what was left of him, was lying on his back. I can still see it. His head . . . you don't want the details.

'Get moving, Pedro,' I said. Then I *was* sick – out over the running board and front fender of the Pierce Arrow.

CHAPTER TWENTY-FIVE

'What've yez got the bags for?' asked Riley as Pedro and I boarded the *Darwin*.

'We're driving up to Frisco after this trip,' I said.

'Yez could've left 'em in yer car.'

'Safer to keep them with us.'

'Suit y'self.' He was a real charmer, Riley.

We stowed the bags below and I went up on deck to catch some air and see whether a touch of the ocean might not induce some happier thoughts. The crew was different from the last time; there was a young Mexican, a tough-looking guy in his late twenties who had only one arm and a negro who looked like a Cuban. He spoke Spanish to the Mexican anyway. They were busy about the ketch under Riley's usual ill-natured directions and all I could do was stand out of the way by the rail, smoke a cigarette and hope for some luck.

We cleared the harbour. The sprawl of Los Angeles faded to a series of bright and dark splotches on a lumpy landscape. The sea was calm and the *Darwin* ploughed along under light sail in fine style. I flicked my cigarette away and faced the difficult task of conversing with Riley.

'When's the meet?' I asked him.

He wound rope with hands that looked like they'd been pickled in brine, the way the old-time bare knuckle fighters used to do, according to my Pa. 'Soon enough and not too long,' Riley said.

'Can't be with Eddy.'

'And why not?'

'He was at a party at my place the other night. He hasn't had time to go anywhere.'

'It's news you're giving me. Parties!' He spat over the side.

'No parties, no rum running. You'd be out of a job.'

He grinned. 'There's plenty of jobs. This one's no prize. Get below, mister, you've played your part.'

A Trappist monk would've been better company on a desert island than Riley, but even those few words were more than he usually allowed. On the previous trip I'd found him more close-mouthed than any man I'd ever met. To see him grinning was very worrying. I went down and played cards with Pedro, losing as usual. He was whistling again and I told him to shut up.

'What's the matter? Sore loser, Senor Dick? You should be used to it.'

'Bugger the cards. Something's fishy here. Riley's acting strange.'

'Strange? How?'

'Just strange. Eddy can't have gone to get a shipment. Riley didn't seem to know that.'

Pedro shrugged. 'He does what he is told. Deal *las cartas.*'

'What *has* he been told? That's the point.'

'He's been told to run rum – that's all he cares about. That and getting his money. You see the Mexican when we came on board? Looks like a smart kid. I'll talk to him. Maybe we can persuade him to help us take the boat to Cuba.'

'Persuade him with your knife? Or with your silver tongue?'

Pedro shrugged. 'Either. Both.'

'When?'

'After we make this trip. Let's play.'

'I'm too restless. I'm going to take a look around.' I went out of the cabin and prowled the below deck area. I wasn't looking for anything in particular, I didn't know what to look for. It was immediately obvious that things had changed in this part of the boat. The arrangement of bulk-heads and lockers looked different from on the previous trip; the effect was less tidy but also larger. On close examination I found that the concealed storage areas were not concealed any more. False panels and other structures had been removed. The *Darwin* wasn't going to carry any contraband cargo this voyage. That left the question of what cargo she *was* to carry and there was only one answer. I hurried back to the cabin.

'Pedro, have you got a gun with you?'

'Si, the .45 from General Domingo. I wonder if that old bastard is dead yet. Why?'

I told him.

He nodded. 'I was thinking myself – who uses a one-armed man to load liquor?' He abandoned the hand of solitaire he was dealing and rummaged in his bag. The .45 came out, big, black and comforting. Pedro checked the action. Then he tested the knife in its forearm scabbard. He was a man of decision again, thank God. 'We've got to take the wheelhouse,' he said.

'Why not pick them off one by one?'

'Because the Thompsons are there.'

I felt the blood drain from my face. Suddenly, the .45 looked like a cap pistol and Pedro's knife didn't mean much. 'Christ, I'd forgotten about them.'

'They are the key to the situation.'

'D'you think they keep them all there? Riley said there were three.'

'I hope so. We're going to have to kill at least one of them if we can.'

'Can't you just wing him?'

'Wing?'

'Wound.'

Pedro shook his head. 'I don't think so.'

'We've got no choice. We're not meant to come back.'

He wiped his hand and took a grip on the .45. 'Okay, let's go.'

We crept up the steps to the foredeck. There was no one in sight. Along the port side to the wheelhouse. Still clear. The boat was making good time, rolling slightly but not enough to throw off aim at close quarters. The one-armed man was at the wheel.

'Good,' Pedro whispered.

I nodded. 'Has to be a handicap.'

'I mean I would rather shoot a gringo than a Mexican.' Pedro jerked open the door. The man half-turned. 'Hands on the wheel, amigo,' Pedro barked. 'Don't . . .!'

One-arm made a dive to his left and Pedro shot him. The heavy gun boomed in the confined space and a spurt of blood covered the windshield. I rushed forward to where one-arm had been heading. The Thompsons were held underneath a bench, suspended by heavy webbing slings. I hauled them up onto the bench; they were heavy, chunky guns with the round magazines attached. *Twenty-one shot clips,* I thought – sixty-three bullets. That put the odds in our favour, but there could be other guns aboard. The man was on the floor, groaning.

'Great shot,' I said.

'Very poor. I was aiming for his chest.'

'Where did you get him?'

'The other arm.'

'Fuck you, you prick . . . you . . .'

'Shut up.' I said. 'Keep still or we'll chuck you over the side.' I unclipped the magazine from one of the Thompsons, opened a side window in the wheelhouse and threw the machine gun into the sea.

'What the hell're you doing?' Pedro yelled.

'We got one each.' I put the webbing belt over my head. 'That should be enough. Another one lying about could get into the wrong hands.' My leg had cramped and I was trembling. There was a bottle of rum on the floor by the wheel. I uncorked it and took a big swig. Pedro did the same. The rough, hot spirit helped but I was still scared.

'Where are they?' Pedro said. 'They must have heard.'

I moved the safety over with my thumb and fired a burst out the window, raking it over the side towards the front. It was overcast and dull with reduced light and the Thompson made a big flame. It bucked and I had to hold it down. 'Riley!' I shouted.

No response. I moved to the back of the wheelhouse and fired a flame-stabbing burst over the stern. 'Riley!'

'Yeah?' The voice came from the stern, down below a locker that held fishing tackle and other gear.

'Don't make me fire this thing again. If you've got a gun throw it out.'

'Now why would I do that?'

'Why would he do that?' Pedro said.

I had no answer; it just seemed like the thing to say. I stared out into the gloom over the grey, gentle sea. The dinghy was hanging above the stern. The dinghy!

'Because I might hit the dinghy and that'd mean I couldn't give it to you and your men and let you go. We're taking the boat and we don't want to shoot you. You can go in the dinghy, or you can . . .'

I was barely coherent with nervousness; the Thompson felt like a ton weight because I was supporting it and not letting the sling do the work. I tried to relax and then jumped a foot as Pedro fired a burst into the air.

'All right, all right,' Riley said. 'We've got no guns. We're coming out.'

Riley, the negro and the Mexican came from behind the locker and stood in front of us – ten feet away with their heads level with our feet.

'One burst,' Pedro said.

'No,' I said.

'How Harry?' the negro said.

'You mean the guy with one wing?' I said.

The negro nodded.

'He's alive. You and Riley drop the anchor and lower the dinghy.' I jerked the machine gun at the Mexican. 'What's your name?'

'Jose, Senor, I . . .'

'Come up here. Pedro, talk to him. We'll need help with this bloody thing. He looks scared enough.'

The negro released the anchor chain. The *Darwin* wallowed and jerked and began to heave on the slight swell. Riley and the negro lowered the dinghy and stood by the stern rail. I came down and moved towards them, keeping well back and watching my feet.

'Watch what you do with that bloody thing,' Riley said, 'if you hit the tanks we'll go sky high.'

'Don't provoke me, then. You, get Harry. Lower him into the boat.' The negro skirted around me and went into the wheelhouse. Pedro was talking quickly in Spanish to Jose who was nodding as if that was the only way he knew to move his head. The negro came out carrying Harry in a fireman's lift.

'Yo' shouldn't't've hit his arm, boss,' he said.

'He was going for the Thompsons, we didn't have any choice.'

He smiled slowly. 'Now how yo' think ol' Harry c'd use him a Thompson gun? How could he?'

'Then he was just plain *loco,*' Pedro said impatiently. 'This one will help us, Dick. Let's get rid of these others and be going.'

Riley went over the stern on a rope and dropped into the dinghy. The negro looped some rope around Harry's waist and lowered him down, then he climbed in himself. The dinghy had oars and a sail; I wouldn't have cared to be set adrift in it somewhere off the Californian coast myself, but Riley and the negro treated it as if they had been shown the door to the street. They stretched Harry out in the bottom and covered him with a blanket Jose threw down from the ketch.

'C'd use some water, boss,' the negro said. 'An' yo' might oblige us wit' d' medicine chest in d' wheelhouse. Ol' Harry don' look too good.'

I nodded and Jose fetched the chest and some bottles of water from the cooler. 'Give them the rum, too,' I said.

Riley caught the bottle. He uncorked it and took a pull. 'Wouldn't like to be you when Eddy catches up with you, mister.'

'He's not going to be too pleased with you either.'

The negro nodded and fiddled with the bolts at the base of the mast. 'Yo' right, reckon we might go to Mexico.'

'Mexico!' Pedro yelped.

Riley's face split into the second grin I'd seen on it – he probably allowed himself three or four per year. 'Now d'yez reckon you'd be able to find your way to Santa Catalina?' He threw off the rope that had been holding the dinghy to the *Darwin* and it began to drift away.

I looked around; the ocean was wide, calm and featureless. There was heavy cloud cover and all directions looked alike. The dinghy was fifty yards off in a minute and the gap was widening fast. The sail went up and the little boat suddenly looked alert and purposeful. It zipped forward, tacked and zig-zagged away playfully.

'You think there's any more rum on board?' Pedro said.

'Si.' Jose was a slim teenager whose face was pock-marked and knife-scarred. He looked as if he'd been fighting from the day he could walk. 'There is more rum, Senor. You want?'

'No,' I said. 'Not yet. Can you start the engines?'

'Si, Senor. An' I can run them if nothing goes wrong.'

'It will,' I said.

'What d'you think, Pedro?'

'About what? I still want the rum.'

'About where we go?'

'Santa Catalina doesn't seem far enough.'

'No, not nearly far enough.'

'You want to go back to Australia, Senor Dick?' I looked at the ketch; forty feet, a mysterious machine of sail and auxiliary engine power. I had no idea of its provisions, fuel or ocean-going capacities.

No knowledge of navigation, radio communications or weather reports. The only sailing I'd done had been on Sydney Harbour where you could see the land all around you. I couldn't imagine myself bringing the *Darwin* triumphantly through the Heads.

'No,' I said. 'Do you know the way to Cuba, Jose?'

He shook his head. 'I know the way back to California.'

'That's no good,' Pedro said. Where's the rum?'

. . .

We went below and Jose got out a case with three bottles of rum in it. We made big drinks with ice from the cooler and a squashed pineapple that Jose produced from somewhere. I watched him closely. He was interested in the Thompsons and the .45 the way a kid in the suburbs might be interested in motor bikes.

'Where're you from, Jose?' I asked after the third pineapple rum whatever-it-was.

'Los Angeles, the *barrio.*'

'You say you know the way back there, how come?'

'We come out fishing this far, further.'

My half-drunk mind was running on impressions, words, fleeting images. *Fishing,* I thought. Salmon, cod, cold water. I jumped up. 'That's it!'

'What?' Pedro said.

'You can take us back to California, right, Jose? I'll give you this if you can.' I tapped the grip of the Thompson.

I never saw someone so excited. Yes! Yes! I can, Senor, I . . .'

Pedro yawned. 'We can't go back to Los Angeles. Los Angeles is Eddy and the Wobblies and . . . Angelica . . .'

'Listen.' I was standing now or trying to stand. I was drunk and happy. Wher you get very few good ideas it excites you to have a real zippity-do one. 'Listen, if you head back to California an' you turn . . . right, where do you get to?'

Pedro thought. He took a drink and lit a cigarette. Jose watched him but his eyes were constantly flicking to the Thompson. He was like a quiz contestant trying to read the answers in the quizmaster's face. The rum and excitement had made Pedro slower than usual. Eventually he sighed. 'Mexico,' he said. 'You crazy bastard. We can't go to Mexico. Domingo would have our balls, or Spring-field or Porfirio Calderon. And Angelica's mother is Mexican. What are you trying to do to me? Mexico! Shit!'

I beamed at him and thumped him on the shoulder. 'Right, right, Pedro my old chum! But what happens if you head towards sunny California and you turn left and keep going left. What happens then, eh? Where do you go then?'

'Where, Senor? Where?' Jose pleaded.

'Canada!' I yelled. 'The British Empire. Hip hip, hooray!'

CHAPTER TWENTY-SIX

Jose squinted around the horizon, looked at the sea and finally pointed.

'California,' he said.

'How far?' I asked.

He shrugged. We'd been at sea for some hours, it was dark, time to think about food and whether we should stay at anchor for the night or get underway.

'Get underway?' Pedro said. 'Are you crazy. We're likely to bump into California or drift down to Mexico or something. I'm not going anywhere until morning.' He was drunk and appeared nervous. I told Jose to check the lights on the side of the ship and waited until he was out of earshot.

'What's wrong?'

'I don't know whether we can trust him. We're going to have to keep watches.'

'Oh, Jesus. Well, I'd better take the first. You're too bombed to do anything.'

'No,' Pedro hissed. 'That's what I want him to think. I'll take the watch and make a show of falling asleep. If he does anything wrong I'll cut him in two.'

'I thought you didn't want to shoot Mexicans?'

'We have to find out now! This could take weeks and we don't want to be sneaking around jumping at shadows. You sleep. Either I'll wake you in four hours or you'll wake up when the gun goes off.'

Comforting thoughts, but I was tired and strained and found I was ready enough for sleep. The motion of the boat helped; I put the Thompson on safety, tucked it between me and the wall and stretched out on the bunk. I thought briefly of Douglas Fairbanks, more lingeringly of Bonnie Dalton, and then I was asleep.

. . .

Pedro shook me awake; my hand flew for the machine gun. I skinned my knuckles on it and swore.

'It's okay. The *chico* is okay. He had a hundred chances and he didn't make a move.'

'He wasn't foxing?'

'Foxing?'

'Like you – playing, pretending.'

Pedro shook his head and yawned. 'No, no. He is not that kind. You see him? He is a *delincuente*. Not subtle. No. He's all right. Get off. I have to sleep.'

I rolled off the bunk and slung the Thompson. 'What's happening?'

'You won't need the gun. Leave it here. He's cooked some beans. Very good. Go eat.'

I was out of the cabin before I realised that Pedro had arranged it so that I had four hours sleep and he could have as much as he liked. I went back to the tiny galley where the juvenile delinquent into whose hands I had entrusted my life was making coffee on a primus stove. He handed me a plate of beans.

'Thanks. Have you checked what food we've got on board, Jose?'

'Si. Have you got a cigarette, Senor?'

I gave him a cigarette and lit it. That was Jose's special trick. He gave nothing for nothing. A cigarette in exchange for information; if you asked for help he got the favour repaid within the hour. I never met anyone so concerned not to be taken advantage of.

'There is some flour, plenty of water. No meat. Some fruit. *Muchos habas* – plenty of beans.'

I ate some of the beans he'd cooked and enjoyed them. Jose smoked and poured the coffee. 'Will you really give me the gun, Senor? The Thompson gun?'

'Yes. You can have both of them, probably.'

His eyes glittered and a wolfish smile came onto his face. With the knife and smallpox scars, the smile completed the picture of a very dangerous young man.

'What will you do with the guns, Jose? Go to Mexico and fight for freedom?'

'Senor?' The wolfishness gave way to puzzlement.

'What will you do with the guns?'

'Oh, rob banks,' he said.

...

Two days before the mast was quite enough for yours truly. If you think that sailing north in a bootlegger's ketch, keeping the coast of California on your right and with two Mexicans for company would be an interesting experience, you'd be quite wrong. It was damnably dull. I was all for starting up the engines and making better times but Jose opposed this.

'Not much fuel, Senor,' he said. 'Engines for *necesidad*.'

'That's crazy,' I said. 'We don't have to outrun anything now. We're not carrying liquor.'

Jose gabbled fast Spanish to Pedro who explained. 'He means emergency – in sailing. We might need the engines to beat a bad wind, to avoid being blown onto rocks, something like that.'

'Oh really? That's different. Right you are – let's conserve the fuel. I don't fancy playing Robinson Crusoe along here.' The coast was very wild in stretches with cliffs coming down to the water and the surf crashing against them and sending spray hundreds of feet in the air. There were bays and inlets of course, but the country behind looked heavily wooded and I had visions of bears and worse.

Towns presented a different problem. The bootleggers had people in their pockets everywhere. They had spies and moonshiners everywhere and the last thing we needed was to be held up in some place on a pretext while the Sheriff got word to 'Tidal' Eddy. So we kept out to sea. This made food a problem. Plenty of beans, Jose had said. And how! I've never been able to look at beans since. The other staple of our diet was fish. Jose was a skilled fisherman and he caught more than we could eat. I can't remember the types and it didn't matter because after a while they all tasted the same. Fish and beans, beans and fish. The rum and what booze Pedro and I had salvaged from Hollywood ran out after a few days so it was fish and beans and water. We all lost weight; I got suntanned from the work on deck. The time I spent not smoking because the cigarettes ran out was the only period I've had off the weed in more than sixty years, not counting serious illnesses.

I suppose it did me good, physically. Emotionally, it did me no good at all. For one thing, Pedro had resumed the schoolmasterly air he'd largely lost in Hollywood. There'd he'd been boozy, skirt-chasing and irresponsible like everyone else. Now he took an interest in navigation and tried to force it on me. He tried to get me to read the *Pacific Pilot* which, along with a battered Bible and a copy of *Don Quixote,* missing pages here and there, were the only books on board. I would have none of it. Mathematics was my weakest subject at school and the charts and figures and calculations gave me a headache just to look at them.

There were a few newspapers and magazines which I read end to end a couple of times. Californian newspapers have never paid much attention to the outside world. It was mostly baseball and what to do with wounded veterans and watermelon trucks tipping over in Bakers-field. I used to be a fair hand at the crossword in the

Australian papers but these left me clueless. 'Who invented baseball in 1839 – 9 letters?'[46]

What international news there was was bad, of course. Michael Collins and his bully boys were refusing to accept the Irish Free State so's they could go on killing people. One item in particular interested me. The Greeks had invaded Turkey with the help of Britain and had got themselves in a sticky spot. There was talk of the Dominions stepping in to help. That maniac Hughes, who was Prime Minister in Australia, pledged his support to protect the graves of the fallen at Gallipoli. Madness.[47] Canada, I was pleased to see, showed no interest. That was encouraging; I was liking the idea of going there better all the time.

We had no real difficulty with the ketch. Each of us knew enough about sailing not to make too many mistakes and the winds and weather favoured us. It got cooler as we went north and we lacked proper clothing. Pedro and I made do with what we had brought in our bags but we'd thought we were going to Cuba so it didn't quite answer. Jose ignored the temperature. He was happiest stripping, oiling and re-assembling the Thompsons which I let him do whenever he wanted. They must have been the best maintained machine guns on the west coast; I must say I was happiest when they were in pieces.

Tempers frayed when Pedro and I were suffering most from the tobacco and alcohol withdrawal. Jose found relief in the guns and in fishing. Pedro eventually settled down to a slow reading of *Don Quixote*. I had almost nothing to do but think and there was little joy in that. I doubted I could sell the yacht although I had the papers. 'Tidal' Eddy must have protected himself there somehow. I had almost no money and had made a mess of my big chance in Hollywood. (Years later, after I'd been back to Hollywood and had done better, well, a little better, a student from one of the film schools asked me about Hollywood in the early twenties. 'It must have been a wonderful time,' this bright-eyed girl said.

'Oh, wonderful,' I said.

'Great fun as well as hard work.'

'Plenty of both.' I've always made it a point to lie to researchers; it's the only way to keep them from coming back and pestering you again.)

Pedro's grasp of navigation became sound enough for him to pinpoint our position after the first six days. A week or so after that he called a meeting on the foredeck. (I told you he'd resumed his schoolmasterly ways.) He spread out a chart and stabbed it with his finger.

'Here we are,' he said.

I looked at the map which could've been of Greenland for all I understood of it. 'Where?'

'Just south of the Juan de Fuca Strait.'

Jose looked panicked. 'Juan de Fuca? I thought we were going to Canada? That sounds like fuckin' Mexico.'

Pedro sighed. 'What did you do? The second grade, with difficulty? That's a strait between Vancouver Island and the mainland.'

'Vancouver,' I said. 'Canada.'

'Brilliant! One side of the water is Canada, on the other the United States.'

'Let me see.' I struggled to comprehend the chart. I didn't like the sound of it. It reminded me of floating down the Rhine with hostile Germany on one side and occupied France on the other. Borders always make me nervous, as I think I've said.

'We can enter the straight and keep to the Canadian side of the waterway,' Pedro said.

Jose shook his head. 'I don' wanna go to Canada. I wanna stay in the States.'

Well, *chico,* that's easy. See here.' He placed his finger near a dot on the map at the end of the strait. The channel was narrow and the dot was on the US side. 'Port Angeles, Jose. We can drop you there. You should be right at home.'

...

We rounded Cape Flattery, entered the strait and headed down the channel, hugging the northern shore. Pedro's charts showed him the rocks and other hazards and he handled the whole operation, at night, practically single-handed. There was an inflatable rubber raft on board and, under cover of night, with the lights of Port Angeles showing faintly to the south, we lowered it to the water.

'Goodbye, Senor Dick. Goodbye, Pedro.'

'*Adios,* Jose.'

I handed down the Thompsons with their magazines. Jose's teeth shone in a wide smile. 'Thank you.'

'Be careful,' I said. 'Keep out of trouble.' Under my breath I added: 'Until you can't be connected with us.'

'*Vaya con Dios.*'

Amazing how these Latins will drag God in at the most inappropriate times. Here's this sweeping of the *barrio,* with two Thompson machine guns in his lap and bank robbery on his mind, and he talks of God. Incredible! We waved to him as he dipped his oars quietly and rowed towards the American shore.

...

Daylight found us moving sedately up the broad Strait of Georgia, which is practically an inland sea, dotted with small islands, between the huge Vancouver Island and the mainland of British Columbia.

'Odd how these northern waterways have southern sounding names, don't you think?'

'Si.' Pedro was hunched over his charts, issuing instructions to me at the wheel. I fancied myself at the wheel and was happy there as long as there were no shoals or squalls or other such things to contend with. I was nervous about our arrival though, and got more so as the weather turned bad and the sea grew choppy. We anchored in the shelter of one of the islands. We adjusted the sail and Pedro went below to check on the engines and fuel. We had no rum, no coffee, just fish and beans and a sort of johnny cake Jose had made with the flour. I chewed on some of this while I waited for his report. He came up smiling and wiping oil from his hands.

'Engines are simple things when you understand them.'

I handed him a plate with the dry food on it. 'And bloody impossible when you don't. Are you saying you can run these engines?'

'Yes.' He pulled a face at the food and pushed it away. 'We have some fuel, enough I think. We can make Vancouver in a couple of hours if the weather does not get too bad.'

I squinted off over the heaving water. There was a ship far away to the north and smoke on the horizon; we'd passed a couple of small boats and one big one. I got the feeling that traffic was intensifying on the strait. I was wearing two shirts, a vest and the jacket of a summer suit. Pedro had on a sweater and cotton pants. Neither of us had solid shoes. It wasn't the way you would have chosen to arrive in Canada. Pedro caught my look and grinned. 'We look strange, no?'

I fished in my pocket and brought out some money. 'I want a steak with potatoes and a bottle of wine. I want a packet of cigarettes and a double whisky. Our money won't look strange. I've got a passport, papers for the ship and the letter we used at the Mexican border. We're legal. What can they do? It's no crime not to have an overcoat. How's the weather?'

'Good enough. We can make it.'

'Let's go.'

Pedro stretched himself and wiped his oily hands on his stained cotton trousers. He looked down at the result. 'I wish I had an overcoat,' he said.

. . .

The weather held and we made good time. The *Darwin's* engines were powerful and smooth and the ship answered the controls easily. I put our .45s away in a locker as any responsible but cautious boat-owner might, tidied up the galley and cabin and went on deck. There were lots of ships around, markers indicating channels for the ones with deep draughts, and various buoys. Pedro set a course for the north side of the harbour where the smaller shipping seemed to be concentrated. It was cold; I shivered and watched the massive mountains behind the city loom up and tower over the water.

When we were still a few hundred yards from the dock a small motor boat shot out and carved through the water towards us. It slewed across our path a few lengths from us and a man on board picked up a megaphone.

'Will you please accompany us to the dock!'

I waved, the motor boat revved up and cut back through its own wake. Pedro followed it in. I noticed that both men on board it wore uniforms. *Well,* I thought, *immigration and customs regulations are a bore everywhere.* Pedro brought the ketch in like a master mariner; she bumped gently against the motor tyres lashed to the pylons. I tossed the ropes onto the wharf and two stevedoring types tied her up under the direction of the uniformed guy, who stood at arm's length from the rail. He'd put down his megaphone and now carried a revolver instead.

'Let me see your papers please.' He was British, thin and ramrod straight, with a toothbrush moustache. Ex-army for sure, confirmed by the service ribbon he wore on his coat a little higher than the top silver buttons. The type to chill your blood and age you before your time. The uniform he wore wasn't army though: blue coat, stars on the epaulettes, high black boots, stiff brimmed hat worn very square. I caught a flash of scarlet under the greatcoat and was puzzled.

I handed the documents over and Pedro and I stood nervously on the gently moving deck. The officer examined the papers and passed them to his colleague whose epaulettes carried no stars. The junior in rank nodded and tapped my passport with his finger.

'Kelly,' he said. 'See that, Inspector? And Australian, or so it says.'

I was getting tired of this. 'What of it?' I snapped.

'Are you a member of the Irish Republican Army?' the senior officer said.

'Are you mad? No!'

'Odd, sir,' the junior said. 'They usually admit it. Boast of it, even.'

The Inspector drew himself up even straighter. 'Do you know anything about one Jose Mineo, an alien, landed illegally on American soil last night with two Thompson machine guns and a quantity of ammunition?'

My knees almost gave out and I grabbed the rail for support. 'Er . . . no, I don't. He . . ., I . . .'

The officer touched his moustache as if it was the only thing in the world he admired. 'I think you do, Mr Richard *Kelly* Browning. I am Inspector Ambrose Chester of the Royal Canadian Northwest Mounted Police and I am arresting you for gun-running and seditious activity, in the name of His Majesty King George V.'

APPENDIX

DOUGLAS FAIRBANKS, RICHARD BROWNING AND *ROBIN HOOD*

Douglas Fairbanks was born Douglas Elton Ulman in Denver, Colorado in 1883. He was the son of a prominent Jewish lawyer and a Southern 'belle'. His parents separated when he was young and he was brought up by his mother. Fairbanks pursued a show business career with varying success from the early age of twelve until around 1910, when he was established as a Broadway star.

By 1916 Fairbanks was popular enough as a movie actor to form his own production company. For the rest of his career he largely controlled the vehicles he appeared in and wisely moved from all-American boy pictures to swashbuckling adventures. In 1919 he formed United Artists with Chaplin and Griffith; he married Mary Pickford in 1920 and in 1921 he produced and starred in *The Three Musketeers*. He was thus at the pinnacle of his popularity and success when Browning encountered him in 1922.

All prints of *Robin Hood* were lost for many years but the film can now be seen in its entirety. No mention of Richard Browning appears in the credits which is not surprising given the nature of their relationship and parting. Having full financial and artistic control, Fairbanks would have been in a position to erase Browning from the picture entirely and it seems that this is what he did.

The story of the mishap during the first take of Fairbanks' curtain descent was effectively suppressed as Browning notes.

Browning's account of Fairbanks is less flattering than most. David Niven describes him as an 'overgrown schoolboy' (see notes) and the only criticism, if that's what it is, director Alan Dwan made about him was that he was 'timid in love scenes'. All agree he was fond of practical jokes and it might be interesting to get opinions on him from some of the people who were the subjects of these jokes. Browning's account of his Anglophilia and athletic skills accords with the contemporary record.

Robin Hood was a great commercial and critical success. Fairbanks backed his judgement with money; the film, perhaps the most costly to date, had the most intensive pre-release publicity yet seen in Hollywood. The results justified the outlay. *Robin Hood* broke box office records everywhere in the world. At Grauman's Egyptian Theatre it ran for so long that the trolley car stop near the theatre was signalled as 'Robin Hood'. The doyen of American film critics, Pauline Kael, refers to Fairbanks' 'beautiful athletic prowess' and describes the film as 'big' and 'handsome'.

NOTES

1. Readers of *'Box Office' Browning* have complained that some of Browning's turn of the century Australian slang is obscure. 'Bolter' may be a case in point. A 'bolter' was a convict who escaped from the penal settlement into the bush during early years of colonisation in Australia. Most 'bolters' starved to death, were killed by Aborigines, surrendered or were recaptured.
2. Exodus 2:22, also 18:3.
3. St Matthew 24.
4. Browning's recollection is inaccurate:
   It is better to dwell in the corner of the housetop, than with a brawling woman in a wide house. Proverbs 21:9.
5. St Matthew 9.
6. 1 Timothy 5:23.
7. Eleanor Roosevelt, wife of the thirty-second President of the United States, an energetic social reformer, lecturer and newspaper columnist, was a homely woman. Browning is probably referring to her lack of physical attractiveness, but possibly also to her liberal and feminist opinions.
8. In Australian slang 'bludger' is a highly derogatory epithet, signifying laziness, a tendency to impose on others and a cadging disposition. But, as is usual with the Australian sense of humour, 'bludger' can also be used affectionately, particularly between men.

9. Thessalonians 3:10.

10. Proverbs 22:1.

11. St John 13.

12. The first battle of the Marne was in September 1914 and resulted in the frustration of German plans to invade Paris. In the second battle, in July 1918, the last great German advance of the war was decisively repulsed.

13. Buff Clayton's brief description of his prospecting in Mexico bears a remarkable resemblance to the story of B. Traven's 1927 novel, *The Treasure of the Sierra Madre.* Traven, a mysterious character in his own right, may have encountered Clayton in his travels and acquired the elements of the story from him.

14. This refers to the casino managements' practice of providing accommodation, meals and liquor (and sometimes female companionship) free of charge to big gamblers.

15. Browning Model 1895 machine gun, so called because part of the mechanism hung down towards the ground while firing.

16. The sewers.

17. This quotation is very astray and we may assume this is due to Browning's mistaken recollection. The lines read:

   I sprang to the stirrup, and Joris and he;

   I galloped, Dirck galloped, we galloped all three.

   Robert Browning, 'How they brought the Good News from Ghent to Aix.'

18. Dog.

19. Drunkard; punishment.

20. The sewers.

21. Where are you going?

22. Shut up!

23. *Hell's Angels,* made in 1930, was the most ambitious and successful aviation picture of its day; it was directed by Howard Hughes and starred Ben Lyon and Jean Harlow.

24. Scullion, dish-washer.

25. Mack Sennett was the leading comedy director of the silent film era. D. W. Griffith was the most innovative director of his day, responsible for such classics as *The Birth of a Nation* and *Intolerance.* Francis X. Bushman abandoned the stage for the screen in 1911 and became Hollywood's most popular leading man. He is thought to have been earning a million dollars a year in the 1920s but he lost his fortune in the stock market crash of 1929. His most famous role was as Messala in *Ben-Hur* (1926).

26. Bartholomew Booth clearly implies that this was not his real name and probably not the one he was known by in Hollywood either. This makes it impossible to check the truth of his assertion that he worked with the leading lights in the profession.

27. Carl Laemmle is credited with devising the star system. In 1910 he lured Florence Lawrence, a leading player with the Biograph company, to his own independent operation. He planted the story that she had been killed in a St Louis streetcar accident, denied the rumour, accused Biograph of propagating it and saw that the press was given plenty of notice when the actress visited St Louis in person. She was mobbed, the result being enormous and profitable publicity for her films with Laemmle.

Laemmle, as head of the Universal Film Manufacturing Company (later simply Universal), confirmed the dominance of southern California as the site for the American movie industry with his establishment in 1910 of the 230-acre studio municipality, University City.

28. In Australian schools, essay-writing was called 'Composition'. Teachers gave students a topic and word length and the pupils were expected to write the piece in class. A perennial topic was 'My Holiday'.

29. H. Elliot Silkstein was the founder of Silkstein Enterprises. A German Jew who migrated to America in the 1880s, he built a handcart business, selling fruit and vegetables, into a street stall selling fruit, vegetables and clothes, and that into a string of street stalls and shops selling everything. He was an early participant in the film business, as a distributor and exhibitor, and moved to California before World War I, establishing one of the first agencies for moving picture actors in the world. He diversified into other fields, as Browning records.

    A man of huge and diverse appetites, Silkstein was married three times and had two sons, one of whom, N. Robert Silkstein, took over the agency part of Silkstein Enterprises. N. Robert Silkstein and his son, N. Robert Silkstein Jnr., were Browning's agents through most of his career.

    H. Elliot Silkstein died of a heart attack in 1925. At the time he was visiting a Hollywood whorehouse which specialised in providing 'look-alikes' for screen stars male and female. One story has it that Silkstein died when in the company of the look-alike Mae West. Another account says that his companion was 'Jean Harlow'. When I questioned N. Robert Silkstein Jnr. about this his answer was, 'probably both'.

30. Harry 'Snub' Pollard was born Harold Frazer in Melbourne in 1886. He travelled to the US with a light opera company in 1915 and remained, making scores of one-reel comedies, at first supporting Harold Lloyd and then as the leading player. A small man with a drooping moustache,

he specialised in 'sad sack' roles. His popularity did not carry over into the sound era and he appeared irregularly thereafter in small parts. He died in 1962.

31. John Gilbert, born 1895, came from a theatrical family and made a rapid advance as a film actor. By the early 1920s he was well-established in Fox productions as a dashing leading man. Three films with Greta Garbo in the late twenties lifted him to new heights of popularity but he failed to make the transition to sound pictures. His voice was high-pitched and did not match his authoritative screen presence, as Browning notes. It also seems that he was not a very good actor and his florid style appeared ridiculous in talkies. Gilbert took to heavy drinking and died of a heart attack in 1936.

32. David Niven, *Bring on the Empty Horses,* (Coronet ed., 1976), p. 196.

33. Alan Dwan has described the chain mail as 'heavy canvas, sprayed with silver paint. It looked exactly like chain mail, but it was flexible, and you could walk in it.' Kevin Brownlow, *The Parade's Cone By . . .,* (Abacus ed., 1973), p. 284.

34. The *Twentieth Century Limited* ran from New York to Los Angeles via Chicago. In 1919, the trip took four days. See Budd Schulberg, *Moving Pictures,* N.Y., 1981, pp. 79-90.

35. Louis Gasnier was a director, mostly of B pictures, whose parties were renowned for their sumptuousness and riotousness.

36. Fear of invasion or mass migration from Asia, particularly China: one of the phobias that lay behind the 'White Australia Policy' which, until the 1970s, effectively restricted migration to Australia to people of European stock.

37. The Hollywood Ten was a group of producers, directors and writers who were subpoenaed to appear before the

House Committee on Un-American Activities in 1947. All refused to testify on their political activities and affiliates, and in 1948 they were tried and sentenced to a year in gaol. They were blacklisted in Hollywood and were able to work in films only by going abroad or by using pseudonyms.

38. 'Movie' was a derogatory name given by long-time Los Angeles residents to newcomers who had come to work in the film industry. Some boarding houses carried warnings that there were no rooms available for 'movies'.

39. The Thompson sub-machine gun ("Tommy gun", the invention of General J. T. Thompson) had reached a sophistication of design by 1921 when the Colt Company manufactured 15,000 units. It fired 45 ammunition and in 1922 would have been a formidable weapon.

40. In fact Browning was aged 26 at this time. A preliminary auditing of the tapes indicates that he either forgot his age, deliberately misrepresented it or was indifferent to dates.

41. The poet was Jonathan Swift, 'My Lady's Lamentation', 1728.

42. As with Bartholomew Booth, it is impossible to identify 'Frank Henry'. In the nature of things IWW leaders sought anonymity. For a brief account of IWW activity in Hollywood, see Brownlow, op. cit., pp. 68-9.

43. In 1977 Polish Director Roman Polanski *(Knife in the Water, Rosemary's Baby, Chinatown)* was charged with drugging and raping a 13-year-old girl. The alleged offence took place in actor Jack Nicholson's home and Nicholson's companion, Angelica Huston, was a police witness in the case. Polanski denied the charge at first and then pleaded guilty to part of it and spent some time in prison on remand. Freed on bail, he left the United States and was declared a fugitive from justice by the court. He now lives in France. See Thomas Kiernan, *Repulsion: the life and times of Roman Polanski,* 1980.

44. Browning refers to Tilden's homosexuality which was revealed after his competition tennis career was over. Tilden was twice convicted for sexual offences and served short sentences in low security institutions.

45. Jack Dempsey was heavyweight boxing champion of the world from 1919 to 1927, when he lost the title to Gene Tunney. Harry Greb, a light-heavyweight who was the only professional to defeat Tunney, was reputed to enjoy the services of two prostitutes in the dressing room before a bout as a means of relaxation.

46. The answer sought would have been 'Doubleday'. Abner Doubleday's claim to have invented the game is now disputed however.

47. The threat to what W. M. Hughes called 'the sanctity of Gallipoli' never materialised and none of the Dominions sent troops to Turkey.

In the same series

'Box Office' Browning

A sybaritic life in the Californian sun, money, women, booze and a career in films: Richard Browning's recipe for happiness. Not too hopeless an ambition, not for a crack-shot, six-foot, all-Australian, ex-private-school horseman. But the films are in their infancy; someone starts the first world war; women and the law conspire to tie Browning up and keep him down. He stumbles from luck to disaster, from Switzerland to Melbourne, from bed to marriage bond. The road to Hollywood is a long and winding one.

'Box Office' Browning is Browning's recollection, from an ungraceful old age, of his early days. Memory unimpaired by booze and drugs and age, a lousy actor becomes a great raconteur, mixing anecdotes about the famous and infamous into his own story.

Also by Peter Corris

Pokerface

In this thriller the player with the best pokerface wins the game –
and it's a dangerous game. Sacked from the shadowy Federal Security
Agency, his marriage tottering, Ray Crawley forms an association
with radical punk Roxy and her friends – and that's his first mistake.

Crawley's former boss Toby Campion is trying to manipulate him
in a game with Canberra. But Crawley is still in the game, and he
won't give up. All the players are holding good cards but will the
best hand win?